DOUBTS AND DILEMMAS

Evita O'Malley

Published 2015 by Shadenet Publishing
www.shadenetpublishing.co.uk

Copyright © Evita O'Malley 2015

ISBN: 978-0-9933040-0-2

Cover designed by Heather Macpherson
www.raspberrycreativetype.com

Also available as an e-book

For my sister, Afra, who encouraged me to write –
because she had run out of romantic novels to read.
You are remarkable, I love you always. Evita.

I wrote this book for my sister, but I am publishing it for my
niece, Shan. Stay strong. Keep fighting – the cancer, not your
mother! Get better. Much love, Evita.

CHAPTER 1

"It is quite indecorous of you to stare at me in such a manner, Mr Darcy," Elizabeth announced pertly.

"And pray," returned Darcy, "why do you suggest I am staring? You sit quite contentedly with your eyes fixed shut."

"Only the fact, sir, were I sitting opposite you while you slept I should be inclined to," she replied with a smile.

"Well, madam, at once you lay before me the very different inclinations of our sexes; I can assure you I did not stare."

Elizabeth opened her eyes to look at her husband. Darcy's retort had been given with his usual measured and commanding tone, but she could see a slight turn at the corner of his mouth, which told the truth of his teasing her. Although only a wife of some hours, she was already acquainted with many of her husband's more subtle expressions. She knew his voice and manner were ever controlled, leaving many with the impression that his imperiousness either provided the whole of his character, or masked a most inscrutable man, but Elizabeth had observed countless reactions that could be read in his face. The slightest curling of a lip or elevation of an eyebrow could speak volumes to someone well versed in the character and countenance of Fitzwilliam Darcy.

ℰℴ

The newlyweds had escaped the raptures of Mrs Bennet and her sister, Mrs Phillips; the overwrought civilities of Mr Collins; the general attention and fuss of the rest of the Bennet family, and were now, alone finally, making their way to Pemberley. When Darcy had announced that business had called him home with some urgency, it produced no small measure of alarm in his wife. Elizabeth pressed him on the matter, fearing this urgent business might take him away from her, but as he looked at her, she saw a rush of guilt colouring his cheeks. When he relayed the sad news to Mrs Bennet, her suspicions were confirmed on seeing a slight twinge at his temples as he explained the matter. He was engaged in a ruse, of that she was certain, and fully appreciating her husband's desire to leave, Elizabeth joined in his apologies and feelings of desolation at having to depart so soon. Both made a sufficient show of their grief to satisfy Mrs Bennet, and provide her with a scene of feeling and emotion to retell to anyone foolish enough to beg of the lady an account of the day.

Though she would feel keenly the absence of her sister Jane's company; in truth, Elizabeth too was glad to quit Longbourn, as Darcy's forbearance with her mother had long been strained and she feared continued marital felicity required at least fifty miles between her new husband and his mother-in-law.

ℰℴ

"You smile rather curiously, madam; might I enquire what amuses you?"

"Oh, nothing of great importance, husband. I am simply wondering how long it will be before we receive a letter from Mama inviting herself to Pemberley!"

Darcy's face fell at the thought of too soon a renewal of Mrs Bennet's company; the last fortnight had been such a trial on his patience and sense of decorum, the only light being his hope that once at Pemberley he would be free from her silliness for at least a twelfth-month.

Upon seeing his expression alter, Elizabeth began to laugh.

"That is a cruel sort of amusement, wife. Have I been so misled as to your character? How could you find such delight in teasing me?"

"Oh, my darling Fitzwilliam, you are too unaccustomed to laughing at yourself, therefore I must do it for you. It is good for the soul to laugh and I warned you before we married that I dearly love to. However, out of wifely deference, I shall limit myself to one laugh a day at your expense. You should thank me, therefore, for fulfilling my duty so early today."

Darcy, distracted by Elizabeth's laughter, could make no reply, and simply sat, mesmerised by her. She was the only person from whom he could accept such teasing; indeed, she was the only person that could have made such teasing not merely tolerable, but pleasurable. He watched as she fussed about in her seat, plumping cushions and spinning her feet. Although her eyes had first drawn him to her, he knew now her smile and the gentle mocking tone she used with him made equal claims on his affections. These happy reflections drew from him a need to be closer to her, the space between their seats suddenly a distance too great to be borne. Desire provoking his actions, he took hold of her arm and pulled her across onto the seat beside him. The surprise of finding herself so suddenly upended caused Elizabeth to laugh again. Her laughter faded, however, as Darcy pulled her to him, her next tease caught in her throat as he gazed into her face. By the time he kissed her, she had completely forgotten what had ever amused her at all.

℘

The journey to Pemberley was to be broken by overnight stays along the route, so as not to unduly exert the new Mrs Darcy, and by the time they reached the first inn, Elizabeth was gladdened by the thought of a rest from the carriage. As expected, the Darcy name ensured them immediate attention and before she had even acquainted herself with her room, Elizabeth was taken to a private bath and left with assurances that her trunks would be unpacked, and her evening clothes ready when she had freshened from the day's travelling. She eased herself into the steaming water, and every muscle that had been stiffened by the exertions of the last few days began to relax. She sighed to the room as her body rested and her mind quieted.

Elizabeth was unsure how long she had lain there. At some juncture, hot water had been added, and when she finally opened her eyes and drew herself out of the water she wondered how Darcy would love her – wrinkled as she was! Her maid opened the door to her bedchamber, which was the adjoining room. Everything she needed for her toilette had been laid out on the small dresser and vanity that sat in the corner by the window. A fire blazed in the hearth, and large bouquets of flowers fragranced the air. Elizabeth stood, exhausted, relieved not to be in the carriage, and uncertain as to what to do next. Convinced no good could come of simply standing there, she climbed onto the bed, determining that five minutes quiet rest might clear her head.

It was several hours before Elizabeth awoke. The bedchamber's curtains had been drawn, and the fire was the only light in the room. Before she had a chance to move and make her waking known, she spied Darcy sitting in one of the armchairs. By the light of the fire, he held a necklace aloft, considering the warmth and depth of the ruby at its centre.

"Fitzwilliam," she said softly so as not to startle him.

He turned to her, a wide smile on his face.

"So, you are awake. I thought you might never stir. Do you find being my wife so tiresome already?"

"You are exhausting, it is true! I had not supposed a man so used to travel would require such constant distraction on a journey. It seems you are quite unequal to making your own entertainment."

"Indeed, wife, I own I have never known myself to be so

agitated, I hope amusing me does not place too great a burden upon you."

"I bear up exceedingly well," she continued. "Still, as recompense, you may present me with the beautiful necklace you seek to shield behind your leg."

"Good Lord, woman! Can I hide nothing from you? This was to be a surprise, something for you to wear at dinner, but dinner was served some time ago; perhaps I ought to simply save it for another occasion."

"Well I have yet to eat," Elizabeth replied, suddenly aware of a gnawing hunger, "and I am famished. I see a tray there, might I have that?"

"Certainly, I called for it for that very purpose; the landlady recommended the sweet tart as a local speciality."

"Well, as I am being treated to a local speciality, I believe this is more than just a simple tray, surely this is something special," she smiled, her hand outstretched, "and so I am dining – my necklace, sir!"

Darcy laughed at the temerity of his new wife.

"I am your servant," he replied, and affecting a crisp bow, moved to her.

As Elizabeth lifted her hair, one side of the gown she wore slipped down, revealing a smooth white shoulder.

Darcy stared at the loosened material as he tried to fasten the necklace, though with the distraction, he fumbled the clasp. He could feel the heat of Elizabeth's body, and his hands lingered over her neck and shoulders as he smoothed the necklace into position. Watching the rise and fall of her chest just below his hands filled Darcy with an unanticipated lust, and before he could take control of himself, he moved his hand beneath her gown and cupped her breast. This move, both swift and unexpected, had the unpleasant effect of causing Elizabeth to cry out in alarm.

Darcy was mortified and at once moved off the bed. As Elizabeth turned to face him, he read the shock in her face and feared his hasty advance had been as unwanted as it was ill received. The sight of her repositioning her gown as she tried to steady her breathing added to his discomposure, and he stumbled out of the room, apologising; begging his wife's forgiveness. The look on her face would not soon be forgotten. He had accosted her, moved only by a need for his own satisfaction. He feared he would struggle to repair the damage his actions had caused. Cursing his rashness, he settled into his own cold, dark room – in expectation of sharing a bed with Elizabeth, he had ordered the fire not to be lit.

℘

Left alone in her room, Elizabeth took but moments to recover, although Darcy was already gone. His touch had not been as unwelcomed as he supposed; it was merely the surprise of it. Elizabeth had for some time been contemplating what becoming Mrs Darcy would mean and though she often considered how she would have to manage a great house, and head charitable concerns, her thoughts invariably turned to the more personal aspects of her life with Darcy, and their upcoming intimacy was often forefront in her mind.

Indeed, she had discovered that since their meeting unexpectedly at Pemberley, where he had shown such civility to her and the Gardiners, and had begged permission to introduce her to his sister, her thoughts in his regard had become altogether pleasant. In the quiet moments afforded her in the wake of her younger sister Lydia's imprudent decamping from Brighton, she often found herself considering Darcy and where once she had recoiled at the thought of attention from him she was, by degrees, increasingly warmed by it, though in the same moment saddened by the realisation it could no longer come to pass. Lydia's ruin would be shared by them all.

This warmth of feeling was enflamed by her discovery of the role he played in Lydia's – indeed in her family's – redemption, and by the time he attended at Longbourn with Charles Bingley, her feelings for him were so altered she could scarcely recall a time when she had not loved Fitzwilliam Darcy.

Still, it was not until he declared his feelings for her were unaltered, that she truly allowed herself to hope for a future with the man. Mrs Bennet's insistence that she distract him so he could not interfere with the courtship of Jane and Charles Bingley had been a source of great amusement to them both. Grateful for the opportunity to be alone with one another, she agreed to walk with Darcy on every occasion he visited with his friend. Though his comportment throughout was beyond reproach, Elizabeth found the sensations that his mere closeness inspired, new and exhilarating. There was an intimacy to his tone and touch that pulsed through her, and she found herself wondering what it would feel like to kiss the mouth that so softly addressed her, and how those hands that so gently brushed her own as they walked would feel when touching her with greater purpose and vigour. As their wedding day approached, and they were at greater liberty to spend time with one another, she marvelled at her increased desire to know the man intimately, to know the feeling of his body against hers, the feeling of his hands on her skin.

With no experience of her own to draw upon, Elizabeth was forced to look for guidance elsewhere. She tried to attend to the lectures she received on the duties of a wife, but in these dry sermons on expectation and duty, she found little to illuminate the passion Darcy inspired within her. Now she wondered whether it was possible that somewhere amidst her ramblings, Mrs Bennet had hinted at moments such as this. Sitting alone in a strange inn, Elizabeth, for the first time, wished she had more closely heeded her mother!

Her first thought was to find Darcy, but she would not call a servant nor could she wander the corridors of the inn knocking on doors; he would not thank her for such humiliation. Indeed, she was not altogether sure he would wish to return to her. She recalled the look on his face as he left: she had embarrassed him. He had sought to be with her, and she had refused him. She reddened as she remembered the childish way in which she had reacted to his advances.

"Foolish, foolish girl," she admonished, catching her reflection in the mirror, "what will he think of you now?"

The next morning, Elizabeth was woken by the sounds of a housemaid cleaning out the grate.

On seeing the lady awake, the housemaid stood, dipped a hurried curtsey, and left to call for a tray.

After a breakfast that brought little enjoyment, Elizabeth was contemplating getting dressed when Darcy knocked and begged admittance. The sight of the necklace still around her neck gave him pause and he stared at the ground.

"Elizabeth," he began, uncertain of how to proceed, "with regards to last night and my behaviour…"

"Oh Fitzwilliam, I am so ashamed of how I reacted," Elizabeth quickly interjected. "What must you think of me? I was surprised by the suddenness, a little startled was all, so silly of me to gasp and carry on as I did."

"My darling," he continued, his shoulders relaxing and his eyes rising to meet hers, "you cannot imagine how I suffered last night. I could only torture myself with what you must have thought of me; such behaviour, forcing myself on you as I did. I beg your forgiveness."

"Forcing yourself on me! Husband, you did nothing of the sort. Indeed, had you stayed but a minute longer you would have seen a gratifying alteration in my reaction. I have long thought upon the feeling of your hands pressed so intimately upon my skin; why it should have startled me when it finally happened I cannot guess, but I can assure you, your advances will not be met with such rejection again. That is if you can forgive my foolishness."

"Elizabeth," he replied, his relief evident, "what a pair we make."

"Indeed, Fitzwilliam," she said quietly, standing by him, stroking her fingers across his forehead and cheeks, "what a pair; each miserable in our own rooms, each tormenting ourselves we had wronged the other, and each entirely mistaken as to the truth of the matter."

Darcy tilted Elizabeth's face to his and looked into her eyes.

He had feared seeing reproach, but there was no trace of disapproval to be seen. He sighed, grateful at finding her so welcoming. Encouraged by her speech, he moved once more to touch her, though with more restraint than before. As they kissed, he allowed his hands to trail along her neck, feeling her body react to his touch. Slowly, so as not to alarm, he trailed the length of her back down to her buttocks, exploring the contours of her body through the linen of her gown.

Without a word, Elizabeth reached round for his hand, and moved it to take hold of her breast. As he gently squeezed her flesh, Elizabeth was lost in the sensation of him.

It was some time before she could draw back from his caress, and he seemed intent on refusing to release hold of her body, but with one hand out to distance him, and the other engaged in steadying herself, she finally broke free.

Before Darcy could object, Elizabeth began to undo her linen nightdress, and in the work of a moment, she stood before him resplendent. She moved across the room and onto the bed, and when there, returned her attention to her husband, holding a hand out to him, inviting him to join her. Mirroring her movements, he walked to the bed, where without a word, he began to remove the layers of clothing now proving to be the only barrier between them.

೮

Elizabeth was convinced that she and Darcy would not be truly comfortable until they were settled at Pemberley, and consequently approached with the idea of their forgoing the planned overnight stay at a second inn, suggesting they simply stop long enough to secure food and a change of horses. "After all, my love, we will do better at home, I feel."

Darcy, mindful for her welfare, countered, "But what of you, my love? You will feel the weariness of such a journey most keenly."

"Is this how our marriage is to be, Fitzwilliam?" replied Elizabeth, her hands set squarely on her hips, her gaze holding fast with his. "Are you to inform me as to how I shall feel, or might I be allowed to decide on such matters myself?"

There was a laugh in her voice, but Darcy recognised the seriousness of the challenge behind it. "No Lizzy, of course you must be your own mistress, as you have always been."

ഇ

The remainder of the journey was largely uneventful with Elizabeth chiefly concerned in concealing from Darcy how fully she regretted not spending the second night at an inn as he suggested. Her endurance of the aching she felt in her body was strengthened only by her resolve not to afford Darcy the victory of knowing what was best for her, even if in this instance, it appeared he had. The final approach to their new home at least provided some distraction, as Elizabeth was full of questions on Derbyshire, Lambton, and the Pemberley estate. Darcy was pleased she took such an interest in the area; however, as the carriage made its final turn onto their estate, she fell quiet.

"It will be well, my love," he reassured her. "You have seen the house, and they are not all strangers to you there."

"But when I was last at Pemberley, it was as a visitor. To return now as its mistress is quite another matter and I am daunted."

Elizabeth dropped her head, unhappy at faltering before her husband.

"My dearest Lizzy, look at me; I have lived at Pemberley my entire life and am, on occasion, overwhelmed by all it entails. You care about what Pemberley means to me, what it means for you and for society here, and that is enough. You will be mistress of this house, and you will conquer it as surely as you have conquered me.'

"Against all will and against all reason, my darling?" Elizabeth teased, looking up at him once more and smiling.

ഇ

With Elizabeth's spirits clearly revived, Darcy relaxed, though before leaving the carriage, he offered, "Know all I want, all everyone here wants, is for you to be happy. Ask for anything and you will have it. Pemberley pleased you as a house; now let it please you as a home."

He stepped from the carriage, and unwilling to relinquish her touch for even a moment, helped her down and walked towards the rows of waiting servants. Concerned her earlier fears might yet weigh upon her, he sought to ease her past the crowd that had gathered to greet them. The entire staff had turned out, as well as many from the village, for a look at the new mistress of Pemberley. Young girls curtsied, and there were cheers of welcome from the Lambton townsfolk. The house staff were pleasant and orderly, under strict instructions from Mrs Reynolds, although many of the under maids whispered, the new mistress did not look quite so frightening a prospect as Miss Caroline Bingley, whom they had greatly feared might one day succeed in overcoming their master's resistance and good sense to become his wife.

However, Elizabeth would not be led away so easily. Knowing these were to be the people of her everyday acquaintance, she was determined that their first impression of her should be a good one. Darcy's concerns for her were quickly allayed as her open manner and easy charm instantly recommended her to the good opinion of all there. Once she had given attention to the townsfolk, praised Lambton, and smiled at the under maids, it was assured she was the firm favourite of all those gathered.

By the time the couple had bid hello to the staff, gratefully received the congratulations afforded them, and had made their way into the hall, it was a certainty. No groom was ever more handsome, no bride ever more beautiful, and no couple ever more deserving of health and happiness than the new master and mistress of Pemberley: Fitzwilliam and Elizabeth Darcy.

CHAPTER 2

The next morning, Darcy drew back the heavy curtain to bathe the still sleeping Elizabeth in early morning light. The room was warm so she had cast off her covers and lay wearing only her shift. The sensible linen garment, a gift from her mother, was doubtless designed not to enflame a husband's ardour, but Mrs Bennet had not taken due consideration of two important things: the ability of sunlight to elicit form from under linen, and the intensity of Mr Darcy's ardour.

"Mrs Darcy," he whispered to Elizabeth, "Mrs Darcy..."

"Yes, Mr Darcy," she replied sleepily.

"You look uncomfortable; can I help you in any way?"

"Uncomfortable? How could I be uncomfortable?"

"Well, your night attire looks a little tight about the throat. Should I perhaps loosen it?"

With a smile perceptible on Elizabeth's face, Darcy reached across and carefully undid the top button of his wife's shift.

"Better, my love?"

"Much."

"Good, for I was concerned."

"For my comfort?"

"Yes. In fact I do not believe one button will be enough; ought I loosen another?"

A third and fourth button followed until the shift fell open to reveal the swell of Elizabeth's breast, who now fully awake smiled at her husband's tender fascination.

"Elizabeth, my love, are you fully recovered from the exertion of travel and of settling here?"

"Indeed husband; fully recovered."

He responded with a kiss, gentle at first, tilting her face to his and laying soft sweet kisses along her cheeks and lips. Then teasing her lips with his tongue, he opened her mouth, kissing her deeply and with greater passion. He pulled her to him and Elizabeth gasped as her body naturally responded to him, her back arched pushing her harder against his chest. Darcy moved, cupping a breast with his hand and running his thumb across her nipple. Now keenly aware of Elizabeth's reactions, he watched and responded to every movement. When she stretched her neck, he kissed it, and trailed it with his tongue. When her fingers brushed across her breast, he licked and gently sucked where her fingers had been. He had dreamed of her like this, hoped she would respond to his passion with passion of her own, and the reality was proving more than he had hoped for. She was warm and inviting, nervous and uncertain to be sure, but most importantly, she was his.

"This cannot be right," Elizabeth murmured.

Darcy drew back, concerned, "Is something the matter? Have I hurt you?"

"No my darling," she laughed, a little giddy from his attentions, "it is…well…it is just this is not what Mama told me to expect."

Relieved, Darcy smiled. "Lizzy, my dear, this is no time to talk about your mother!"

∽

Darcy lay on the chaise soaking up the early morning sunshine. He had been determined that Elizabeth would be entirely his for as long as possible, and had given instructions to the staff accordingly. As a result, he and Elizabeth took a bath only when the bath was filled and their robes laid out; their meals were set out as they bathed or dressed; their room was tended to while they bathed or ate, and Elizabeth's personal maid had been told not to disturb them until she was called for. The couple had a bedchamber comprised of three adjoining rooms: the bedroom, a private bathroom, and a breakfast room, and for the first two weeks at Pemberley, these were the only rooms occupied by them.

Elizabeth saw no one but Darcy, and although she enjoyed it, she was aware such seclusion could not last. Darcy would have business to conduct and she would have to adjust to her new position as Mrs Fitzwilliam Darcy. More importantly, Georgiana was to join them and it would not do to continue to indulge such selfish isolation. It was for this reason she broke her husband's silent morning reverie with the question, "Are we to venture out into the world today, my darling? Or are you so assured I shall embarrass you that you wish to hide me here forever?"

"You begin your teasing very early, madam. Am I no longer enough of a diversion for you?"

"Oh, you are excessively diverting, darling, but I shall be thought wanton if I do not emerge from this room, and if you continue to neglect your duties, I fear Lady Catherine's prediction that I would ruin the family might prove founded!"

Darcy moved to the bed to be closer to her. "My dear, if you were in any way concerned by the opinions of my aunt, we would not be sitting here. I just wanted you to myself, Elizabeth; tell me, was I unreasonable? When we leave this room, there will be a hundred things that will call upon your attention and take you from me. Was I selfish?"

"Selfish indeed, but I shall not fault you for it. I realise too, that when we leave there will be a hundred things that will call your attention away from me, but that is as it should be, for we cannot be too lost in ourselves. Besides, if you are always about me how can I bemoan your absence, and if you do not leave me, how can I anticipate your return?"

℘

Although Darcy accepted that Elizabeth was correct, he was not willing to forgo her company immediately. Instead, he proposed that in order to protect her reputation, and ensure his estate was not falling to ruins in his absence, they would venture out into the world together. Elizabeth would need to become better acquainted with their lands and the surrounding areas, their tenants and the houses that relied on them. Darcy would conduct the tour himself, ensuring her education and his pleasure.

Elizabeth, who had been as unenthusiastic for their separation as Darcy, had readily agreed. Although, by half past eleven, they decided that they had already lost too much of the day, and so determined it would be best if their adventure began the following morning, leaving them forced to tolerate one more day of delicious seclusion wrapped up solely in one another, without distraction.

℘

The following morning saw the Darcys rise early, keen to take advantage of the good weather for their tour of Pemberley. As the estate was vast, Darcy suggested a phaeton would be the most suitable means of travelling; assuring Elizabeth there would be ample opportunity for walking, particularly around some of the beauty spots. As Darcy had not determined how long their excursion was to be, Mrs Reynolds – the estate's long-time housekeeper – had the foresight to order a picnic lunch so they need not be forced by hunger to return too soon. Darcy thanked her for the excellent thought, and set off in high spirits for what the day would bring.

"Tell me about growing up here, Darcy," Elizabeth began, once the horses had settled into the easy rhythm of a gentle trot. "Did you play in that copse on the left of us? Did you climb those trees?"

"I did not play, as you so gently put it, in that copse," he replied with derision. "I fought great battles there! It was no mere game. Cousin Richard and I spent an entire summer defending that patch from invaders; it was exhausting and brutal!"

"Exhausting and brutal? Good Lord! And pray, husband, who were the invaders you so bravely fought off?"

He smiled as he responded, "I believe it was an army comprised of three bears, a china doll, and a cavalry."

"A cavalry?"

"Yes, we dragged the old rocking horse from the nursery – nurse was furious of course, the damage we did pulling it across the grounds. Still, Richard felt it only proper that we would have to best a cavalry to claim victory truly as our own. Even then, he was set to be a military man; you should have seen the strategies he devised."

Elizabeth laughed at the thought of a young Darcy romping about the grounds they now toured, dirty and battle hardened. As he told tales of boyhood adventures, she was surprised by the carefree child he described, and wondered, not for the first time, if it was the death of his mother, and later, his father, that inspired the solemnity and seriousness he was so often associated with now.

As they approached a small group of cottages, Darcy slowed so Elizabeth might be introduced to any of their tenants that were at home. Not satisfied with simply waving from a height, Elizabeth was soon out of the phaeton and paying a call on the women and children. She gratefully received the congratulations of all, and on hearing that it had at one time been a tradition to celebrate the marriage of a master with a peasant's ball, she assured such a wonderful tradition would be maintained and she would speak to her husband directly.

"You mentioned nothing of a peasant's ball to me, husband," she began when she took her place by him once more. "What is this tradition?"

"Oh, it is nothing. I believe my great-great grandfather initiated the organising of a large party for the staff and tenants of the estate to celebrate family occasions, such as marriages and births. It was not something I wished to burden you with, Elizabeth; there has not been one in years and I doubted many would even remember."

"Fitzwilliam, my love, surely the purpose of a tradition is that it is repeated and remembered! Good Lord, what must everyone think? I take it you have no objections to the party beyond the burden that will fall upon me and you would not mind if I asked Mrs Reynolds to help in handling the arrangements?"

Although she had asked whether her husband had any objections, before he could voice his assent, Elizabeth was already making suggestions as to where the party would best be set up, and asking where they might secure a small band. Darcy sat back in his seat and allowed her to excitedly talk through plans and pose questions, delighted at how wholeheartedly she was embracing her role as mistress of Pemberley.

"Well, we can make no further plans until I talk to Mrs Reynolds," said Elizabeth, finally drawing breath. "She will, I am sure, be the best placed to help with the details of the thing. Lord, when I think the best that Hill and our servants could hope for was a bowl of punch in celebration."

As she finished, she looked from her husband, who had been the sole focus of her attention for a full quarter-hour, to the place where they had stopped.

"Fitzwilliam, it is beautiful!" was all she could manage on seeing the secluded spot before her.

Darcy, pleased by her reaction, stepped down from the phaeton and led her towards the rose garden that had been his mother's. The garden was perfectly situated between a small wood and a wide, open field; the trees on one side offering shelter from the worst of the wind, and the open space on the other ensuring the flowers always had light. The garden was enclosed by a wall of large grey stones built up about waist high, with a small gate. There appeared little order to the manner in which the planting had taken place, although each bush was allowed sufficient room to grow large and full, without being crowded or overshadowed by its neighbour. A sea of large full red blooms spread out before Elizabeth and Darcy as a vibrant offset to the pale silver bark of the birch behind them, and in front of them, the green of the field with its small delicate spots of yellow and purple wildflowers.

"This was my mother's private garden; she planted and tended it herself growing only red roses. During my father's time, there were no plans to farm this area and there were no cottages nearby, so she could find solitude for a time here when she needed it. When she told my father of her plans to grow her own garden so far from the house, he resisted, but as in all things, he succumbed to her gentle persuasion. When he saw the great joy it brought her, he determined the land would never be used for any purpose that did not suit my mother, and so it has remained until now. After my mother's death, the only people to visit this part of the estate were the gardeners, who maintained the garden as my mother had, and my father. In those early days after her death, he grieved, and…well…he would…that is…we would often find him here…"

Darcy fell silent. Elizabeth, moved by the intimacy of what he was sharing with her, felt for once unequal to the task of conversation, but the gentle squeeze she gave his hand and the tender attention she gave his every word told him she understood.

"I often laughed at the villager's talk of the ghosts that must haunt Pemberley, scaring children with imagined tales of phantoms stalking the halls of the great house, but there have been times I would swear this place is haunted. Even now, there is a small part of me that fancies I might yet see my mother here among these flowers."

He fell quiet again, lost in memory, so Elizabeth offered, "Did you share this garden with her, Fitzwilliam?"

"Not as I should. I was such a young boy and not designed to tend flowers. I was more interested in battle and adventure, and my mother could not have hoped to draw my attention with planting and pruning. If I could but have appreciated how important those hours were when she brought me here; if I could but have known how later I would wish for that time again."

Darcy withdrew from her, the sting of old wounds, and the sudden rush of long ignored feelings of loss and grief calling his attention away.

"Such sombre recollections!" he laughed at length, shaking himself free of the past and half looking at his wife, "I had not meant for this to be such a maudlin affair; forgive me."

"Are you embarrassed, Fitzwilliam? Why do you hide your face from me?"

Darcy drew back his shoulders and stood straight and tall. "Such a mawkish display; what must you think?"

"I think, Fitzwilliam," Elizabeth responded, taking his hands in hers, "there is no shame in love, and certainly no shame in the remembrance of a loved one, but the remembrance need not sadden. I would wish for you a happy memory here, no grieving father and lost mother. Might you remember a time of joy here to replace the sadness?"

"I believe I might," he smiled, the half-forgotten recollections of sunny days and his mother laughing as he darted about her flowers now coming to the fore, banishing feelings of sadness and the memory of a stricken father lying prone among the bushes, the earth swallowing the sounds of his grief.

"Yes, I believe I might be able to do just that..." he continued "but, now! I have been self-indulgent enough for one day. We must turn our attention to far more pleasing matters, to the reason I brought you here. It is my intention to offer this garden to you as a wedding present, a small part of Pemberley that is yours and yours alone. You can make of it what you will, replant or alter however you see fit, although I would ask that the first rose bush my mother planted be allowed to remain untouched by any changes."

After all that had been shared, this was the last thing Elizabeth expected, and so moved was she by the generosity and true feeling of the gift, it was some minutes before she could reply.

"My darling, is there no end to the ways in which you will surprise me? I could not have imagined such a perfect spot as this in all the world, let alone in our home. That you would trust me with it is beyond expectation. There are but two alterations I would make, and that is the inclusion of a seat in the shade over there and your promise you will share it with me."

ℰℱ

As arranged, Georgiana Darcy arrived at Pemberley a month after the married couple. She attended the wedding and then, in order to provide the newlyweds a measure of privacy, had gone to their house in London's Grosvenor Square. Her journey to join them in the country, however, had been fraught with concern, not with the journey itself, but with what she was to encounter once she returned to Pemberley.

Georgiana had found Elizabeth quite wonderful when they met. Her brother had such regard and admiration for her that she was certain they should be friends and that Pemberley would be as much her home as it ever had been, but during her time in London, Caroline Bingley warned her that changes must be expected. Elizabeth was no longer a guest at Pemberley, but its mistress and would have things arranged in her particular way. Caroline, out of concern for her dear friend, felt it necessary to remind Georgiana – often – that she would likely no longer find herself at liberty as she had been in the past.

Georgiana ventured to suggest that she did not believe her demands too excessive: time to play her music and the pleasure of some friendly society were all she really craved. Caroline immediately assured she did not mean to imply Georgiana was in any way demanding, but that they must both accept that life at Pemberley would forever be altered by the admission of this relative stranger into their circle.

"I shall, of course, endeavour to protect you from the worst excesses of the new mistresses' changes and you must share with me the details of all goings on," Caroline offered sympathetically. "Indeed, we must work together to ensure Pemberley remains the happy home we have both become accustomed to. Do you not agree?"

Georgiana's unwavering trust in her brother would not allow

her to even imagine she would need to apply to Caroline for protection from any attack on her liberty at home, but certain her companion's interests were well meant, she agreed to remember Caroline's kind words.

So, it was with a head filled by imagined threats, and a heart filled with apprehension that Georgiana stepped from the carriage to be greeted by Elizabeth with a warm smile and open arms.

"At last; we have all been waiting for you," called out Elizabeth upon seeing her sister-in-law descending the carriage steps.

Georgiana, afraid she had delayed everyone, began an apology, regretted her late start, and begged forgiveness for any inconvenience caused.

"Nonsense! There has been no inconvenience; it was simply our excitement at your arrival that plagued us. You have been missed."

Georgiana was gratified by the welcome and smiled meekly. "I would not wish to be a burden, but I own I have been anticipating my visit."

"A burden? You could never be a burden. Now come inside, I hope you will not find your home too much altered."

They stepped into the hall and at once Georgiana saw the ways Pemberley had been changed: there were large vases of flowers adding fragrance and colour to the entryway, and some of the paintings had been moved. Dark family portraits were replaced by light landscapes depicting Pemberley, Lambton, and the surrounding area. In the centre, in a place of prominence, hung Georgiana's own portrait.

"Oh, my!" she exclaimed on seeing it.

"I do hope you will not object. It is such a wonderful portrait and I thought the light in here suited it so delightfully."

"But people will see it once they enter the house and what will they think, but how terribly proud I must be?" whispered Georgiana, fretfully.

"People will think as I do; it is a wonderful painting. It is best suited to hanging here, and despite all its charms, it does not quite do you justice. Now, will you not deny me this little indulgence? I could not bear to rehang the painting of your great aunt."

Georgiana stood enthralled by Elizabeth. She was beginning to sense a little of what had drawn her brother so completely to his new wife. There was something in her manner, beyond charm and ease, and although she could not explain it, it seemed that Elizabeth's magic was just as effective on her, for she simply could not say no.

Darcy was as surprised as Georgiana by her acquiescence. He had assured Elizabeth, his sister would not countenance the portrait being such a prominent feature and yet when he joined them for lunch, the portrait was still there, and Georgiana, with unusual animation, was declaring she could only agree to its remaining in the hall if Elizabeth was certain no better place could be found.

He sat during lunch watching the two women he loved most dearly in the world as they chatted and laughed, as though they had known each other a lifetime. Georgiana joined Elizabeth in the conversation, and was full of observations from her weeks in London. Whenever timidity or uncertainty seemed to cloud her thoughts, Elizabeth was reassuring and interested, posing questions or interjecting with stories of her own, ensuring the easy flow of conversation. Darcy had never seen Georgiana so comfortable in society; he thought he could not love Elizabeth more, but on seeing the transformation she was effecting in his sister, he felt his heart would burst for the limitless talents of this women.

"You amaze me," he sighed. Meaning the comment only for himself, he was disconcerted when both women stopped talking and turned their attention to him.

Embarrassed by his public display, he added, "You amaze me, ladies, in the way you succeed in filling a full half-hour with talk of nothing!"

He instantly regretted his barb, as Georgiana's face fell. A blush spread across her cheeks and her lips tightened, all ease and lightness gone.

Elizabeth merely arched a brow and countered, "And yet

there you sat for the same half-hour fully engrossed by such nothingness! Should I call for the paper if we bore you?"

Georgiana raised her eyes a little on hearing this and Darcy thought he could discern the hint of a smile.

"I can assure I was not as engrossed as you might suppose. What interest can I have in the latest sleeve lengths, in Mrs Turlington's new terrier or whether Mr Romane's ices surpass Mr Burdock's?"

Elizabeth smiled impudently, and responded, "For a man with little interest, you display excellent recall, Fitzwilliam!" before turning her attention back to Georgiana and carrying on as before.

ఈం

After lunch, Darcy and Elizabeth stood alone in Georgiana's music room while she went to retrieve some new pages she wished to play for them.

"Thank you for your intervention earlier," he stated, the earnestness in his voice causing Elizabeth to turn to face him. "It was a foolish thing to say. I did not mean it, and I could see Georgiana immediately withdrawing. I would not hurt her for the world."

"Fitzwilliam, you worry too much; she is well. A minor setback, but we recovered admirably. Georgiana ought to become more accustomed to the world; we must bring her out into it. You cannot hope to always protect her from unpleasantness, but we can show her every slight need not wound too greatly, and that she need not sit defenceless."

"You would teach my sister to be as outspoken as you?" Darcy posed, somewhat incredulously.

"That, my darling, is beyond even my abilities, but I will encourage her confidence. I assure you, if we can persuade Georgiana to look straight and bold into the face of any foe, with her share of the Darcy countenance she need never utter a word to silence them."

CHAPTER 3

The household quickly fell into a routine, with Darcy up before either Elizabeth or Georgiana so he could attend to estate business. The two women were left to breakfast alone. Elizabeth used this time to draw out her sister-in-law, engaging her with planning the peasants' ball. Georgiana was hesitant, but Elizabeth's openness overcame her reserve, and with preparations for a party to focus on, the pair were soon more comfortable with one another than either had thought likely for so short an acquaintance. Georgiana, it emerged, had a talent for design, and she was delighted when the drawings she produced for table displays and flower arrangements were readily taken up. Though at first she thought the use of her ideas due to sisterly affection, she was gratified to overhear Elizabeth sincerely praising her to Darcy.

It was decided the ball was to be held within a week of Georgiana's arrival, to take advantage of the unseasonably good weather, warm evenings, and clear skies. The lawn was to be laid out for a picnic; there would be large blankets and banks of cushions for groups to come together and sit, set out around three large tables, which would be piled high with fruits, meats, and sweet treats. Mrs Reynolds had consulted with cook, and a variety of dishes were already being planned and prepared: the crowning glory of which would be a rich fruit cake, known to be cook's speciality.

Elizabeth and Georgiana were so distracted with arrangements for musicians, table decorations, and games to engage the children that neither could quite believe when the week was up and the day of the ball before them.

"Do you think all will be ready by this evening, Fitzwilliam?" Elizabeth asked of her husband that afternoon. "We have only a matter of hours. Can everything possibly be in readiness when it must be?"

"Lord, Elizabeth, I had not imagined you would take so much care for a peasants' ball. I am sure all will be well; you have everything running with a military precision even cousin Richard might envy!"

"Must you tease me even now when my nerves are so rattled?" an exasperated Elizabeth cried out, swatting at Darcy.

"Yes, I must. You have been so seriously engaged in these preparations that I am afraid you have forgotten the importance of laughing at yourself! So, as you kindly once did for me, I must do it for you," he teased in reply, gently flicking at the papers she shuffled in her final check of all preparations.

Putting the pages down, Elizabeth smiled at Darcy. "I suppose I have only myself to blame, then; I have been too good an example to you. I see the error of my ways, sir, and will right myself accordingly."

Darcy pulled her to him and kissed her, his fingertips tracing her lips as he released his kiss long enough to say, "If you have ever loved me, Lizzy, never change."

୧୦

As soon as she was at liberty, Elizabeth joined Mrs Reynolds and Georgiana in the garden to oversee the progress of the work there. Despite Elizabeth's certainty that not all could be done in the few short hours left to them, Georgiana had the great pleasure of assuring her that, in fact, all was ready. The musicians were on hand, and in good spirits, as cook had seen fit to provide them a small feast of their own to ensure them strength enough to play all night. The food was ready, waiting only to be laid out when wanted. Indeed, for all her concern, there was nothing left for Elizabeth to do, but dress for the evening.

Although the main of the plans for the evening had been undertaken by Elizabeth, she felt it necessary to consult with Darcy as to how he would have seating arranged for Georgiana and themselves. She had a small table in readiness should he desire it, but was happy when he agreed no separate table be set up, they must of course enjoy the picnic with their guests on blankets and cushions.

"Husband, I could not have imagined the Fitzwilliam Darcy I first met at a ball in Hertfordshire would ever deign to throw a party such as this, and to join his servants and tenants in so informal a manner. I have known for some time that my initial prejudices against you were unfounded, but to have been so misled as to your nature, well it unsettles me. I have always prided myself on being a good judge of character, how is it then that when I needed it most, my good judgement failed me so completely?"

"You were not as mistaken as you suppose, my love. Before I met you, I had lost my way; I was in very real danger of allowing priggishness and conceit to mould me into a man I ought never to have been. Your challenging of me – indeed, even your rejection of me – forced a self-examination I was not accustomed to. I am a proud man, Elizabeth; I thought I regulated that pride through good sense and reason, though I see now I was not always successful. Your good influence will, I believe, help me to be better. Still, here among those I have known my whole life, I was always most at ease, and even without your influence I would have always been comfortable breaking bread." Finishing with a low bow, he smiled at her. "Now what do you say to joining me outside, Lizzy, for an evening I am certain none of us will soon forget!"

ℭ

By the time the family had joined their guests downstairs, most of those due to attend were already gathered, and there was a great cheer when Darcy and Elizabeth stepped on to the lawn. Darcy thought it necessary he mark the occasion with a speech, but on seeing how eagerly the children were gathered, anticipating a beginning to the evening's sport, he settled for a few simple sentiments.

"Thank you all for your warm reception. Mrs Darcy and I are pleased you could join with us in celebrating our marriage. You will be grateful to know, I will not bore you with long speeches. Mrs Henderson has created a feast and we should not delay the pleasure of it a minute more. All I ask is that you join me in welcoming your new mistress: my wife, Mrs Elizabeth Darcy."

The garden resounded with cries of celebration and congratulations to the new Mrs Darcy, and the evening began with glasses raised high for the health and prosperity of the happy couple.

℘

In all her planning and preparation for the evening, Elizabeth had given little thought as to how she would fare for so many hours with the people who in daily life tended upon her needs, and ensured the continuity of both the great house and the estate, and she was struck by the sheer number of people in attendance.

"Fitzwilliam, do all the people here work on the estate or have we invited others from the village?"

Darcy gave the crowd a cursory glance before responding. "Not everyone is here, to be sure, but most of the staff and tenants are. All those about you work for us or farm the estate. Why?"

"I had not realised it to be so many, that is all. How is it we can need so many servants for a family of three?"

"It is my great hope, Elizabeth, that our family will be increased before long," he replied, gently stroking the curve of her hip, and smiling playfully. "Besides, it is not the family that requires such assiduous attention, but the house and estate, unless you have a sudden desire to learn the minutiae of grate cleaning, silver polish, animal rearing, or crop growing."

"There are some mysteries in life, Fitzwilliam, I am content never to unravel, and the secret to a perfect polish is one of them!" she jibed before turning her attention back to their guests, and to the need for the second ham to be brought out.

The early evening passed with unprecedented success. There was music, food, and entertainment enough to ensure the satisfaction of all. As the night began to draw in, large torches were lit to lighten and warm the garden. Many of the younger children, exhausted by excitement, slept wrapped tightly in blankets, cradled by those too old to join in the dancing. Darcy and Elizabeth opened the evening's chief entertainment by leading the first dance, but thereafter sat back to allow their guests to enjoy themselves without too much concern about the presence of the master.

Leaning into a small sturdy hedge, Elizabeth close beside him, Darcy was struck by the space which propriety always required between them. He watched other couples, relaxed by wine and the enjoyment of the evening as they held firmly to one another, wrapped in each other. He longed for such liberty with Elizabeth. In that moment, he could think of no greater pleasure than to take her onto his lap and wrap her body with his, their shared heat fighting off the chill of the evening.

He smiled at the fantasy of such freedom, knowing that not even here, not even where he felt most comfortable, would he flout convention so blatantly. Still, as he sat, seemingly en-grossed in watching the dancing, he allowed himself the indulgence of imagining them both later, when in the privacy of their bedchamber he could freely explore the delight of having her body wrapped in his.

His happy diversions were unceremoniously interrupted by a loud yell from a far corner of the party. Such was the violence of the shout that it forced the attention of all there to the couple involved, and even the small band ceased, momentarily, to play. Darcy, on seeing the man who had been the cause of the disturbance, rose at once and made his way over, instructing the musicians to play on and the revellers to dance, as he passed them.

"Mr Martin! What is the meaning of this? If you cannot hold your tongue, or your drink, I will ask you to leave."

At once, Mrs Martin was in front of her husband seeking to calm him, and assure Mr Darcy that beyond a minor disagreement, all was well.

"I heard your minor disagreement from the other side of the garden, Mrs Martin!" replied Darcy, tersely. His anger not directed towards the woman herself, but the man to whom she had the misfortune of being married.

"It's a private matter, sir," Mr Martin shot back, alcohol emboldening his natural insolence.

"And had you been content in keeping it private, I would not be standing here. As it is, I believe you have been here long enough, it is time to go."

Turning to Mrs Martin, Darcy continued, "You and your children are of course welcome to stay."

Mr Martin, incensed by this slight, briefly appeared to forget whom he addressed and almost squared up to his master, then just as swiftly he recollected himself and stepped away, swearing heavily under his breath. Grabbing a bottle, and the remains of a large pie, as he passed the table, he staggered away from the party, heading off in the direction of his cottage.

ℂ

"What in heaven's was that?" Elizabeth asked upon Darcy's return.

"A domestic disagreement, it would appear. I have sent Mr Martin home; hopefully, he will sleep through the worst of it."

"Who is this Martin? I do not know him or his family."

"His wife's family have worked this estate for generations. When her parents died, the land passed to their son, Edward, but he was not well suited to a country life and rather than have the property forfeited, I offered the living to his sister, and simply paid Edward off. Sadly, Mrs Martin – or Miss Brown as she then was – did not choose wisely when she chose her husband and he has been a bane since he arrived here."

"If he is the cause of such misery could you not just evict him? It is within your power, surely."

"It is, and if I could be certain that in evicting him I would not also be forcing out his wife and children I would do so. As it is, she defends him still, and I will not see her or the children punished further."

Once Mr Martin had been seen off, all those gathered returned to the enjoyment and gaiety of what remained of their evening with alacrity, though their enjoyment was not to last long. The change began innocently with one of the children sitting staring into the night sky. On noticing the child's attention so taken with something, one of those who kept watch turned their attention to the same patch of sky. On seeing nothing, but knowing her eyes were not as sharp as they once were, she enquired of the boy what interested him so. The boy continued his gaze and said he was watching out for shapes in the sky.

"Shapes in the sky, boy? Have you quite lost your senses?"

"In the smoke; I'm looking for shapes in the smoke."

Old Mrs Maybury's eyes shot back to the sky on the mention of smoke, just in time to see the first lick of flames reaching into the night. The alarm was raised in an instant; all merriment ceasing in the same moment. The men immediately sprang into action and raced in the direction of the fire. The women, under the supervision of Elizabeth and Georgiana, gathered the children together, and followed behind at a safe distance.

The cottages on the east boundary were on fire.

℘

By the time the men arrived, the Martin's cottage was completely ablaze and two other roofs glowed bright. In the middle of it all stood Mr Martin, swaying heavily and clutching his hair. He was roughly pushed aside as Darcy and several of the others acted with the common purpose of stopping the spread of the fire. Darcy took command of the scene and those who had followed him were quick to respond, the dread of the fire spreading to the other cottages and nearby crops focusing the actions of all. The women and children were ordered to move away and told to fetch blankets and anything that would carry water.

Elizabeth took control of this venture, forcing herself to remain clear-headed and calm in the wake of the chaos, knowing she could be no use if panic were allowed to take hold. Giving orders in a clear and steady voice that belied her fear, it felt but minutes before the needed supplies were at hand.

Two lines were arranged running from the nearest well, with the women passing pails and jugs of water up to the men who ventured closer to the fire. Nothing could be done to save the Martin's home, so Darcy directed the main of the effort to the other two houses and in stopping the spread further. Small fires that sprung up away from the main blaze, as burning embers were carried by the wind, were stamped out by the older children, and those who were able were sent on to the roofs of the nearest buildings, pails of water being passed up to wet them. The fires on the roofs of the Martin's neighbours were attended to by the men, with water and water-soaked blankets used to beat out the flames. A small band of men, led by Darcy, saw to the Martin's cottage, for though it could not be saved, it posed the greatest threat to the surrounding area as the fire burned fiercely within it.

"It has to come down, sir," one of the men yelled to Darcy. "We must tear it down and control that fire."

Darcy agreed, and they immediately set about gathering tools and rope to help safely bring the burning building down. Mrs Martin, on hearing this, looked briefly at Elizabeth, a momentary plea on her face, but both knew there was no saving what remained of her home, and the best that could be done was to protect the rest.

Mr Martin, suddenly aware of what was passing, stumbled up

to the men attempting to secure hooks to exposed awnings and loose brick. "The devil take you!" he bellowed "Get away from my house!"

One of the men pushed him away angrily, hoping the shock of finding himself landed heavily on his rear might do enough to dissuade further interference, but Mr Martin was drunk and easily incensed, and attacked the man with greater conviction than before. "I said, away from my house, damn you!" he yelled, this time following his outburst with a bevy of punches.

As pathetic a drunk as he was, Mr Martin still posed a danger, and two of the men turned on him; fear and anger increasing the savagery of the beating they meted out. Already humiliated by his earlier behaviour, Mrs Martin suffered the further indignity of watching her husband be dragged away mewling like a babe. Within minutes of his being tossed roughly over the nearest hedge, the cottage that had been Mrs Martin's home since the day of her birth came crashing down.

All those gathered worked tirelessly, and as the fire was extinguished, thick black smoke polluted the air around the cottages. Darcy ordered the women and children be removed to a safer distance while the men attended to the last of the flames. Elizabeth and Georgiana gathered everyone and moved them back, staying as close to the men as possible, but ensuring the air was cleaner. Some were sent to the house to gather blankets and food. Groups huddled together for warmth, and in that manner, in complete silence, they waited.

It was yet another half-hour before the first of the men was seen stepping out of the clearing. Blackened by smoke and bent over with fatigue, he was followed shortly by the others. Wives and children raced forward, carrying blankets and refreshments.

Elizabeth and Georgiana scanned the men as they approached, and on seeing that Darcy was not among them were immediately apprehensive. Elizabeth spotted Mr Foster, one of Darcy's gamekeepers, and ran to him with urgent enquiries as to her husband's whereabouts.

"He is by the cottages still, my lady," was all the man had time to reply before Elizabeth was racing towards the clearing.

Elizabeth slowed to catch her breath as she approached, so that she might be capable of speaking when she found Darcy. Silhouetted against the clearing, she saw her husband leaning against a nearby oak, his head hung low, and his breathing ragged. There were only two left by the cottages: her husband and Mr Martin.

Mr Martin, sore, but sober now, had made his way back once he believed everyone else had left. He was surprised to find Mr Darcy still there, and for some minutes all the men could do was stand in the clearing next to one another, each too exhausted to speak.

Mr Martin, believing he had the measure of Darcy began eventually by saying, "It will have to be rebuilt, of course. Though heaven knows where we will find the money to do it – without your generosity, that is, master – but you won't see us put out. Too good and worthy a master for that, I reckon! Not for a mistake, sir."

He paused to give Darcy a chance to reply, but was not quickly rewarded by a response.

Slowly, Darcy drew a deep breath and pushed his body away from the tree that until that moment had been the only thing stopping him from collapsing. "A mistake, Martin? You think allowing yourself to become so drunk that you start a fire that destroys your home and threatens the destruction of the homes of those around you is aptly called a mistake?"

"It was an accident, sir, you must believe me. I tipped an oil lamp, and before I knew anything about it the cottage seemed ablaze – but you will rebuild it?"

"It will have to be rebuilt and I will see to it."

Mr Martin smiled, but his satisfaction was short-lived.

"It will be rebuilt, though you shall not be here to see it," Darcy continued.

"You will not turn us out, not the children and all, sir? I did not think you so cruel, so heartless. What would your father say to it? What would your father say?"

Darcy drew himself up, suddenly reinvigorated, and Mr Martin shrank back before him. "Do not talk to me of my father! You did not know the man, so do not dare to lecture me on what he would say. My father would have had you whipped for what you did tonight, so you may be grateful for my lenience."

Starting to whimper, Mr Martin pleaded, "What of the children, master? What will become of them?"

"Your children will be cared for, your wife will be cared for, and the cottage will be rebuilt with no expense to your family – under the very simple condition that you leave tonight and never return. I will provide you money enough to get out of Derbyshire and what you choose to do and where you choose to go beyond that I care not, but you will never return to this county, and you will never impose yourself upon Mrs Martin again."

"You cannot ask a man to abandon his wife and children, surely you cannot? You might as well rip out a man's heart as ask that of him!"

"There are many men who are forced to leave their family and they survive it – as will you. I have no doubt of your being able to find some solace in life – as long as that solace is elsewhere."

"And if I refuse? What will you do if I refuse?"

Darcy stepped up to Mr Martin on this challenge, so close that their chests touched as he breathed – deep, even, and controlled. "Understand me, I will have you gone. I would prefer to see your family safe and protected here among the life they have always known, but if you insist on remaining with them then all is lost. The choice is yours."

Mr Martin knew there would be no arguing, there would be no quarter given, there was no mercy to be found here. He could stand his ground and his family would lose everything or he could walk away. He looked at Darcy once more, "What have I done, master?"

"You know the answer to that, Martin, and you will have to live with it. The question now is, what will you do?"

"I will go, provide me money enough to leave and I will do it, but promise me they will be safe and looked after when I am gone."

"I swear it, Martin, you can trust in that."

Mr Martin stepped back from Darcy and the two men regarded one another with more respect than either had ever shown previously. With a resigned nod, Mr Martin agreed to wait at the village where money would be sent to him, and on that, he turned and was gone.

Elizabeth now stepped from the shadows and approached her husband. "It is done then, Fitzwilliam? He will trouble you no more?"

"It is done, and though I believe it to be the right thing, I can take no pleasure in such an ending."

Elizabeth, unwilling to dwell on the unpleasant scene she had just witnessed turned to the cottages and continued, "And what now for the rest of the Martin family? Will the cottage be rebuilt here or will they be moved to another part of the estate?"

"I doubt there will be anything to be salvaged from the remains of the house, though if there is anything that might be saved, we will find it. There is damage to the roofs of a number of the cottages and repairs will begin tomorrow. The Martin's cottage will be rebuilt where it once stood; I will not see Mrs Martin removed from her close friends and neighbours at a time when she will be in greatest need of their support. I take it you overheard the full of my conversation with Mr Martin?"

"I did."

"And do you approve of my actions?"

"Do you need my approval, Fitzwilliam? If I were to disapprove of what had been done, would it change anything?"

"No. I neither need your approval nor would your with-holding it cause me to alter what has been done, but nevertheless I wish to know, Elizabeth, was I just?"

Elizabeth took a minute before replying. "I am struck by the hardship this family must now endure. That Mrs Martin and her children should be deprived of their home, her husband, their father, and all in one night, seems a burden few could bear easily. I wish with all my heart that they should not have to suffer such loss. Still, on further considering the man they are to lose, compared with all that will be gained by their continuing to remain here among their friends, and the life they have built, I must find justice in all that has been done. Mr Martin's punishment will be great, but his own stupidity and intemperance has been his downfall. I find no fault in what you have chosen to do, husband."

Darcy, exhausted as much by physical exertion as by the responsibility of being a master, sighed, "I am so tired, Elizabeth. I need to wash off this night and long only for the peace and comfort of your embrace."

Elizabeth said nothing, but taking Darcy's hand in hers, led him home.

CHAPTER 4

On the fifth morning after the peasant's ball, when the family had largely returned to their usual routine of Darcy being gone before the others were up, the two ladies were left to breakfast together. When conversation could turn to something other than the events of that fateful night, and a consideration of how the new build works were progressing, Georgiana began a most unexpected conversation with Elizabeth.

"Do you know of my involvement with George Wickham?"

The question was tentatively put, and Elizabeth was aware of how difficult it must have been for her to raise the matter.

"Your brother told me a little of the affair, but in the strictest of confidence, I assure you, and only with the expectation I would not make it generally known."

"I believed myself in love with him. He was so charming, and I so at ease with him, having known him all my life. I did not think it possible he could use me so abominably."

There was an awkward silence, as neither seemed to know how to proceed. Eventually, Elizabeth spoke.

"My father once told me, next to being married, a girl liked to be crossed a little in love. He teased, of course, but being disappointed need not be cause for shame or embarrassment. In this instance, you were young and worked upon by a man whose manner has fooled most. Your dalliance is little known, indeed, only among those of our closest acquaintance, and our sole concern is for your continued happiness."

"And that is what pains me the most! For I am not happy!" exclaimed an uncharacteristically unguarded Georgiana. "How can I trust myself to be out in society? How can I trust I shall not shame or embarrass the family? Is it any wonder my brother keeps me at home?"

With this remark, Georgiana grew quiet, fearing she had spoken too freely, even for Elizabeth, and feeling how ungrateful she sounded. "Forgive me, I have misspoken. I am being silly; no doubt an hour at the piano will lighten my spirits," she finished, while rising from her seat.

Before Elizabeth could say another word, Georgiana was gone and in the wake of her absence, Elizabeth was left with much to ponder.

☙

"Fitzwilliam, do you realise Georgiana has been home for two weeks and we have yet to dine out, engage another party here, or so much as set up a table for cards?"

"If I am not mistaken, we held a ball here but nights ago, or do you suggest I imagined that!"

"Do not feign obtuseness, Fitzwilliam, it does not suit you," Elizabeth replied tartly. "You know perfectly well what I mean. Georgiana needs opportunities to meet young men and women of similar standing, or is it your intention that your sister find a husband among your tenants or servants?"

Darcy continued to wash his arms, but a slightly elevated eyebrow, questioning the appropriateness of the conversation while he was still in his bath, was evidence enough that he had heard her.

"And do not raise your eyebrow at me, husband. I think it is shameful we have not done more to entertain her; she must feel terribly neglected. What do you think she does all afternoon while we keep to our room?"

"Are you complaining about my attentions, Lizzy?" Darcy said, flicking water at her. "I was unaware you found your afternoons with me so onerous. I judged you rather enjoyed them – or do I mistake that rising blush?"

"Fitzwilliam Darcy! That is a fine way to talk to your wife!"

"I might be inclined to believe your coyness, madam, had you not spent the last few minutes eyeing me in a decidedly lascivious manner. You put me in mind to delay this evening's business and to lock myself in here with you!" and with a quick movement, he reached for Elizabeth and pulled her screaming into the bath with him.

Darcy's man had been moving towards the bathroom door with a fresh robe when he heard the scream. He paused: the sounds of spilling water, Elizabeth's laughing, and then the low moan of "Fitzwilliam" convinced him that now would not be the time to make an entrance. Rather, he determined, the proper course would be to seek out Mrs Reynolds and arrange for a late lunch.

֎

"Do not think you have distracted me from my purpose in coming to you earlier," Elizabeth warned as she dried and fixed her hair. "I am quite determined we are to do more for Georgiana."

"I assure you, Georgiana is by no means wanting for stimulation. She has new music, which always engages her. She reads, and always manages to get through the newest additions to the library, and then for additional company, I usually invite the Bingleys for a few weeks. We have our routine and are both perfectly contented."

"Oh I see – perfectly contented – then whom did I observe this morning, pacing the music room, not settled to music, reading, or anything else?"

Darcy stopped and turned to her, finally paying attention. "Are you certain? This has always been how we spent our time here, and Georgiana never seemed unhappy."

His obvious confusion at this sudden upset to his and Georgiana's routine elicited a gentler response from Elizabeth.

"She is growing up, Fitzwilliam; you cannot hope to always keep her at home, so isolated. She is a young woman and will be in need of the same distractions as any other. She needs younger society. There must be girls her age in the county, and perhaps a few young gentlemen, some people capable of forming a party for outings and entertainments?"

"I do not like the notion of men entertaining my sister. She is too young, and I am sure she could not want it."

"She is seventeen, Fitzwilliam, and that is exactly what she wants! I do not suggest we simply allow her to gad about, but some measure of fun must be afforded to her."

Darcy was hurt by the implication he prevented Georgiana from enjoying herself and sought to counter the slight with almost sullen declarations regarding what Georgiana considered fun.

"Fitzwilliam Darcy, is that petulance I read on your face?" Elizabeth replied, scolding him. "I am not denying the wonderful way you have loved and raised Georgiana; no brother could have done more. I simply wish you to see she is growing up and we must encourage her."

"And how do you propose we do that?"

"Well, my love, I believe we should start with dancing!"

෨

Elizabeth and Georgiana stood within the small drawing room, waiting for Darcy to conclude some business with his steward.

Georgiana was fretting over the party they were attending that evening. Would she be expected to talk, or to dance? How would she represent the family? Would she be a disappointment? The Cramonds held a yearly party to celebrate the beginning of the season. In the weeks thereafter, many of the families left to go to London to attend a whirl of parties and social engagements. Darcy usually contrived a reason for them to refuse the Cramonds and as he and Georgiana visited

London infrequently, they would generally be left to spend their time in the peace and comfort of their own society. She could not understand what had prompted him to accept the invitation this year, and could only conclude that he intended to use the opportunity to introduce Elizabeth to the families of the county, but that did not explain why she needed to attend. In her distress, she turned to Elizabeth and appealed, "Must you dance tonight, Elizabeth? I am sure my brother should not mind if you were not to. He does not often stand up and I do not believe it would be a hardship for him if you did not; that is, if you were to tell him you did not wish to."

Elizabeth laughed. "Would you wish me to sit for the evening? Do you think me so deficient?"

Georgiana was shamed by the question, and meaning no criticism of Elizabeth, hastened to add, "Of course not. I only mean, if you dance, I shall be left alone. I am sure my brother will not have you dance with anyone but him, and who will I stand up with?"

Elizabeth observed Georgiana closely. There was distress in her plea: she was not crying off to be awkward or to gain attention, but was simply and desperately uncomfortable at the thought of having to be on her own. Her isolation was now painfully obvious. Elizabeth had always been surrounded by friends and family when out in social settings, often in a way that appalled her when it came to Lydia, Kitty, and her mother, but she had never been alone. There had always been the comfort of knowing that her sister, Jane, or good friend, Charlotte, was close at hand. If she and Darcy were to stand up together for a set, then who would Georgiana be left with?

"Georgiana, you shall not be left alone for a moment if you do not wish it, but will you not be bored? Would you not like to join in some of the dances? Do you have no friends attending with whom to meet?"

Georgiana looked away from her before replying quietly, "No, I have no friends attending tonight. My brother has introduced me to some of the young ladies, but I do not feel well enough acquainted. I would not like to impose without an invitation and I would much rather stay with you."

"Of course, you shall stay with us," replied Elizabeth, who was struck by the panic in the request. "I would not have you upset, so do not fret. You and I shall pass the evening together. I shall comment on the number of dances and the crowds, and you on the selection of music and the size of the rooms."

"You tease me so, but you will not mention this to my brother?"

The reply came, but not from Elizabeth.

"Will not mention what to your brother?"

Georgiana blanched at the sound of Darcy's voice, and looked pleadingly at Elizabeth.

"Georgiana was asking me not to tell you how she was scolding me, before you came in."

"Scolding you, indeed!" said Darcy, his surprise evident "And what cause would she have for that?"

"I had just informed her that I planned on behaving shamefully this evening. I feel quite giddy with it. I may dance, flirt, and give my opinion far too freely! What do you say to that, sir?"

"Only, Mrs Darcy, if you plan on drawing such attention to yourself, you had best be properly adorned while doing so."

On that, he drew from behind him a large jewellery box, which opened to reveal the most exquisite yellow diamond either woman had ever seen. Neither Elizabeth nor Georgiana spoke, nor could they look away from the brilliant stone.

"Speechless? At last!" Darcy smiled.

ℰℒ

The Cramond's home provided the perfect setting for a party. It was as if the architect had expected just such a use for the property, and designed the lower floor accordingly. The foyer was large and open, with high ceilings, and there was an ornate staircase in the centre, with two chandeliers on either side. In addition to the light provided by an array of candelabras, these chandeliers sent shafts of coloured light down the hallways, along which, guests moved from the foyer to the grand dining room. The dining room had large windows and glass doors, which both afforded a spectacular view of the grounds, and ensured the room was always cool enough on the one side for those wishing to dance; while a large fireplace on the other ensured it was warm enough for those wishing to watch. The large dining table was removed for the first party of the season and small sets of chairs and love seats were placed around the edges and into cosy corners. The two adjoining rooms were opened: one laid out with refreshments, and the other for cards.

Darcy exhaled slowly as they entered, and Elizabeth squeezed his hand in appreciation of the sacrifice he was making. She had come to learn that while he relished the company of an intimate set, he was far less comfortable in a large crowd. Elizabeth could only hope that Darcy's discomfort would be lessened by the presence of some of his acquaintances who were also expected to attend that evening. For her own part, she was determined to be pleased. They had been promised an extravagant affair, and she believed Mrs Cramond was liberal enough with Mr Cramond's purse that it would be just so.

Elizabeth had been given the opportunity to sketch the character of her hostess when she arrived at Pemberley, thus enabling her to deliver personally their invitation.

Mrs Cramond was an interesting woman with good intent, but rather brash execution. She approved of the changes to the house, but recommended different flowers for the vases: the mixed bouquets favoured by Elizabeth should be replaced by roses, as altogether more elegant. Elizabeth was as beautiful as had been rumoured, but she must take pains to maintain her bloom by the daily use of salts. The new rug in the small front room was delightful, but would hardly prove to be practical when the Darcys started a family. These observations were offered with such warmth and enthusiasm that Elizabeth could find no fault with her guest; indeed, she was so sure there was no real criticism intended, she believed any remark suggesting as much on her part would have been acutely felt by Mrs

Cramond. So, through it all, Elizabeth smiled pleasantly, nodded when required, and assured that she would certainly take consideration of all Mrs Cramond's excellent advice.

The introductions began at the moment they entered the foyer, and Mrs Cramond could not contain her excitement at being the first in the county to play host to the new Mr and Mrs Darcy: she was by their side immediately. Elizabeth feared the effect that Mrs Cramond's officious attention would have on her husband's mood, but he smiled, and bore with exceeding grace, her almost endless declarations: her delight at their attending, her joy at being able to introduce the new Mrs Darcy to the best society in the county, and her hope that they all enjoyed the evening.

Mrs Cramond's usual excessive civility was emblazoned by her delight at the coup of getting the Darcys to her party. She had, rather unfortunately, overheard one of her guests complaining, the previous year, that there was nothing new to excite at these parties, casting doubt on whether she would even continue to attend. From that moment, Mrs Cramond had worked to ensure that the next party would be the event of the season. Although, she had thought not to invite Mrs Thurgood, who had been so unfortunately overheard, she sent the invitation, realising her success would not be complete if her detractor was absent. That the Darcy's had chosen this year to attend was simply more than she could have anticipated, and she showed little restraint in her excitement as she introduced them to those gathered.

Mrs Darcy had been the subject of much speculation in the weeks since her arrival at Pemberley and there was a great deal of interest among the ladies as to what she would wear, how she would dance, and whether she would prove as proud as her husband was generally thought to be. Mrs Cramond's exuberance at the triumph was such that she could be heard calling, above the noise of a crowded room, which boasted at least seventy guests, twenty servants, and a small band playing a lively tune in the corner. "Mr Markham, Mr Markham, I will have you here, for I must introduce you to the new Mrs Darcy, this instant."

Although Elizabeth had taken a liking to their hostess, she was nevertheless grateful when Mrs Cramond was called upon to quit their company by an emergency, which hastened her elsewhere.

Darcy, Elizabeth, and Georgiana breathed a sigh of relief at her departure, finally at ease to explore their surroundings in relative peace. It had been agreed the party would remain together for the evening, although, while taking a turn about the room, Darcy's attention was quickly drawn to a man with whom he had the greatest desire to speak concerning the sale of a parcel of land at the outer boundaries of Pemberley. With a rushed apology and a determination to be but a moment, Darcy disappeared.

Unfortunately, for Elizabeth and Georgiana, Mrs Cramond returned all too soon, and set about quickly casting all those around her aside in order to claim the prize of having Mrs Darcy at her table. Elizabeth spent the next quarter-hour being rigorously scrutinised by those in attendance, after which they appeared to have collectively determined that they liked her. Her dress was exquisite, but tasteful, expensive but not ostentatious. Her manner was charming and pithy; she was clearly a woman of insight and intelligence who would add greatly to their circle. Naturally, the wife of Fitzwilliam Darcy would never have been refused admittance to their society, but there was relief in learning she would be a boon and not a burden.

"And so, Mrs Darcy, can we expect you to join us more regularly, now we have been properly introduced?" began one of the ladies. "We meet almost every afternoon and are most busy with various charitable concerns and projects to improve the villages in the county."

Elizabeth smiled at the thought of what Darcy would say if she chose to exchange their afternoon activity for tea and cakes with the county ladies. "Well, of course, I am most anxious to involve myself with your good work, but I must consult with Mr Darcy, as he likes to have me at home in the afternoons."

"Well, you must not allow him too much of a say in what

you do; we ladies must have our freedom too. I was sure to put my mark on my husband very early in our marriage and I have never regretted it!" announced Mrs Cramond forcefully, before remembering Georgiana was still among their party.

Certain such conversation would best not be heard by young ears, she continued, "Georgiana Darcy, you are simply the most exquisite creature I have ever beheld, and you are far too young and gay to be stuck here with us old married women! I must see you dancing and enjoying yourself."

Both Elizabeth and Georgiana tried to assure her that Georgiana was perfectly comfortable, but Mrs Cramond was of a personality that brooked no opposition once she had determined the course of events, and so neither could sway her from the resolve that Mrs Darcy was to remain with her circle and Miss Darcy was to join the other young people at cards or dancing. She called over a girl and instructed that she and Miss Darcy were to be the closest of friends before the end of the evening, and with one last glance at Elizabeth, Georgiana was led away.

Georgiana silently crossed into the other room, not only because her general disposition led her to be quiet, but because the young lady who had been charged with her welfare did not draw breath long enough to allow her to speak. Georgiana, however, learned two important things about her companion before they concluded their walk: her name – Isabelle Mary Hunt – and the fact it was unlikely they would become confidantes. Georgiana had listened with disdain as Miss Hunt talked disparagingly of several of the other women in attendance: the girth of one was cause for ridicule, while the lack of trim on the dress of another was pitiable. Therefore, as soon as she could, without causing offence, Georgiana left the company of Miss Hunt, claiming a great desire to play cards.

She approached a small group, and in her eagerness to be rid of a most unpleasant companion, had no scruples in advancing herself and seeking an invitation to join them. The party, she learned upon introduction, was made up of two ladies: sisters Mary and Ann Trevelyan, their cousin John Trevelyan, and his friend William Grey, all of whom with politeness, and eagerness to expand their company, welcomed her to the table.

"You are just what we need, Miss Darcy! A fifth, for we are at an impasse and desperately need another vote."

Georgiana smiled in response to the welcome, although she was apprehensive as to what she might be called upon to do.

"Do not be alarmed," laughed Mary, "we have been discussing the latest work of Henry Fields. Ann and I argue it is a wonderful edition worthy of acclaim, while our cousin and Mr Grey will not have it. What do you say? Have you read Henry Fields?"

"I have indeed, and fear I must agree with your cousin and Mr Grey in that I did not enjoy his latest work."

"Ah! There you have it. You are bested, Mary, and must admit I am right in decrying Mr Fields a pretender in the literary world," smirked John Trevelyan.

"Oh you misunderstand me, sir," Georgiana interrupted. "I agree his latest work is flawed, but only by comparison to his last, which surely must be hailed as a work of great standing in modern literature."

This response was the source of much amusement around the table. John Trevelyan feigned displeasure as the others teased him mercilessly; Mary even threatened to force him to read a chapter from the book every evening as a punishment. Georgiana quickly joined in with the general gaiety of the party and did not notice how long she had been separated from Darcy and Elizabeth, so it was with some surprise when she realised the dancing had already begun.

"Have I been here an hour?" she asked.

"I do hope our small group does not bore you, Miss Darcy?"

"Quite the contrary, Mr Grey, I had not expected to be so pleasantly engaged this evening. I am not much used to such varied company and was unsettled at the thought of attending a ball where I had no particular acquaintance."

"Well, I very much hope you will not leave us tonight without considering yourself to have four particular acquaintances among your set, now, Miss Darcy. For I believe it true to say we would be honoured to count you among our friends."

Georgiana blushed and turned away from Mr Grey's deliberate gaze. When she returned her eyes to his seat, he had risen and his hand was extended to hers.

"Might I be so bold as to claim the honour of your hand for the next dance?"

With another, deeper blush, Georgiana accepted.

☙

Darcy and Elizabeth had taken up a position at the top of the room to join the next set. When they had returned, they looked for Georgiana, but found her engaged with new friends. Fearing any intrusion might break the magic of the moment, they returned to the main hall and sought the seclusion only a dance at a ball could offer.

Their surprise at seeing Georgiana, also in the line and conversing most cordially with her partner, was the cause of much pleasure for Elizabeth and much discomfort for Darcy.

"Do we know who he is? Who are his people? And what are his intentions?"

"They are dancing, husband; you jump rather hastily from dancing to marriage."

Darcy laughed. "Once, at an impromptu dance, I commented on the delight to be found in the face of a pretty girl, and Caroline Bingley made a similarly hasty jump, presuming to ask when I could be congratulated on my marriage!"

"Oh, and just whose face so delighted you?"

"That is exactly what Caroline asked; you can imagine her surprise when I told her, yours."

"Indeed. Only a pretty face then?" was all Elizabeth could respond before moving away from him to circle the next couple in the dance.

"You improved upon acquaintance," was Darcy's reply on returning to her.

"You are shameful!"

"You are beautiful."

"You are forgiven."

Their intimate conversation continued until they met with Georgiana and her partner. There was a brief introduction and Georgiana had just enough time to assure them both that she was having the most wonderful time before they moved on.

"Mr Grey seems a pleasant fellow," ventured Elizabeth. "Handsome, but not overly so, with enough attention to dress to show him conscientious, but not vain. He has a polite manner and dances very well. I am inclined to like him."

"You sound like Jane."

"Were it true, it would be a compliment, indeed. I fear I shall never be quite so good as Jane, but I might try to learn from her example. She always defended you."

"Well, I always felt Jane was a sensible girl," he smiled, "but you are far too willing to draw a person's character from a few moments shared at a dance and you are not always right. Allow me the comfort of admitting that while I see no cause for alarm, as yet, I reserve the right to make a fuller judgement at a later time. Should he make a formal introduction, I will take the measure of the man."

℘

At the other end of the room, Georgiana was equally absorbed in an intimate conversation of her own. Mr Grey had praised her grace and declared a better dance partner could not be found in the county. In response, all Georgiana could do was blush and glance away.

"Do I embarrass you? I would not make you uncomfortable, but you cannot be unknowing as to your natural abilities. Never could a lady be so unaware of her talents and charms, surely?"

"Mr Grey, I beg you to stop, for I fear the blush will never fade from my cheeks if you do not!"

He moved briefly to her ear, and whispered, "I rather like the blush."

In an instant, he moved away again and stood opposite her as if no such delicious intimacy had ever occurred.

Georgiana, however, was reeling from his closeness: the heat and the smell of him, his breath on her face and the low deep timbre of his voice. She feared she might be overcome, but her hand in his for the last turn of the dance steadied her, and although aware of only him, she completed the set with such grace and poise that anyone watching would not have supposed her affected at all.

Such was the effect of Mr Grey's attention that Georgiana was delighted to dance again, next with Mr Trevelyan, and then with the Cramonds' son. Although no partner could quite compare to her first, she was pleased to see he watched her dancing. When she stood up with Mr Cramond, Mr Grey walked the length of the room with them. Though making conversation along the way, Georgiana often noted his eyes upon her instead of his companion.

When finally summoned to leave, Georgiana was forlorn, but assurances from the party they would meet again gave her hope that the pleasure of the evening would be repeated. In the carriage on the journey home, she spoke enthusiastically of the ball and her new friends.

Darcy had never seen her so animated; it both pleased and worried him, and although she made equal reference to "Mr and the Misses Trevelyan", he was concerned that the greater part of her pleasure lay with her new connection to Mr Grey.

ℂ

"Fitzwilliam, my love, I have been thinking about Georgiana."

"Hmm…" was all the response Darcy could manage.

"I do not think it is wise for her to be always so alone."

"She is not alone. Did we not just spend an evening surrounded by more company than one could wish for. She has us, and Mrs Baxter will start with her next week," he yawned in response.

"I think she should have a confidante: a girl her own age to spend time with, and share secrets with."

There was no response from Darcy.

"I was thinking I ought to write to Papa and invite Kitty to stay."

Darcy was suddenly very much awake, sitting up in bed and staring down in disbelief at his wife. "You cannot seriously mean to suggest we should invite Kitty? Please, Lizzy. Kitty! What possible good could come of it?"

"I believe they could be good for one another. Georgiana will help to temper some of Kitty's more wayward tendencies, and Kitty will help enliven Georgiana. We could invite her for a month."

"No!"

"No?"

Elizabeth smiled at her husband and reached over to stroke his chest, swirling her fingers along his torso in smooth rhythmic patterns, holding his gaze with her own, daring him to continue to refuse her. "No?"

"No!"

She drew down the sheet that covered his lower half, and smiling still, ran her eyes from his face down the length of his body, her hands moving on to his thighs, never ceasing in their long slow strokes as she reached over and began to kiss his neck. "No?"

"No…" he replied, although with less conviction.

Her mouth moved from his neck as she licked and sucked the soft flesh of his ear.

In response, Darcy let out a shudder and his breathing grew rapid as a delicious heat arose within him.

"No?" she whispered now, still touching and teasing.

"Perhaps,"

"For a month?"

"Perhaps…"

"For how long?" Elizabeth queried, moving away from him.

"A month," Darcy moaned as he moved to reach her again.

"And so we are in agreement?" she asked, still out of reach and slowly removing her nightdress.

"Yes…agreement…of course…" he mumbled.

Elizabeth dropped the nightdress to the floor and sat before him, dressed only by the candlelight that cast light and shadow across her body. "You see, my darling, that was easy! You always give in to me. Really, why do you fight me at all?"

"Because, my dearest Lizzy," Darcy began, while pulling her across him, "I do so enjoy having you make me surrender!"

CHAPTER 5

A letter was dispatched to Mr Bennet the following day, who replied, with uncharacteristic promptness, that he would be delighted to have Kitty join them. In a separate note to Elizabeth, he added that Mary, however, could not be spared, lest he be left alone with Mrs Bennet.

Kitty accepted the invitation with a mixture of anxiety and eagerness. Her anxiety came from the thought of being too much in the company of the severe Mr Darcy; whom, she was certain, must have required a great deal of persuasion to consent to her stay. Her eagerness for the social possibilities that a stay with them offered, however, lessened her fears, and in truth, she was eager to reacquaint herself with Miss Georgiana Darcy, whom she fancied would prove a more interesting companion than Mary.

Within two weeks of the plan being agreed, Kitty found herself at Pemberley, being ushered into a small morning room, while a distressed housemaid went in search of Mrs Reynolds. The young lady was a day early and the housemaid was quite at a loss as to what to do, as neither Mrs Darcy nor Miss Darcy was at home to greet her. It fell, therefore, to Mr Darcy to welcome his houseguest, and Kitty, could scarcely have been more uneasy when he entered the room, without her sister. To her surprise,

Darcy was pleasant; she might almost have thought him amiable were it not for the sternness of his brow. He enquired after her health, after the health of her family, and listened with apparent interest to her account of the journey.

Darcy even reprimanded himself for selfishly keeping her from being rested and refreshed. For his part, Darcy too was surprised by their encounter. Kitty was quite charming, her manner not excessively silly, and though she spoke with great animation of her travels, she did not run on or become giddy. He began to fancy this lively young girl might be just the companion for Georgiana, after all.

Kitty was shown to her room by an apologetic Mrs Reynolds, and was not half an hour in getting settled before she was joined by Elizabeth and Georgiana. The conversation turned to family and travelling, and at the earliest juncture – when Georgiana and Kitty were comparing the state of the roads, the inns frequented, and the variety of cold meats and ices to be had along the way – Elizabeth excused herself and sought out her husband.

ॐ

"So, she has arrived, husband," Elizabeth began, having found Darcy in the library.

"Yes indeed, and much improved since our last meeting. I venture that a prolonged separation from your sister, Mrs Wickham, has been beneficial."

"We shall see how she fares over a month, although I do believe Kitty and Georgiana were fast becoming friends even as I left them."

"It is a good thing, Lizzy," responded Darcy, "for you were right: Georgiana needed somebody. Although I tease, I do believe Kitty might have just the spirit to help coax Georgiana out."

"Well, I am certainly glad you approve, Fitzwilliam, as Kitty was so fagged by the journey we could not have returned her to Longbourn for at least another fortnight!"

After a moment's silence, Darcy queried, "Should we hold a party here at Pemberley?"

"A party?" Elizabeth stared at her husband, uncertain she had heard him correctly. "You wish to throw a party here?"

"Is it such a preposterous notion? You look quite overcome at the suggestion. If the idea does not suit, by all means let us forget it and never speak of it again."

"I am simply surprised you would volunteer to host a party. You are not renowned for your love of them, Fitzwilliam. Surely Kitty has not managed to exert such influence already?"

"Beyond thinking it would be a good opportunity for both Georgiana and Kitty to become better acquainted with some of the other young ladies in the county, she has nothing to do with the suggestion," he smiled. "A man may change, and I wish to celebrate. There is not time enough to organise a grand affair, but I believe we could manage a party, attended by a select group."

"You do not need to sway me, husband," Elizabeth said as she took a seat on his lap. "I would be delighted."

Darcy wrapped his arms round her waist and pulled her to him. He dipped his head, kissed her throat, and then the swell of her breast. "What would I do without you, Lizzy?"

"That, my darling Fitzwilliam, you will never have to know."

℘

The preparations for the party began the next day. Kitty was delighted, never having hoped that the social engagements should begin so soon after her arrival. Her immediate concern was to who would be invited.

"Lizzy, shall there be a great many people at the party, do you think? Does Darcy have a large acquaintance, or shall it be a small set?"

Elizabeth understood what lay behind her questions. "There will be no men in regimentals if that is what you really wish to know," she replied, but on seeing the forlorn expression on Kitty's face added, "although there are several young men and women invited, the sons and daughters of the best families in the county."

Kitty cried out, clapping her hands in delight.

"And so you must exert yourself and display some sense of decorum. You cannot fly about, as you and Lydia so liked to do. If I hear one screech of laughter, Kitty…"

"Lizzy, I am not a child. Really, what must you think of me? I do not screech, and I can be perfectly proper." Kitty was defiant, and wishing to prove herself an adult, maintained her ground, adjusted an errant curl, and gave her sister the most withering look she could manage.

ɞ

"What do you know of the guests who shall attend the party, Georgiana? I simply must know more about them or I shall die! Truly, never was a girl more in danger of death from curiosity than I."

Georgiana laughed at the dramatic manner in which Kitty had entered the room and thrown herself upon the couch. "I do not believe one dies from curiosity, Kitty, but I shall take pity on you and tell you what I know of our guests."

Kitty cheered up instantly, and adopting a most serious manner, adjusted her seat to provide Georgiana her fullest attention.

"Mr and Mrs Cramond will no doubt attend. She loves the season and informed me herself that only the worst fit of ill health would be enough to keep her at home when there is the opportunity to join with neighbours—"

"Georgiana," Kitty interrupted, "how old are Mr and Mrs Cramond? For unless you can tell me they have children of a near age, I am not inclined to care whether they attend."

"They have a son; he is four and twenty, and gaining quite a name for himself in politics. I have heard him speak on agricultural reform and he is most impressive."

"Is he handsome? Does he ride well? Has he a horse and four? Really, Georgiana, what are his particulars?"

"Kitty, you must be calm. He is considered handsome, though I have heard his eyes criticised as being set too closely together. He rides and hunts very well, but I have no notion as to his carriage." She waited for a moment, and with no further interruptions from Kitty, continued. "The Trevelyans shall also be present with their two daughters: Mary and Ann. I vouch they shall become firm favourites of yours, as they are mine. They are charming and gay, love to read, and dance, and enjoy, above all else, teasing their cousin, Mr John Trevelyan, who will also join the party. He is a fine fellow, tall and broad, and although he looks quite heavily set, he has a light foot and is very good company. When I met the Trevelyans, they were with a Mr William Grey…I hope he may join them again. He is a most charming man and I believe you will agree him to be handsome, but as to his skill with a horse, I can offer no clue."

"You like this Mr Grey! I am sure of it. I see it as clearly as I see the nose on your face. You are alight just at the mention of him. Tell me all; I have a passion for romance, and having none of my own I beg a share in yours."

"Kitty! How you run on. There is no romance to speak of. I admit him to be agreeable, but we had only one dance at a ball…although he did brush my fingers with his in the most delightful way when we walked to take our place, and he was very attentive."

"Oh Lord, what a lark!" laughed Kitty. "I fancy myself in love every time a handsome man turns my head with some attention and flattery. I am endlessly in danger, but Georgiana, tell me plainly: do you think this could be a real sort of love?"

Georgiana considered her response, before admitting, "I do not know, but I dearly hope to find out."

CHAPTER 6

Georgiana and Kitty had spent much of the week planning what to wear, how to have their hair arranged, and where they should be standing so as to appear to the greatest advantage upon the arrival of Mr Grey.

Georgiana was tasked with attending to the young ladies and gentlemen, and to her surprise found the role was not as daunting as she had expected. This, she believed, was due to the presence of Kitty: there could be no awkwardness when there was the need to introduce her. Indeed, her ease in company was such that Darcy was moved to comment on how altered she was.

It was not until the announcement of the Trevelyan's arrival that any hint of agitation was evident. Kitty was immediately by Georgiana's side, positioning herself so that she might observe Mr Grey's approach; to determine if he took notice of Georgiana, and whether he showed any degree of affection.

"Well, he has come!" Kitty whispered. "And truly he is handsome, though I maintain a weakness for a man in a red coat, just like my Mama – but quiet yourself now, the party approaches and his eyes have not strayed from you for an instant."

"Miss Darcy," began Mary Trevelyan, "how delighted we are

to see you again. Ann and I had been trying to determine the best afternoon to engage you to join with us, when your beautiful invitation arrived."

"Indeed," Ann added, "it is just as my sister says! I cannot believe it is two weeks since we were last in company. I shall not be happy, this evening, until you have agreed to join us for tea in town next week. Two weeks' absence among friends is too great a separation and I will not risk it again."

"Well, I would not wish to spoil your evening, Ann, so if you can agree to tea on Wednesday I would be delighted to accept, if you have no objection to my friend, Miss Kitty Bennet, joining us?"

Kitty could see why the Trevelyans were such favourites with Georgiana: they were warm in their greeting of her, and most insistent that no tea party could possibly take place without the addition of Miss Bennet, who, as a friend of Miss Darcy, was assured to be a friend of theirs. Their cousin, John Trevelyan, protested there was not enough tea and cake in the county to induce him to join them; two women around a table was trouble enough, but as for four! His jest was taken with good humour, as it was meant, and soon the party were talking and laughing as though they had known each other a lifetime.

When Georgiana was called away, Kitty saw her opportunity to further acquaint herself with Mr Grey and to discern whether he had any partiality for her friend. Within minutes of Georgiana's absence, Kitty approached him with seeming despondency.

"I declare, Mr Grey, the party seems duller when Georgiana is not here, would you not agree?"

"It is true, Miss Bennet; Miss Darcy has a gentle charm that must benefit any gathering."

"Oh, she is charming indeed! And I do not know a more well-read or interesting woman."

Mr Grey smiled at Kitty's obvious stratagems. "That is also true: Miss Darcy has a fine mind and eloquence of thought."

"I believe you danced together once. How did you find her?"

"As graceful and light of foot as any I have had the pleasure to dance with, Miss Bennet. I hope to have the satisfaction of a second dance this evening, and if I might request your company for a set also, I might very easily call myself the happiest of men."

Kitty smiled with satisfaction and accepted the invitation, although she insisted that the honour of the first dance must be Georgiana's.

Mr Grey agreed. He would be remiss in not first seeking out the hostess to the party, and with a short crisp bow to Kitty, he went in search of Georgiana before the first of the dances began.

℘

"Well, Mr Darcy," enquired Elizabeth, when they found themselves alone in a quiet corner, "how do you find this evening?"

"In truth, madam, I would wish this rabble gone from here and our doors closed against them and the night."

"Fitzwilliam! What way is this to speak of our friends and neighbours?"

"Well, they have been inconsiderate enough to keep you from me for at least three-quarters of an hour so I owe them no civility!" He glowered, "Do you know how you torture me as you give your smiles and attention to others?"

Elizabeth brushed the collar of his coat. "Would you have me all to yourself this evening, Fitzwilliam? Would you have me ignore our guests?"

Darcy pulled her to him and crushed her body against his. "I would have you to myself always, Lizzy; our guests be damned!" he replied, and with unexpected desire, kissed her deeply.

Elizabeth yielded to his kiss, her body pushing against his, but the announcement of the first dance caused Darcy to remember where he was.

"And so they call you from me again."

He stepped from Elizabeth, and though to most he would look no different from usual, she could see a colour at his temples and hear a pull on his breath that betrayed him.

She moved in close and took his hands in hers. "Your sacrifice for the good of our guests will not go unrewarded, husband."

Her closeness, the feeling of her smooth skin beneath his fingers, and her hot breath against his neck caused Darcy to colour further. "Step away, woman!" he begged, "While I possess the power to let you go."

Elizabeth, alive at the nearness of him, as he to her, stepped back. "I look forward to your lack of restraint when we are alone, Fitzwilliam," and with one last smile, she turned and was gone.

ॐ

It was some minutes later before Darcy felt recovered enough to rejoin the party. The dancers were arranging themselves on the floor to begin the first set, and there was a general call for Mr and Mrs Darcy to lead. Darcy declined, declaring that the distinction must fall to his sister, in whose honour the party was being held. In truth, Darcy was moved more by his need not to be in too close contact with his wife, than with a desire to promote Georgiana, but he was gratified to see how well she looked as she was escorted to the top of the room by William Grey.

Georgiana was delighted when Mr Grey approached and asked for the honour of her hand for the first dance. Her inherent modesty told her that the request likely came from his feeling an obligation to her as hostess of the party, rather than any particular partiality. However, obligation, if any existed, could not explain his insistence on claiming the second dance also, and such was her continued happiness in his company, she did not consider the impropriety of accepting him for both dances.

This partiality was not lost on Darcy, however, who observed William Grey's attentions to Georgiana, and her enthusiasm for them, with displeasure and suspicion.

From across the room, Elizabeth noticed the beginnings of a

scowl forming on her husband's brow. With alarm, she followed the path of his gaze to determine the source of his disquiet, and laughed out loud when her eyes settled on Georgiana and her dance partner. The sound of Elizabeth's laughter caused Darcy to look away from his sister. The brief look he received from his wife was chastisement enough to stop him from striding out among the dancers and calling William Grey to account.

On the completion of the second set, Darcy went in search of the couple and requested his sister's hand for the next. His cold, but civil, dismissal left William Grey in no doubt that his dancing with Miss Darcy was at an end. He, good-naturedly, thanked her for the honour and pleasure of her company, congratulated Mr Darcy on a wonderful evening, and set off in search of Kitty Bennet whom he had promised to engage for a dance also.

Darcy's decision not to dance, initially, had been noted by Kitty, who judged his lack of enthusiasm as a terrible slight on her sister. She observed that he did not dance at all throughout the first set, or the next, and so Elizabeth was left on the side to watch the dancing. He did not even stand with her, leaving her at the mercy of Mrs Cramond and the ladies of the charity board. Indeed, when he did finally stand up, it was with Georgiana and not with Elizabeth. Kitty was incensed at this affront. Emboldened by wine and the high spirits of her company, she began to decry his behaviour loudly during a brief interlude before the third set.

"I cannot think what Mr Darcy means by ignoring his wife so. I declare he does not dance or talk with her, or even so much as look at her! Poor Lizzy! Well, I can assure you, when I marry, it will be for love and passion; I don't give a fig for fortune."

"Kitty, be quiet!" exclaimed Elizabeth, who had just made her way over to the group. "You know little enough of the world to be giving your opinion so forcefully."

Elizabeth, angry and embarrassed by her sister's declarations, was determined to end all such conversation. Kitty turned to argue with her, she did not care for public chastisement, especially when she believed she spoke no untruth, but the fury on Elizabeth's face warned her that any argument would be in vain. With an audible huff, Kitty spun on her heels and left the room.

William Grey returned to the group just as Kitty was departing dramatically. Uncertain as to what had occurred, and unable to fulfil his promise, he turned his attention to Elizabeth, begging her not to leave him standing there when he dearly loved to dance. Elizabeth, pleased at the chance to dance and learn more of the man, accepted with enthusiasm.

"Mr Grey," she began, almost as soon as they had taken up their positions on the floor, "I feel I must warn you: as a rule, I like to converse while I dance. Do you think you are up to the task of being both witty and graceful?"

"Well, madam, my grace has never been found wanting. As for my wit, I cannot vouch, though I shall certainly endeavour not to bore you!" he responded with a smile.

"Excellent news," she replied, "it is just as I had hoped. In truth, I could bear being bored far more than being trod upon."

The dance began, and it was well known to the pair that there was no need to guide or explain the movements. As a consequence, they could allow their conversation to turn to other things.

"I saw you dance earlier with my sister-in-law, Mr Grey," Elizabeth began. "You danced beautifully together. I do not believe there was a single person who was not enthralled."

"Well, I must refuse any part in such praise; I judge any adroitness on my part to be a reflection of Miss Darcy's grace and elegance. May I say, meaning no insult to your own ability, she is the finest dancer that I have ever had the pleasure to partner."

Elizabeth laughed. "Oh, I take no slight at that; I am too aware of my own deficiencies to take any umbrage at your notice of them. I have no doubt, Georgiana's light step would make her a delight to dance with. Are you very fond of dancing, then?"

"Do you attempt to draw me out, Mrs Darcy?" Mr Grey replied. "Would you have me admit to being fond of dancing, or of the company of my dance partner?"

"Oh, my apologies if I was in anyway obscure. Please, I would wish there to be no misunderstanding as to my meaning. I have no real interest in how you feel about dancing; how you feel about my sister-in-law, however, is an entirely different matter!"

Elizabeth's response caused Mr Grey to misstep and he coloured as he felt her eyes upon him. "Really, Mrs Darcy, not even your husband was so forthright in his approach to me. I am a little undone by the boldness of your questioning."

"Well, Mr Grey, I hope you can forgive any impropriety on my part. Know that my questions come from concern for my family and not from any particular distrust of you or any desire to meddle in your affairs. Recent romantic entanglements have caused me to exercise a greater inclination towards prudence, and protection of those I hold dear, particularly when it comes to their attachment to charming young men with a passion for dancing."

"I cannot fault your desire to protect Miss Darcy," he admitted, "and while I was taken aback by your boldness, I admire it. For the moment, would you be satisfied by knowing I dearly love to dance? I have had numerous dancing partners, but none whom I have asked for a second, before Miss Darcy. As to my intentions, I enjoy Miss Darcy's company; I am aware of her fortune, but am not in need of it, and I hope to gain your husband's permission to call on her."

Elizabeth nodded. "I am satisfied, sir, and I thank you, but be warned, my husband may not prove so easily persuaded!"

§

Her cheeks still burning with indignation, Kitty knew she could not return to the group at once, but neither could she hide in her room, fearing Georgiana would seek her there. Instead, she ventured up to the picture gallery where she could find a quiet alcove to nurse her wounded pride in peace.

The candles had been lit earlier in the evening so that the

party could admire the newly hung painting of Darcy and Elizabeth, although the candles had burnt down now, so their light did not reach beyond the middle of the gallery.

Kitty sat in the alcove at the farthest end of the hall, a large curtain and the darkness of the corner shielding her from view should anyone enter. She considered the earlier conversation, her belief in her own innocence growing at every reimagining. Elizabeth had not been justified in admonishing her so. Kitty could hardly be blamed for the fact that Elizabeth's marriage to Darcy was more comfortable than passionate. What was wrong with her determination for romance? She believed, unlike her sisters, that Lydia had been right in choosing George Wickham, who although not wealthy, had evidenced his passionate nature most clearly in their elopement. She did admit, however, that although justified in her opinion, she had perhaps been misguided in voicing it so loudly, and in company. With a slow exhalation of breath, she fixed her hair and dress, determined that she would apologise to Elizabeth, and not allow the indiscretion to spoil what was otherwise proving to be a most enjoyable evening.

She was just ready to return to the party when the echo of footsteps caused her to stay her departure. Opposite her, in the shards of light cast from behind a closing door, she saw a man's figure moving up the gallery. He stopped at a new painting upon the wall, and gazed upon it before stepping back into the darkness.

Kitty was uncomfortable, sitting alone with this stranger, and was wondering if she could move away quietly enough not to be seen, when another person entered the gallery. This time, the figure of a woman, who Kitty recognised as Elizabeth, was visible in the shadow cast, before the door closed again.

"Dance with me, Mrs Darcy," the man's voice called out.

"I do not think my husband would approve of my dancing with a stranger, and certainly not in such a secluded setting," Elizabeth quipped, her response echoing into the gallery.

"What cause can he have to complain when he refused the opportunity to dance with you earlier? A foolish man, your husband. Perhaps your sister, Kitty, is right: perhaps he lacks true feeling and passion."

Elizabeth made her way towards the voice. "I warn you, sir, do not mistake the reserve my husband displays in public for a lack of passion. I certainly do not!"

"Dance with me, Elizabeth."

"Step into the light and let me know who makes such a request."

Kitty was surprised to see Darcy step forward. "Oh, so you pretend not to know me. You may cease your teasing, for I believe you know me as well as I know you."

"And how do you know me, husband?"

"I know you by sight. I would know you just from your eyes; were I to have to pick you from a thousand women, I would recognise those eyes that have so totally captivated me. I know you by sound: I can discern your voice first and foremost among all others; I listen for it when I am not by you. When we are apart, I know how it feels to hold you and how it feels to have your body next to mine. I know the smell of your neck, and the hollow of your bosom where you trace lavender water. I know the taste of your kisses and the saltiness of your skin," and placing her hand over his heart, "I know you here."

Elizabeth reached to hold Darcy's face in her hands. "My darling, I wish I could express so eloquently how I love you. I had never dreamed it possible to find such fulfilment in marriage. I thank God, I had the sense to see beyond my prejudice against you and that you had the heart to continue to love me long after I deserved it. I believe I could not have found such happiness with another. Know my love, as you have found me worthy of your heart, I shall guard and protect it as truly as it were my own."

"And will you dance with me?"

"Always."

From her corner, Kitty could hear the gentle hum of a tune. She watched as Darcy stepped closer to Elizabeth, placed one hand at her back, holding one of her hands with his other, and drew her in to face him.

They danced together, slowly, heedless of proper form, their bodies moving as one. As they moved, one of Darcy's hands remained at Elizabeth's back, securing her body next to his, but the other released its hold so he was free to touch her and she him.

It seemed to Kitty, who continued to gaze at the couple, that their touch was not lustful, not designed to provoke, but gentle, almost reverential, as if they sought to trace the very soul of their beloved. She had never witnessed such a display. Their love for one another could not be doubted, but neither, Kitty suddenly realised, could the esteem and admiration they felt for one another. Though she had always loved to share tales of passion and romance, she had never conceived such an all-consuming devotion could be possible.

The couple stopped when they reached the end of the hallway, just by the alcove in which Kitty had hidden. She felt wretched now; a trespasser to such an intimate moment.

Darcy tilted Elizabeth's chin so he could kiss her, and Kitty closed her eyes, feeling that even looking was too great an intrusion.

Elizabeth broke the silence that followed. "Come now, Fitzwilliam, it is time to return to our guests. Is there anything you need before we do?"

"There is only one thing I shall ever need, and that is for you to love me; just love me, Lizzy."

With that, Kitty heard the door open and close. The portrait gallery was silent and hers once more. She remained where she had hidden, and although she did not fully understand why, she began to cry.

૪ૃ

Once the party was done, and the last of the guests seen safely off, Darcy lay on his bed, exhausted; his mind still absorbed with thoughts of William Grey and his intentions towards Georgiana. He did not hear Elizabeth enter their bedchamber and it was not until the gentle smell of lavender announced her presence that he looked up.

When he did, he was greeted by the welcome sight of her standing naked, tracing lavender water from the hollow at her neck to her navel. He watched as she turned to the glass to fix her hair, allowing curls to tumble down her back. Every movement was deliberate, all attention to her nightly ablutions undertaken slowly, affording him the opportunity to gaze upon every inch of her at his leisure.

"Do I meet with your approval, Fitzwilliam?" she asked, turning to face him.

"Need you even ask, Elizabeth?"

He moved to raise himself off the bed, but Elizabeth stayed him. "I must make amends for the lack of attention shown to you this evening, dearest. It is my intention to more than recompense your patience and your sacrifice."

She moved onto the bed and sat across his upper thighs, allowing herself complete access to his chest. She undid the buttons on his shirt one by one, and as she slid it from his shoulders down his back and arms, she allowed her body to brush against him. Then, sliding lower down his legs, she began to remove his breeches, gently teasing the fabric from his body.

Darcy relaxed as he lay back, relinquishing complete control to Elizabeth. He knew what would come next: his trousers would be dropped carelessly to the floor and then Elizabeth would begin to massage his feet and calves. Her nimble fingers would work his tense muscles before her hands moved up to his thighs. He felt the familiar thrill course through him as Elizabeth's hands began to knead his lower legs. A smile broke out as he anticipated the touch of her hands on his skin, knowing she would briefly, and tentatively, make a sweep across his inner thigh before moving her hands to his sides so she could sweep upwards across his chest with wider strokes and circles.

He was so immersed in what he knew would happen, he did not notice the change in Elizabeth's hand movements, until she failed to sweep around by his side. Before he could utter a word, there was a burst of heat within him, as her hands moved deeper into his inner thighs and masterfully grasped the very core of him.

"Elizabeth," Darcy gasped, "what are you…?" He tried to sit forward, but her lips now followed her fingers and the sudden explosion within him caused him to throw back his head and lie deeper into his pillow.

He was lost to the feel of Elizabeth's fingers and lips, aware of little else but the pleasure and heat pulsing through him. Never had her touch been so sure, and never so decidedly well placed. All tentativeness was gone; she knew his body and was leading him to sensations he had never expected. Just as he feared he could take no more, she stopped, and slid her body up along his. He felt her breasts push into his chest, felt her thighs secure themselves around his, and felt the heat between her legs match the heat between his own.

Darcy turned their bodies, relishing the feel of Elizabeth's softness beneath him. Her arms reached up to his head and she drew him into a vigorous kiss, while her legs wrapped around his thighs and pulled him deep within her. She moved her body in unity with his, their natural rhythms in perfect time with one other. He knew she had been innocent on their first night together, so he was amazed that she could surprise him with such passion and inventiveness in their lovemaking. He had been an experienced lover before they met, but with Elizabeth, he found himself looking for greater ways to please his wife, knowing no greater thrill than the sound of her moaning, and the feel of her body as it shuddered in the wake of the pleasure he brought her.

Their bodies merged. Their arms and legs intertwined, their mouths leaving their deep kiss just long enough to release the cries, which passion called forth. With one final thrust, Darcy claimed Elizabeth completely, holding her body tightly to his, feeling her final release.

Afterwards, he collapsed on his side, exhausted, and completely satisfied. He looked across at Elizabeth, and catching the glisten of sweat across her breasts, leaned forward to taste her, enjoying the saltiness of her skin.

In response to the feel of his tongue, Elizabeth giggled, and playfully said, "My darling, I hope you are beginning to feel the sincerity of my desire to make amends for earlier."

"Beginning, my love?"

"Oh, do not think we are finished; indeed, I have only just begun!"

Darcy moved his head from her breast, took a deep breath, and with feigned supplication raised his hands in surrender, replying, "Madam, I am at your mercy. Do with me as you will."

CHAPTER 7

The family were slow to rise the next morning. When Kitty and Georgiana made it down, they found Elizabeth alone. She had only been up long enough to pour herself a cup of tea and ascertain that Darcy had been gone at least an hour. While Georgiana helped herself to ham and eggs, Kitty called Elizabeth aside to speak to her privately.

"Lizzy, I must speak with you about last night and my unfortunate outburst," she began. "I wish to apologise for any disrespect you felt. I am sorry for it and I will not speak so out of turn again."

Elizabeth regarded her closely. She was surprised to find Kitty genuine in her apology, and sincere in her declaration that she would be more guarded in the future.

"Well then, Kitty, we shall speak no more of this, and continue as before, but I warn you, I will have no further talk regarding Darcy and me."

"You have no reason to fear, Lizzy. I know I have no cause to speak so unkindly nor so unjustly of your husband; it will not happen again."

Elizabeth was puzzled as to Kitty's meaning, but before she could question her further, Georgiana rejoined them, and the conversation turned to the success of the evening, the dancing, the company, and what they would do to entertain themselves once the others had left for London.

"Well, I shall be desolate," announced Kitty.

"Oh Kitty, I am sure we shall make do," teased Georgiana. "We shall make entertainments enough between us to pass the time until our friends return."

Elizabeth could hear a slight wistfulness to her tone.

"You do not think they will forget us?" Kitty cried out, suddenly alarmed at the length of time they would be separated from the Trevelyans and Mr Grey. "Our acquaintance is so new; you do not think they could forget us, surely?"

"Kitty, though I make no bold statements as to myself," answered Georgiana, "I assure you, you are quite unforgettable! Fear not, the Trevelyans and Mr Grey will not forget us. We will meet them on Wednesday for tea, and no doubt learn when we shall see them again."

"I am afraid you will have to cancel your plans for tea," declared Darcy as he strode into the breakfast room. "I shall need the carriages." Detailing his reasons no further, he headed straight for Elizabeth, kissed her good morning, and helped himself to a piece of cold ham.

Georgiana was clearly confused and distressed by the news. Kitty was distraught at the thought of missing their friends, but Elizabeth had spotted a gleam in Darcy's eye as he made his pronouncement and knew he would not deny his sister a chance of socialising without good reason.

"Fitzwilliam, I had planned to go to town that day. Shall I be walking? I do not object for myself, for as you know, I love to walk, but I wonder what our neighbours might say if I am seen traipsing about the countryside."

"Georgiana, I am sure your friends will not mind you changing your plans; you can arrange to meet them another day. As for you, Elizabeth, I fear you will be too busy for a trip to town," Darcy replied, his usual composure preserved.

Kitty could bear being silent no longer. "We most certainly cannot make new arrangements with our friends for they go to London directly and we shall not see them for Lord knows how long. Now all happiness shall surely be ruined by your needing the carriages! I declare I shall walk to the tea shop if it takes all morning."

"That would be an unfortunate use of your time. How will your packing be done if you are not there to instruct?" was all Darcy offered in response.

All three women sat, bewildered.

Kitty spoke first: "You are sending me home?"

Followed by Georgiana: "Brother, you cannot! Please do not!"

And lastly, Elizabeth: "What are you about, husband?"

"Oh," Darcy finally declared, "have I not mentioned that we are going to London?"

℘

By Wednesday morning, Darcy, Elizabeth, Georgiana, and Kitty, all found themselves packed neatly into the largest of the carriages, beginning their trip to the house in Grosvenor Square. The Trevelyans had been contacted and their disappointment at the cancelation of their date for tea was acute, until the news that they would all be reunited in London by the end of the week was offered as solace. Ann and Mary's excitement rivalled Georgiana and Kitty's, and in a flurry of notes passed between their houses, plans were quickly put in place that would see them all together again by the Saturday in one of London's finest tea houses, where the season's entertainments and engagements could be planned in earnest.

Once the journey had begun, Georgiana and Kitty's attention was quickly drawn to each other and their hopes for the excitement that London would offer. Kitty had never been to the city, so it fell to Georgiana to tell what she knew of the parks, galleries, tea houses, libraries, theatres, and shops. She admitted that she had little real experience of many of the enter-tainments London had to offer, as she had been too shy to indulge in society, but she had seen a play at a grand theatre and been in several of the larger houses, so many hours were filled with her detailing the minutiae of all she had encountered.

As their sisters were happily engaged, Darcy and Elizabeth could direct their attentions towards one another. When they were not talking, Darcy was distracted by memories of their first long journey in the carriage on their return from Longbourn after the wedding. Sadly, with company this time, he would not be afforded the pleasure of pulling Elizabeth onto his lap and passing the tedious hours in kissing her. As he turned to look at his wife, he noted the wicked smile on her face and realised that her thoughts had been as delightfully engaged as his own. He began to regret not sending Georgiana and Kitty in a carriage of their own.

"Husband," Elizabeth whispered, "do you recall the last journey we made in this carriage?"

"As it happens, wife, I was just this moment lost in the memory."

"What a shame we have company this time."

"You read my mind, witch!" he joked. "I suppose it is too late to send them to the other carriage?"

"They might find such behaviour suspicious; would you care to explain to your sister why you needed the privacy?"

"I believe I would spare her innocence a little longer, if you please."

₭𝄞

Once Georgiana and Kitty had exhausted their conversation in relation to their knowledge of London, they began to question Darcy and Elizabeth. Darcy was surprisingly forthcoming and the girls hoped his willingness to talk about London's entertainments might yet be turned into a willingness to enjoy them and to allow them to join him.

"Mr Darcy, I do hope you have not come to London solely for business. You will make time to enjoy the city's delights," posed Kitty, with little or no subtlety.

"Well Kitty, I would think it a shame to miss out on all the pleasures London can afford. I hope to spend time at the theatre, and may even be persuaded by Elizabeth to take a turn about a ballroom. Your thoughtfulness as to my entertainment is gratifying – thank you."

Kitty was concerned that neither she nor Georgiana had been mentioned in his plans and looked to Georgiana.

Georgina continued, "Oh yes, brother, you have been so busy of late, it would be good to see you enjoy yourself. Of course, if you were out, I think it would be little trouble if Kitty and I were to join you." Her tone had risen at the end, making her statement half question, half hope.

"Oh, I might see my way to including you in our outings," he added innocently, leaving a long enough pause to tease the girls about details that may follow. "There is a ball on Saturday that I thought could provide a sufficiently grand start to our time here, and so I secured four tickets to that very end."

Darcy sat, both satisfied and horrified by the high-pitched squeals of delight his announcement inspired, and though Georgiana and Kitty were profuse in their thanks, all the gratitude that really mattered, he found in the smile of his wife.

ℴ

The following morning, almost as soon as their bags were unpacked, Kitty considered the gowns she had brought. All were found wanting and she was determined something would have to be done. While she would never approach Darcy to ask for something new to be bought for the ball, she had no such scruples in accosting Elizabeth with an impatient plea.

"I simply cannot be expected to wear these dresses to the ball on Saturday, Lizzy!" she opened with, before even uttering 'Good morning'. "Really, I have nothing that is not a hand-me-down, or at least a season old. I think you would be embarrassed to be seen with me!"

"You could always stay at home," Elizabeth coolly replied, refusing to indulge Kitty's hysterics.

"Elizabeth, how can you be so cruel? You know perfectly well I mean for you to buy me a new dress," protested Kitty.

"Kitty, that is rather presumptuous of you. I should have hoped for gratitude for all that has been done for you, and yet still you expect more."

Kitty was a little chastened by the remark, but any good which could have resulted was quickly undone by the entry of Darcy, announcing loudly to the room that he would be off to town in an hour and if the girls wanted anything new to wear they would have to be ready. There was a loud screech and a flash of muslin as Kitty raced for the door, followed by a calmer and more dignified Georgiana who stopped as she passed her brother to thank him for generosity she could not possibly deserve.

"Well, what a fine start!" exclaimed Elizabeth. "I was attempting to school Kitty in being grateful and making do, when you stride in with talk of trips to dressmakers."

"Do I spoil them, Lizzy?" he answered. "Would you have me be as Kitty thinks me to be, cold and unfeeling?"

"Kitty, it seems, for reasons known only to herself, has changed her opinion of you, husband."

"Well, perhaps all that was ever needed was a trip to the city," he laughed.

"No; indeed, it was before you mentioned this trip. She talked of being unjust and unkind. I was taken aback by the sincerity of her apology. That you offered a trip to London has undoubtedly secured her favour, however. As for this, well, I fear we may never get her to leave."

"You know, I can scarcely believe it, but I have taken something of a shine to your sister, Lizzy, and I would not be unduly disturbed if we were unable to convince her to leave. She has brought such liveliness to Georgiana; it gladdens me. Did you see Georgiana's face when she thought I was sending Kitty home? I have never seen her look so crestfallen. You were right when you said she needed somebody, and Kitty has proven to be just that somebody."

"Husband, you seem to forget, I am always right!" Elizabeth teased in response, and placing herself in his lap, she added, "Although, I am perfectly willing to forgive you if I am to be included in your trip to the dressmakers."

Laughing once more, she kissed him with such intent and intensity that Darcy forgot his plans for the day, and Kitty and Georgiana were left waiting two hours before the couple appeared downstairs ready for the excursion into town.

ℰꝋ

The time for the Saturday ball was upon them before Kitty and Georgiana had hoped possible. They had met with Ann and Mary Trevelyan earlier in the day, and plans were made to meet again later that evening. Without Georgiana ever having to ask, Ann offered that Mr Grey and their cousin, John, would be joining them, and Mary declared the Mr Grey had requested the honour of dancing with both the young ladies of Pemberley. Although both girls had been mentioned, Ann and Mary smiled knowingly at Georgiana, giving rise to a deep blush on her part and some gentle well-meant teasing on theirs.

Extra attention was given to every detail of their hair and dress in preparation for the ball. Georgiana doubted that she had ever been so conscientious, and Kitty's enthusiasm for Georgiana's perfection had meant her hair being redone three times, but finally, with pale pink flowers and a chain of pearls woven through perfectly placed curls, Kitty was pleased, and Georgiana was ready to, once again, meet Mr Grey.

As they dressed for the evening, Darcy's attention was also focused on Georgiana, and the possibility that she might encounter William Grey once more. Despite having engaged Georgiana for several dances now, and displaying an obvious partiality for her, he had failed to make any formal approach to Darcy, and this, he did not like. The moments he had managed to snatch with William Grey were too brief to allow any real consideration of his character and this unsettled Darcy further. He had made some discreet enquiries as to the boy, and discovered that he was the second son of a good family, whose fortune and land holdings were solid. He stood to inherit a sizeable fortune, though no land of his own. He was not linked to any scandals and was generally found to be a well-liked gregarious fellow. Still, Darcy did not like it!

"Husband, I can see the vein on your brow throbbing. Stop thinking on William Grey and Georgiana and let us enjoy the evening. If I am not mistaken, your snooping turned up no great scandals or skeletons in relation to the boy. Can you not now be easy and allow Georgiana to enjoy the attentions of a well-educated, well-respected, jovial, pleasant, and perfectly handsome young man? Or do I ask too much of you?"

"I resent the implication of my having snooped! I made discreet enquiries Elizabeth, as any concerned guardian would."

"And you found nothing amiss, my love, so let it be. Let your sister enjoy herself. After the time she had with Wickham, I should have thought you would be pleased that her next romantic entanglement would be with someone so much more worthy."

Darcy sighed and sat on the bed. "I worry Elizabeth; I remember how delicate she was after her involvement with Wickham, and I fear the consequences should she face disappointment again. Do you think me foolish?"

"How could your love for Georgiana ever be foolish, Fitzwilliam? Seeing you with her, your care and concern for her, was one of the things that first endeared you to me, but you must take pains to ensure your love does not smother. She is a young woman and needs some freedom. If her heart be broken, we will be here to nurse it better. She is not fifteen now; she is not the same young girl worked upon by Wickham. You love her, I know; now learn to trust her."

Darcy smiled at his wife. "As ever, you will be my guide, Elizabeth. I will do as you ask – well, I will certainly try – though perhaps if you see me scowling, you might take pains to remind me."

Ⅎ⁍

After all of the excitement and worry of their preparation, both Darcy and Georgiana found themselves at last making their way up the grand steps to the ballroom, each with different anticipations as to how the evening would go. Darcy took solace in Elizabeth's presence by his side, and her assurances all would be well. Kitty's high spirits could barely be contained. In truth, Elizabeth feared that any impropriety exhibited would be on the part of her sister and not the more reserved Georgiana, who was, for the third time since they had left the house, assuring her agitated companion that there would be dancing, and young men enough to share. If there were not, she would forgo a partner or two so Kitty might dance the entire evening.

"Not if the partner is Mr Grey!" teased Kitty in return, much to Darcy's displeasure.

On hearing the comment, Elizabeth nudged him playfully, and silently prayed the evening would pass without incident or embarrassment.

Once inside, Kitty and Georgiana were impatient to meet their friends, and before Darcy could utter a word, the two entered into the gathered throng and were lost from sight.

Darcy stood perplexed by their sudden absence. "It feels strange," he said, his voice tinged with sadness, "not to have Georgiana by me. She did not even look behind her as she left."

Elizabeth drew closer to him and curled her arm around his. "Will you make do with having my arm this evening then, husband? I cast not the elegant figure of your sister, nor do I possess her grace, but I flatter myself to think I might nevertheless be a suitable companion."

"You are many things, Lizzy, though I doubt suitable is one of them," he replied, earning himself a prod to the ribs as rebuke. "It will be my honour, as you well know, to have you with me. Lead on, Elizabeth, and let us hope tonight brings the enjoyment it should."

৪৩

Darcy's sadness at the loss of Georgiana was quickly overcome by his delight at Elizabeth's reaction as they entered the ballroom. Her eyes widened in an attempt to take in the opulence of their surroundings. This affair made even the grand private balls she had attended with Darcy seem like simple country dances.

The room was lit by large crystal chandeliers that sent flashes of colour dancing across the deep red walls. Large, red velvet curtains framed the windows, the long folds of material held back by heavy gold braid wrapped around ornamental golden dragons. The rich reds and golds of the furnishings added depth and warmth to the dark wood of the floor and the furniture, all of which had been waxed and polished, giving a high sheen. Impeccably dressed staff served drinks from golden trays, and platters of fruits, tarts, and meats were piled high on tables. Adding to the decadence of the room were the whirls of coloured silks worn by the women attending, the light from the room reflected in the glitter of their jewels.

Elizabeth had never witnessed such a display, and Darcy smiled at her excitement, though he had never been one to overindulge in the pleasures of London society. He had attended his share of high society balls, but never had he delighted in them so much; Elizabeth's enthusiasm proving infectious.

"Fitzwilliam, have you ever seen anything like this?" she exclaimed. "I do not know whether to revel in the spectacle, or mock its excesses! Such needless extravagance; it is quite wonderful!"

"I have attended this ball in previous years, and although I was never unduly taken by the garish display, I thought you might enjoy the theatrics of it."

"I can honestly say, tonight will provide me with enough wanton ostentation and silliness to distract me for months to come at the mere recollection. I shall have to write to Charlotte, though I fear she will not believe half of what I tell her."

℁

From across the room, the Darcys were surprised to hear a familiar voice calling out: "Darcy! Good Lord, is that you, man? Is that Fitzwilliam Darcy I spy attending a ball and in London no less?"

On hearing the salute, the couple turned to be greeted by the welcome sight of the Bingleys making their way towards them.

"Jane!" called out Elizabeth, her delight in the evening now complete. "We had no notion as to your being in London. We thought you recovering from an illness at home."

"Oh, dearest Charles will fret so," Jane replied with a smile. "My condition was not so serious and a few days' bed rest was all that was needed. I am fully recovered and excessively pleased to see you here this evening. Charles was certain you would not come to London, and we had planned to arrange a stay at Pemberley."

"Indeed, Mrs Darcy," interrupted Charles Bingley, "I am much in awe of your power of persuasion over my friend. I cannot tell you the number of times I tried, and failed, to convince Darcy to attend these functions with me. However did you manage it?"

"Oh, do not look to me, Mr Bingley, I was as surprised as you when Fitzwilliam volunteered the plan and secured tickets to this ball without any consultation."

The Bingleys looked at Darcy incredulously.

Despite being aware that three pairs of eyes stared at him intently, Darcy managed to maintain an air of disaffection. "Really, Bingley, I fail to see why you make such a show of surprise," he offered at last. "You must admit Elizabeth makes far more attractive company than you."

❧

The couples fell quickly into the comfort of family and friendship, and taking a position on the edge of the main ballroom, were rewarded by the sight of Kitty and Georgiana dancing gracefully among London's high society.

"Is that truly Kitty?" queried Jane. "She looks the very picture of refinement. I can scarcely believe my eyes!"

"She has settled in well at Pemberley, it is true," replied Elizabeth. "Georgiana's influence has been great. Mama and Papa will be quite shocked when she returns to them as a young lady instead of a silly girl. Fitzwilliam declares she benefits from an extended absence from Lydia."

"Well, if such a separation be the reason for the improvements I bear witness to, long may it continue. Though you know, I could never be unkind to Lydia, and I should be grateful if we can prevent another sister succumbing to the seductions of a man such as Wickham."

"Jane," declared Elizabeth, "that smacks of disapproval! Can it be you have seen the light where Wickham is concerned and are willing to accept he may not be all we might have wanted in a brother?"

"I have had quite a change of heart when it comes to Mr Wickham. Indeed, Lizzy, such new information has come to light, I can hardly believe I ever defended him."

Elizabeth was surprised at Jane's honesty, and concerned at what had so hardened her resolve. Moving out of the hearing of Darcy and Bingley, she encouraged her to continue.

"Oh Lizzy, you know how I dearly wished Wickham to be the man we believed him to be upon our first acquaintance. I defended his actions, even in the face of growing concern surrounding his honesty and integrity. I held out hope he might yet prosper as a newlywed with a new commission, but I have received such accounts of his profligacy that I fear he is beyond redemption."

"This is most serious news," declared a shocked Elizabeth. "Where do you get your accounts? Can they be trusted? Remember, Jane, there are those who preach gossip as if it were the word of God, and take pleasure in the pain that results."

"How I wish I could attribute all I know to malicious gossip, but my accounts come from a most trusted source. They come from Lydia herself!"

At length, Jane detailed all she knew of the activity of George and Lydia Wickham since they had left Longbourn to join his regiment in the North. Lydia wrote of parties and balls, new hats and dresses, a carriage and four, and all manner of delights. "But how is such a life to be maintained and on a soldier's wage? He has no other source of income that would support such extravagance. You should see how Lydia relishes the recounting of the monies spent, never thinking about how bills are to be paid. She simply maintains a blind faith in her husband."

"Wickham will have profited somewhat from his agreement to marry Lydia," agreed Elizabeth, "but even Fitzwilliam's generosity will have had limits. If Lydia's tales are to be believed, they will quickly be insolvent if they are not already so."

"It is not just the money that concerns me, Lizzy. Lydia talks of Wickham being out at night without her, claiming that the politics of military service in the North requires him to attend functions, an obligation, she calls them, but why he is obliged to attend without his wife, I do not understand."

"Poor Lydia," was all Elizabeth could offer by way of consolation. "Do I speak too harshly when I say at least it is a mercy she does not see all the failings of the man she is betrothed to?"

"No," laughed Jane, "I think for once we can rejoice in Lydia's silliness and hope she remains happily ignorant."

"I will send her some money," Elizabeth resolved, "and counsel her to set it aside – though I know the temptation of a new hat or pair of shoes will likely see it spent."

"Well, if you will send her money," Jane said, "do not send it up North, for I received a note from Mama just yesterday: Lydia and Wickham are expected in London in two days."

∞

News of the anticipated arrival of the Wickhams was not greeted warmly by Elizabeth. She did not mind for herself: Lydia was merely tiring, and George she had learned to manage with casual detachment, but she was less certain of how her husband would respond to the news and so was determined he would hear of their coming from her.

"Husband, do you think I could persuade you to a dance?" she began, just before the beginning of the next set.

"Wife, I believe you could persuade me to anything," replied he, smiling warmly. "A dance with the most handsome woman in the room could surely be no punishment."

"Handsomest woman in the room? I believe there was a time you found me only tolerable."

"And if I am not mistaken, there was a time you promised your mama that you would never dance with me."

"I have always said: too good a memory in matters of love is an unforgiveable thing! I shall forgive your foolishness if you forgive mine and dance with me," Elizabeth laughed, taking hold of Darcy's hand.

The couple were watched as they picked their way through the gathered guests on their way to the ballroom floor. There had been much talk of Elizabeth, and those attending were keen to get a glimpse of the woman who had succeeded in securing the attachment and fortune of Fitzwilliam Darcy.

There was a general agreement that her figure was pleasing, and her face, though not as handsome as her sister's, would certainly be described as pretty. Those who had spoken to her added to the general gossip that she was intelligent and witty, and though she tended towards a certain outspokenness, she had enough of the manners of a gentleman's daughter to prevent coarseness in manner or conversation.

Those who were free from the disappointment of not having secured Darcy for themselves, or their daughters, observed the man as well as the wife. He had never looked so at ease in company as he did escorting Mrs Darcy, stopping to wish hello to friends along the way. When they reached the line and took their place among the dancers, his attention could scarcely be drawn away from her, and one woman observed, with a degree of alarm, that Fitzwilliam Darcy was smiling!

To their being the centre of such attention, the couple were completely insensible. Their attentions were given over to the other, and as they made their way through the dance, all else seemed to fade away, leaving them alone in a crowded room.

"I have some news to share with you, husband; news, I fear, that will not please you, but which I would have you hear from me and not from another."

"Such drama, Elizabeth; pray, what is the matter?"

Elizabeth looked at her husband square in the face, so as to observe his true reaction before responding. "The Wickhams are coming to London."

There was an immediate clenching of his jaw, and a furrow across his brow was briefly evident, but before Elizabeth could comment, these tensions were gone and Darcy looked unconcerned by the news.

"You are not displeased by the news of their coming to London then, husband?" she queried, surprised by his calmness.

"Wickham and I shall never be on good terms, but I am tired of the man and I refuse to allow him to interfere again in my happiness. We will, of course, extend some manner of courtesy to your sister; if you wish to see her or have her to dine, you would not find me unwilling. Her husband, however, may not enter our house."

"I had not thought to invite Lydia to the house at all. I intend to send her some money and perhaps I might meet her in town. I confess I have little enough desire to spend too much time with her myself and am even less inclined towards spending time with her husband. Oh, I am truly awful, Fitzwilliam. What sort of a woman casts aside the bonds of sisterly affection with such ease?"

"Do not upset yourself, Lizzy," Darcy whispered. "Lydia relinquished any strong claim to sisterly affection when she ran off with Wickham and almost ruined your family. She gave little heed to any scruples in regards to you when she acted so recklessly. You owe her nothing."

"Still," Elizabeth returned, "she is my sister and foolish and selfish as she may be, she will always be my sister. There is no malice in her; her actions were borne out of impetuousness and the imprudence of youth, not from a desire to do harm. I am certain she never so much as gave a thought to the devastation her indiscretion could have wrought."

"That hardly excuses her, Elizabeth."

"No indeed not, though it softens my feelings towards her, nonetheless. I will send her some money. I may meet her. I shall see. I believe I have it in my heart to forgive her impulsiveness even if I may never forget it, for in the strangest of ways she helped bring us to one another, and that is a gift I will ever be grateful for."

CHAPTER 8

Despite Darcy's earlier concerns, the ball passed very well. Georgiana danced with William Grey, but only once. Kitty's high spirits were suitably regulated, and although her vivacity was commented upon, it was by way of compliment rather than criticism. Elizabeth was an absolute success; her manner winning over men and women alike, even those closely associated with Lady Catherine, grudgingly admitted the elegant and well-spoken woman before them was not what they had expected. The addition of the Bingleys, being the best possible company, added greatly to their general enjoyment. Even the news that the Wickhams would soon be in London could do little to dampen Darcy's satisfaction in the evening, and as they journeyed back to Grosvenor Square, he congratulated himself on such a propitious start to their stay in London.

৪৩

Darcy's self-congratulation was not long lived. It ended at the instant the first mail was received on Monday morning, for sitting among the expected letters of business lay two letters penned by the same hand: one addressed to him, and one to Georgiana. He handed Georgiana her letter, and the instant she and Kitty spied the wax seal, the cheeks of one flushed, the other paled, and neither stayed at the table long enough to finish their breakfast.

"I passed Georgiana and Kitty in the hall," said Elizabeth as she entered, "and they were most flustered. Is everything well? Good Lord, Fitzwilliam, what is the matter?"

"We have received a letter."

Elizabeth sat, expecting the worst possible news. "Good heavens, Fitzwilliam, what is the matter? Is someone hurt? Dead? Tell me at once, what is the matter?"

"Now, Elizabeth, please do not worry. To my knowledge, everyone in the family is in the fullest of health. We have both received letters from William Grey. He asks permission to call today on Georgiana."

"William Grey? William Grey is to call on Georgiana and that is the cause of your obvious distress? Oh, for pity's sake, Fitzwilliam, you scared me half to death because a man wishes to call on your sister? Really, husband!"

Elizabeth swatted his arm as punishment for his silliness and ignored his protestations as to the seriousness of the matter, turning her attention to breakfast and finding the freshest piece of toast.

ℂ

To Darcy's relief, when William Grey arrived that afternoon, he was not alone, but accompanied by the Trevelyan sisters. His greeting of the two women, whom he found pleasant, charming, and most suitable companions for Georgiana, was cordial and inviting. His greeting of Grey was not. Before his treatment of the young man could rise to the level of incivility, Elizabeth made an excuse to call him from the room and insisted he leave and not return until the party had quit.

"Fitzwilliam, what do you mean by sitting there and scowling at the boy? He did not come alone, which must alleviate some of your distress. I doubt very much he intends to propose to Georgiana today. If you continue to stare at him with such blatant hostility, he may never, and if that be the case, Georgiana may never forgive you."

"Do you seriously intend to remove me from my own house, Elizabeth?" he uttered.

"No, darling, of course not; just from the drawing room!"

She smiled as she answered, kissed him lightly on the cheek, and turned about to rejoin the others, leaving Darcy standing bewildered in the hallway. There seemed little else for him to do, but to return to the library and continue his regular business, trusting Elizabeth would be vigilant in her attention to his sister and her suitor. With a sigh of resignation, and the grudging admission that Georgiana looked quite the young lady playing host to her friends, he left her in peace, determined not to reappear until he knew their guests to be gone.

Almost as soon as Darcy and Elizabeth had left the room, William Grey saw his opportunity to speak, finally, with some degree of privacy, to Georgiana.

"Miss Darcy, would you be so good as to tell me the history of the charming figurine I see on display over there," he said, pointing to the other side of the room. "It puts me in mind of something I have been looking for as a gift for my mother."

"Certainly, Mr Grey," she replied. "Come, let me show it to you, so you may more readily judge it."

William Grey was pleased at her willingness to follow his ruse to separate them from the group, and though they would still share a room with Kitty and the Trevelyan sisters, the space between them was sufficient to allow a greater degree of intimacy to their conversation.

"I hoped to come alone today, Miss Darcy, but once Miss Ann and Miss Mary knew of my plans, they refused to hear of their not accompanying me. I trust you are not too disappointed?"

Georgiana reacted just as he had hoped with shy smiles, light blushes, and expressions of "Oh, Mr Grey". He stood watching her, doubting he had ever seen anything as beautiful as the face of Miss Georgiana Darcy tinged pink with a blush.

"I enjoyed our dance together last night; I have enjoyed all of our dances together. I would have asked you for another, but I feared your brother would not approve. He is a most forbidding fellow, but I dare say he has cause to be, with the attention and favour you must garner wherever you go."

"Mr Grey!" Georgiana exclaimed.

"Do I speak too plainly, Miss Darcy? Forgive me, but surely, you must know how difficult it was for me when you danced with those other men at the ball last night? The thought of their being able to hold your hand and converse so intimately with you tortured me."

"I talked of horses and hunting with Mr West, politics with Mr Cramond, the weather with Mr Armstrong, and nothing at all with Mr Wayburn. You need not have been distressed," Georgiana offered by way of consolation.

"But you held their hand and gave them your attention, nevertheless, and I envied them," he continued, moving his fingers across the figurine she held, to lightly brush her, smiling with satisfaction as the blush spread further across her face, her breath quickening at his touch.

ଫ

Forcing himself to focus on something – anything – Darcy picked up the remaining correspondence from the morning and began to look through it. He stopped at a small letter that drew his attention due to the unfamiliar hand. Drawing it out, he reached for the letter opener to break through the heavy wax seal on the back.

He read the short note contained within, the colour draining from his face as he did so. He slumped into his chair upon finishing, the paper crumpled inside his tightly clenched fist.

Dear Mr Darcy,

We are not acquainted, but I write to you concerning a woman with whom we are both connected: my sister May Sinclair. It is with considerable grief, sir, that I must inform you of the death of my beloved sister some weeks ago.

I will not here detail the circumstances of her passing, as I do not believe it proper, but I must speak with you regarding a matter of great importance concerning my sister and her relationship to you.

I would be grateful if you could meet me, at a time and place of your convenience. I am staying at the lodging house on Breakmore Street, and you may send any message to me at that address.

I await your reply.

Yours sincerely,

John Sinclair

For several minutes, Darcy could do no more than sit and stare blankly, shock completely overwhelming his usual sense of action. May Sinclair dead! He had not thought of the woman in some time; to hear now that she was dead was disturbing news. As to the matter they needed to discuss, he could not imagine what Sinclair was hinting at. He sat for some minutes, remembering May and how important she had once been to him. A half-smile broke out on his face as he pictured her sitting by her dressing table listening patiently to him as he recounted his day and talked out his frustrations. As a woman, she had been attentive, attractive, and quick-witted. As a lover, she had been passionate, engaging, and creative. Indeed, May offered him everything he required in a mistress, and he had been grateful to her.

His smile faded as he thought of how he had ended their affair; how cold and unfeeling it must have seemed to send a letter. He did not even show her the courtesy of paying her a call. He regretted this action now; May deserved better.

Darcy ran his fingers through his hair and roughly shook his head, as though forcing his fugue state to clear. If he was to handle this matter appropriately, he had to think. Above all else, two things were certain: he must meet with Sinclair, and he must ensure Elizabeth never learned of it. He most certainly did not relish the thought of having to explain his relationship with May to her.

With a course of action in mind, he wrote a note to Sinclair detailing his intention to meet with him the next day at his club.

Darcy would ensure that they had a room where they could talk privately. With hopes of a speedy conclusion to the matter, he had a boy deliver the note to Breakmore Street and await a response.

ℂ

Darcy was sufficiently distracted by the correspondence that he forgot his earlier concerns surrounding William Grey's apparent courtship of Georgiana. His distraction was observed later that evening, although those who noted it accounted for it differently.

Georgiana assumed his reluctance to speak on the matter was a sign of his disapproval: he had left the drawing room abruptly, and had not been seen again until dinner. This was surely evidence enough that he disliked Mr Grey. If this was the case, then what hope could Georgiana have for any future with him? These thoughts subdued the gaiety that the afternoon's visit had inspired.

Kitty failed to notice any change in Darcy. She was completely consumed by concern for Georgiana's despondency, and creating all manner of fanciful romantic reasons for it. Perhaps her separation from Mr Grey was at the heart of it. Perhaps in their quiet moments, alone at the other end of the room, he had proposed, and Georgiana feared that Darcy would refuse to allow it? Whatever the reason, it was plain that he and Georgiana were passionately in love, and she would do all she could to further their cause.

Elizabeth's concern was the greatest of all. She could make no account for Darcy's distraction. He had said little to her while they dressed for dinner, displayed no humour as she teased him about William Grey, and had, most worryingly, failed to respond with a suitable degree of passion to her kisses.

ℂ

After an uneasy night, Darcy was glad to leave the house early to attend his meeting with John Sinclair. Elizabeth's questions, as they had retired to bed, proved that she had not been fooled by what he thought was a valiant effort to appear as though nothing were amiss. He mentioned receiving a letter with unsettling news and claimed his distraction was due to a matter of business. He apologised, and assured her that it would be dealt with. He suffered a slight twinge of guilt over referring to the matter as a problem of business, but in truth, he had no idea what Sinclair wanted, so he assured himself, while trying to assuage his conscience, his lie had been innocent enough.

Darcy had intended to arrive early at the club to breakfast and prepare himself for his meeting, but when he arrived, Sinclair was already waiting and this troubled him. The matter must be one of either great seriousness or potential financial gain for him to attend an hour early. After initial greetings, the two men sat down to an uncomfortable breakfast, neither really possessing the appetite for food, but eating, nonetheless. As soon as the room was cleared and the gentlemen finally left alone, Darcy opened the conversation.

"I think it is time we attend to the business which has drawn us both here out of our beds so early. You said you had a matter you wished to discuss with me, well get to it and let us both be gone."

"You really are quite formidable, Mr Darcy, just as my sister described. I will do as you ask and cut straight to the heart of the matter, though you may not thank me for my frankness. As I mentioned in my letter, my sister is dead. She died several weeks ago of a malevolent fever. I was out of the country at the time of her death, and having no one to claim her she suffered the indignity of a pauper's burial."

"I am sorry to hear that, Mr Sinclair. I had no notion of her even being ill. If she had reached out to me, if I had known of her death, I can assure you I would have done what I could, but I do not understand your purpose in coming to me now."

"I am not here to speak to you about May directly; it is rather in relation to her daughter…"

Darcy turned sharply to him, his full attention given over to the man. "Her what? May had no daughter!"

"May did indeed have a child, named Maria, after our mother."

"I cannot fathom May failing to tell me she had a child. Where was she kept while May lived at Bow Street? I know she was never there. Was Maria with a family, or sent away to school? "

The questions were tumbling from Darcy in rapid succession. When Darcy finally drew breath, Sinclair could answer. "You seem to be under the misapprehension, sir, that the child is of some age. She is not; she has months, not years to her. The fever which eventually killed my sister sprang from a frailty born in child birthing."

"Can it be possible?" Darcy interrupted. "Who is the father?"

Sinclair simply smiled.

Darcy rose to his feet, sharply. "No! That is not possible. I cannot be the father. I cannot. I took every precaution…"

Sinclair said nothing in response to the denial, but simply continued to smile; after all, he had not expected Darcy to own the child immediately.

The two men stared at each other, a heavy silence between them, until Darcy pulled himself up to his full height, smoothed his waistcoat, and simply left the room.

℘

Elizabeth wondered at Darcy's early departure. She understood some pressing matter of business was calling urgently upon his attention, but she had not anticipated such an early start to his day. She too had risen early, feeling unwell, and was disappointed to find him gone. She had wanted the comfort of his arms and the reassurance of his presence beside her. She had only now to take solace in the notion that once his business was attended to, his distraction would be at an end.

Continuing to feel unwell, Elizabeth chose not to go to breakfast at her usual hour and so was still in the bedroom when Darcy returned from the club. He presumed she was in the breakfast room, and was entirely unaware his entrance was observed from the bathroom door. Darcy strode into the bedroom, his face flushed with agitation, muttering something beneath his breath. Before Elizabeth could say a word, he ripped the coat from his back, threw it against the wall, and swore in language that Elizabeth had never heard him use.

"Fitzwilliam, what is the matter?" she cried out, standing just behind him, shaking at the violence in his voice.

Darcy turned, surprised at seeing her there. "Elizabeth! I thought you were at breakfast," was all that he replied.

CHAPTER 9

Despite Elizabeth's efforts, Darcy refused to speak further on his outburst. It was just business, he promised, nothing to be concerned about. He laughed at his anger, calling it a silly response to a minor upset.

"You would tell me if it was anything more serious, wouldn't you, Fitzwilliam? Elizabeth asked. "You know you can share these things with me."

"Of course, my heart, it is nothing. Business, that is all."

Taking her in his arms, he drew her close to reassure her, a tightness appearing across his brow as he realised that he had lied to her for the second time. As he held her, he swore to himself that it would be the last.

∞

The boarding house that John Sinclair had listed as his lodging looked a dismal run-down affair. Darcy was not sure what he had expected, but standing outside, he felt that the setting added to the sad and distasteful nature of the business he was there to conduct.

The landlady who responded to the bell could not disguise her surprise at the appearance of a gentleman of Darcy's standing. She was certain that he could not mean to enter her home, and it was some minutes before Darcy could convince her that he was at the correct address, and that he did mean to stay, if she would be willing to admit him. He was then most cordially invited in, and the landlady, an elderly widow named Mrs Undergood, showed him to the small drawing room where he could wait upon the arrival of Mr Sinclair.

Although the building was run down and the furnishings worn, Darcy could tell that Mrs Underwood did what she could to keep her rooms clean. Her own appearance was neat, so he regretted the discomfort and embarrassment his presence clearly brought her. She apologised for the smallness of the room, feared she had nothing but tea to offer as refreshment, and at all times kept one hand over a patch in her sleeve where the material had completely worn through.

Darcy was conscious of the difficult position she was in, and, with intentions he attributed to the good influence of Elizabeth, sought to alleviate her discomfort by saying, with as much warmth as he could manage, "Mrs Undergood, please do not concern yourself; this room is perfectly comfortable. If it would be no trouble to you, I would be most grateful for some tea. I found the streets dusty today and I can think of nothing better than tea at this moment. I find nothing refreshes quite like it."

Mrs Undergood looked grateful for his politeness and with a promise of a "brew like no other" went to leave the room.

"Mrs Undergood," Darcy added as she was leaving, "I cannot help but notice how spotless your mantel is – I have some staff who could learn something from you."

The landlady beamed at the compliment. "Well, I thank you indeed, sir, I can only imagine the fine surroundings you are accustomed to, but I do my best to keep my own as proper as I can. I am heartened by your notice of my efforts."

With that, Mrs Undergood she set off to the kitchen, pride and gratification adding a lightness to her step, not felt in many years.

ℰℭ

Darcy did not have to wait long for the arrival of John Sinclair. The presence of a gentleman at the Breakmore Street lodgings was news, which spread quickly into the back streets and public houses. It found Sinclair deep in his cups, soliciting the company of a young local girl, Bessie Hargreaves, for the afternoon. He had known Darcy would reach out to him: a newlywed of his standing would not risk damaging his position or reputation, but to arrive so soon, and in person at his lodgings, spoke of a desperation that he hoped would prove profitable.

Unwilling to forgo the pleasure of either his ale or his bit of muslin, Sinclair arrived back at the lodging house, a jug in one hand and Bessie in the other. He swayed slightly as he entered the room, and it was clear to Darcy that the young girl holding his arm was keeping the man standing tall.

Sinclair bowed clumsily, pushed Bessie in the direction of the nearest chair, and turned to his visitor.

"Well, Mr Darcy, I hope you have returned ready to conduct business – you will find me reasonable."

"I would conduct this business, as you put it, in private. I must ask your companion to leave," Darcy retorted, with such command that the young girl was almost to the door before Sinclair caught her arm.

"She will remain until I decide otherwise!" he bellowed, his ire at Darcy's manner invoking sobriety. "Talk with me now or I might find myself more inclined to talk to your wife. The decision is yours."

Darcy's equanimity had never been so tested, but he was quickly resigning himself to the fact that, for the moment, Sinclair had the upper hand. Though it pained him, he signalled capitulation and allowed the other man to proceed as he wished.

Bessie, showing more discretion than her social betters, quietly moved to the furthest corner of the room, and concentrated on tracing the pattern of the paper on the wall with her finger.

Sinclair, pleased with his victory, cleared his throat and began, what Darcy assumed, was a well-practised speech.

"As May's closest remaining relative, the care for her daughter has fallen to me. I do not resent the burden, but you must understand I am a man of limited means. If I am to meet my obligations to the girl, I believe it only right her father do the same."

"You seem very certain I am the father; might I enquire why?"

"Come now, Mr Darcy, we are both men of the world, are we not?" Sinclair replied, emphasising his point with a wink in the direction of young Bessie. "We both know of the services my sister provided you. She was handsomely rewarded and well looked after for her efforts. In fact, I thank you for your care of her. I was not at home when my father cast her out and her situation could have been graver."

"And it is because of this relationship between us, you believe me the father?"

"I know my sister, Mr Darcy. She would not have risked all the benefits of being your mistress for a simple rutting."

Darcy winced at the continued coarseness of the man who, although he bore a physical resemblance to May, lacked the refinement and gentility of her nature. "Mr Sinclair, as you insist on your companion remaining with us, I must insist you temper your vulgarity."

"What, Bessie there? Are you concerned for her innocence?" Sinclair laughed. "Oh, she won't mind, will you, girl?"

"I mind, Sinclair," glared Darcy.

There was a flash of hostility between the men, though Sinclair resolved it would be to his advantage to avoid antagonising Darcy. "I will mind my tongue if it so offends you," he smirked. "Now, back to why we are here. I have made discreet enquiries. I know at the time the child was conceived, May was living in the house you provided for her on Bow Street, and was within your employ. If you will accept your responsibility in the matter, I see no need to make it public knowledge."

"You are determined to pronounce me the father if I fail to comply with your demands, I take it?" stated Darcy.

"I would be left with little choice; you must understand my

position."

"I fully understand your position, Mr Sinclair," Darcy replied in a tone, half acknowledgement, half threat, "but now understand mine! I know I am not the father of Maria Sinclair, and I will not have my reputation tarnished by lies suggesting otherwise. If you will seek compensation for taking on your niece, I suggest you look to her real father."

Sinclair had no time to respond to Darcy's denial of the girl, as he found the man suddenly standing in front of him. "You seek to threaten me, Mr Darcy, standing as close as you do?"

"There is no threat, Sinclair. Mrs Undergood was correct, though: it is a very small room." Darcy smiled, but there was no warmth to it. "As you are content to investigate no further, I will uncover the truth to Maria's paternity. All I ask is, you give me time to do so."

"I can ill afford to wait indefinitely for you, Mr Darcy," Sinclair replied, increasingly unnerved by the closeness of the man.

"Give me two weeks. If I have discovered nothing within that time, we will come to some other arrangement."

"Two weeks it is, sir. I have it on your honour, I shall hear from you again?"

"You have my word, Sinclair, and in the meantime you will not reveal your suspicions as to the paternity of Maria?"

"On my honour."

Darcy sighed and looked across the room. He doubted much stock could be placed in the honour of Sinclair but the direct look and quick nod he received from Bessie at least promised that her silence was guaranteed.

ഇ

Upon entering his club, Darcy took a chair in the furthest corner of the room. He turned it to face the nearest window, affording him a perfect view of the street below, with a hope that his position would suggest to others that he wished to be left alone. His demeanour was such, in fact, that no one but the waiter dared to approach him, only interrupting his solitude long enough to determine what he desired to drink. Once the brandy had been supplied, Darcy was left alone to mull over what was to be done.

Knowing that he was not the father of May's child was not enough; he had to prove that the claim be entirely baseless. He would not subject Elizabeth to the rigours of social judgement and mockery, which he knew the women of London were particularly adept at! There were some, chiefly those influenced by his aunt, Lady Catherine De Bourgh, who even now maintained a polite distance from her. Although none had been so foolish as to display obvious rudeness or disrespect, he had heard the chatter regarding her low connections and her sister's dubious marriage, from behind their fans. He would not give them fuel to make an outright attack on Elizabeth or their marriage. He would protect her from that.

He had secured some time from Sinclair, but the difficulty in identifying the real father remained. As he sat, sipping his third brandy, Darcy forced himself to think of May properly, in a way he had not done since they were last together.

He recalled spending time with her, following his return from Hertfordshire. Once there, he had been determined to return to his old life and to forget any possible infatuation he had developed for Miss Elizabeth Bennet. He smiled as he thought of all the ways he had tried to convince himself that she meant nothing to him. Such stubborn foolishness: for all his conviction that he was unaffected by Elizabeth, he was nevertheless unable to be unfaithful to her.

He had visited May, but his passion for her was gone. He could not be with her, knowing it was Elizabeth he craved. There had been no intimacy between the pair since he had returned to London, and when he sought her out, it was solely for the purpose of conversation.

When a letter had arrived from his aunt, informing him of the presence of guests at the parsonage of Rosings, he was gone the very next day. He never saw May again, maintaining, and then ending, their relationship by letter.

He had since come to regret his treatment of May: his leaving her alone, realising such isolation could not have been borne easily by a woman he knew to be fond of society and generally gregarious. He could not blame her for eventually taking a lover.

On thinking of May being alone, Darcy remembered her speaking fondly of a friend, a Miss Natalie DuPont, who had come to Bow Street shortly after her, and who had taken up residence two doors along. In Miss DuPont, she had found an engaging companion for the days or weeks that Darcy was away and a source of much needed female companionship. Perhaps, he hoped now, that May had found comfort in the bond of friendship when his abandonment of her was all too clear.

Amidst the haze his fourth brandy was inducing, Darcy was aware something important had just occurred to him: May had a friend, a confidante! Why had he not seen this before? Surely, if May had confided the identity of her lover to anyone then Miss DuPont would be that person. Darcy smiled for the first time since receiving Sinclair's letter: he was no longer at the mercy of others, but had a course of action to follow. He would find this Miss DuPont, certain that if she knew the identity of May's lover, he could convince her to reveal it.

CHAPTER 10

A few days later, Darcy found himself at liberty to pay a call on Miss DuPont. He hired a hack to take him to Bow Street, preferring the relative anonymity of a hire to walking or taking his own carriage.

Bow Street was renowned for two things: its beautiful houses forming a crescent around a well-maintained park, and the fact that almost all of its residents were the highly paid mistresses of London society. While he had never been embarrassed to be on the street when he was single and visiting May, Darcy felt less inclined to be seen in the area now that he was happily married. Although many of the mistresses on the street were supported by married men, Darcy would not have himself linked to such a distasteful practice. He found no fault with a man who maintained a mistress, once he was wealthy enough and unencumbered, but he had little tolerance for it among those who had promised fidelity and unity to one woman.

Upon admittance to Miss DuPont's home, Darcy stood within the upstairs drawing room while the maid informed her mistress she had company. He took notice of the surroundings as he waited. The room was perfectly placed to capture the early morning sun, and everything in it had been designed to enhance the feeling of light and space the room naturally afforded. Small watercolours depicting the English countryside adorned the walls. There were no heavy draperies or overstuffed armchairs to draw the room in, but four perfectly proportioned, comfortable chairs, with a small elegant table. Above the fireplace hung a large mirror, adding to the light and space in the room. All of the colours were muted creams, warmed by flashes of gold from embroidered upholstery and decorative frames.

When she finally entered, Darcy was as impressed by the woman herself as he was with her room. Miss DuPont was a tall, slender woman, with a striking Roman bearing; her dark curls pinned and positioned to frame her face, drawing attention to her eyes, and elongating an already graceful neck.

"I believe you wish to speak to me in relation to a friend of ours, Miss May Sinclair."

"Miss DuPont, what do you know of me?" began Darcy, using a tone he always found particularly effective in soliciting the compliance of others.

Unaffected, Miss DuPont initially flashed a smile in response. Her profession having schooled her to handle all manner of men, she was little swayed by Darcy's demeanour. She followed her smile with, "Mr Darcy, or may I call you Fitzwilliam?" Her tone teasing, her manner playful.

Darcy was somewhat bristled by the response. Few women were so audacious in their treatment of him. "No, madam, you may not!"

"Well, Mr Darcy, beyond knowing you were once a particular friend of May Sinclair, I know nothing of you at all. I fear we have little to talk about, unless you care to strike up a friendship with me…"

Miss DuPont paused, allowing Darcy sufficient time to either take the chair at the table opposite her, or quit her room entirely. As it happened, he did neither, maintaining his determined stance by the fireplace.

"I come here on a matter of great importance, not only to myself, but I believe to May, also. I realise your profession requires the utmost discretion and loyalty and I have no desire for you to compromise yourself in any way."

Darcy paused for a moment to allow Miss DuPont to interject. Accepting her silence as assent, he continued. "I believe, in our time together, May was loyal to me and discreet in all our dealings, but I also believe, should she have had a secret, she would have confided it in you. Did she ever speak of us, of our time together?"

Miss DuPont sighed. "She did not, Mr Darcy, so whatever you came here in search of, I fear I shall be of little assistance to you."

"Did you know she bore a child? A daughter? Did you know her brother seeks to libel me the father?"

"Mr Darcy, May only had one acquaintance at any given time, you surely know that as well as anyone. I know you supported her well; she had no need to be disloyal. Indeed, it would have been against her interest to do so. If she had a child during your time together then I, like her brother, would assume you to be the father."

"But I know the child cannot be mine. At the necessary time, May and I were no longer intimate."

There followed another pause as Darcy considered how much to divulge to this relative stranger.

"Am I to believe, sir, you continued to support May, without any demand upon her time or affections?"

"I had fallen in love, Miss DuPont, and although I feared I would not succeed with the woman in question, I felt my acquaintance with May was a betrayal of her and my hopes for a life with her."

Miss DuPont considered this. "But if your relationship had ended, why does her brother believe you to be the father?"

"My love was not easily won. Foolishly, I needed to know I had the comfort of a woman available to me. I maintained May's upkeep for several months after our last meeting, before finally releasing her from our arrangement. I am not the father."

Although not inclined to doubt the truth of anything Mr Darcy had said, Miss DuPont admitted there was such conviction in the last statement that any doubt would have been laid to rest.

"Do you know of anyone else? Was there anyone else?" continued Darcy.

"I cannot help you Mr Darcy," she began, before a slight hesitation crept into her tone, "I cannot…"

"You remember someone!"

Darcy moved suddenly forward, crossing the room in three easy strides, taking up the earlier offered chair.

"No, and yet, yes. There was someone. Not an acquaintance, you understand, as she remained yours until you determined otherwise. However, there was a gentleman who pursued her – a love match. I thought nothing of it, knew she would not risk your arrangement, but if you were not with her, did not see her, and she believed herself to be in love, well I cannot be sure…"

"His name…the gentleman's name?"

"I do not remember. With all my heart, I wish I could help you, but I do not remember. Give me time, it may yet return."

Darcy sighed and leaned back in the chair. "Time, madam, is the one thing I do not have."

When Darcy took his leave, he was heavy in heart. Although Miss DuPont had assured him that she would contact him if she could help him further, he began to fear it might all come to nought.

At the front door, he took stock, drawing himself up, determined not to succumb to defeat. He walked out on to Bow Street, and stood momentarily, at a loss for what to do or where to go. It was only upon hearing his name that he focused his attention in time enough to see something being dropped from an upstairs window. Catching the object deftly in one hand, Darcy looked down to see a piece of paper woven neatly through the teeth of an ornate woman's comb.

With the piece of paper clasped firmly in his hand, and the name of May Sinclair's lover revealed, Darcy strode on with renewed purpose. He walked on, oblivious to the pair of eyes that watched him with great interest from across the street; oblivious to the presence of Mrs Lydia Wickham.

CHAPTER 11

Lydia had intended to write to Elizabeth almost as soon as Jane had let it slip that the Darcys were at the Grosvenor Square residence. She was sure that her sister would want their company; George's charm and her own spirited nature would be a solid addition to any gathering. She had delayed in the matter, however, after receiving a note with some money from her sister. Although Lydia was always pleased to add coin to her purse, she was piqued by the lack of invitation to dine, dance, and play cards, or so much as take a carriage ride through the park, in the accompanying note. Still, on allowing some days to pass, Lydia guessed that it was perhaps a simple oversight, or the result of the note being hurried on the insistence of Mr Darcy, who was no doubt always rushing about between engagements. So Lydia determined to be patient and await further communication from her sister, but after a week of patience, her hopes remained unfulfilled, and resentment began to creep upon her.

This resentment was strengthened by the reports she had received from acquaintances of the many outings and gay parties her sister attended; the fact that Kitty seemed to profit from Elizabeth's attention was the cruellest blow of all.

"Is it fair that Kitty should be allowed to join them when we do not? Why must she be singled out for advantage?" Lydia complained loudly to her husband.

"My darling Lydia," said he, "did not you take decided pleasure in escaping to Brighton with Colonel and Mrs Forster? Did not you tell me of Kitty's wailing and crying at the injustice of your getting such an advantage? Surely now, after all your success, you would not deny your sister her chance?"

Lydia paused to consider, and pouting, still argued, "But must she be advanced at such a high cost to me, indeed to us, my darling? Just think of the fun that must be had with such varied society and in such surroundings. The tales I have heard of the parties they have attended, and beyond the simple delight I would have for myself, might not you benefit from an introduction to the society there?"

The appeal to his interest caught Wickham by surprise, and he finally gave Lydia a measure of his notice.

"Indeed, husband," she continued, emboldened by his attentiveness, "just think how your cause might be promoted by the sorts of people we could engage at the society balls and private parties Darcy and Elizabeth no doubt attend, or at least have an invitation to. Your career and our elevation in society could both be aided by the friends we should make, if Lizzy would but afford us the opportunity."

Wickham blinked and shook his head a little, as though to be certain it was indeed Lydia standing there placing so solid and well-reasoned an argument before him, for even he had not been so bold as to count on the advantage that their relationship to the Darcys ought to yield. "Darcy will hardly be willing to invite us to join his party, Lydia, have you considered that?"

"I have, husband. Darcy is surely a force to be reckoned with, but I have no doubt as to his being most sincerely attached to Elizabeth, and that attachment might yet be used to our advantage."

"You will not be offended, I think, if I point out that your relationship with your sister has been tried somewhat by our elopement, so how do you suppose Darcy's attachment to her will be of any use to us?" he asked in amazement at his wife's newly expressed cunning.

"Well, it is but a simple thing, husband: we must ingratiate ourselves with Lizzy. I know full well you were once a favourite of hers, and the sting of your choosing me must have wounded, but I am certain she loves me too well for any lasting disregard of sisterly affection."

જ

It was not until the day on Bow Street that Lydia finally found a way to insinuate herself into her sister's favour. Elizabeth was proud – of that, Lydia was certain. She would not take kindly to being cuckolded by Darcy. Though the knowledge of his activities might lead to some disharmony between the couple, the service of exposing the truth of Darcy's infidelity would leave Elizabeth in Lydia's debt.

So it was with no small measure of delight that Lydia finally sat down to write to her sister:

My dearest Lizzy,

It is with deepest regret I write to you with an account, which I fear will grieve you greatly. I had cause to be out in the area of Bow Street this morning. I was on my way to the milliner's, contemplating a new hat I was to purchase. I was trying to decide whether I might choose blue ribbons, or green, to add to the look of the thing, for although a pretty hat, it would really be too plain without some ribbon, when I half spied a man of familiar build and manner exiting from one of the grander houses on the street. Though I paid little notice; my thoughts being otherwise occupied.

It was not until I heard a name being called out that I truly took account of the gentleman. He was called from an upstairs window, where a woman held out her hand and dropped something to him.

She called out "Fitzwilliam", which, naturally, gave me cause to look again. Oh, dearest sister, how it pains me to tell you, it was indeed our Fitzwilliam Darcy, my dearest brother-in-law,

*your dearest husband, whom I witnessed being called by a lady
from one of the grander Bow Street houses, and by his first name.*

*Well, I need not tell you, but I hardly knew what to do; I did
not know what to make of it or how to account for it. Indeed, I
was so affected when I reached the milliner's, I took my hat with
no ribbons at all!*

*I remain hopeful of an innocent explanation for Darcy's
presence on the street, for what token passed between him and the
lady, and for her obvious familiarity…*

> *Your sister,*
> *Lydia Wickham*

Although Lydia, in recounting the sorry tale to her husband,
would proclaim her great struggle in determining whether to
send the letter to her sister, she had not in fact struggled long,
for within half an hour of returning from the milliner's, the note
was written and awaiting delivery. Lydia smiled; so, Mr Darcy
was not fully satisfied with his new wife, and still sought to
purchase pleasure from 'London's Ladies'. Her husband smiled
too; so, the righteous Darcy was flawed after all.

Lydia sat stroking her husband's hair, knowing he would
never be found leaving a house on Bow Street. In this, at least,
Lydia was correct, for Wickham would never pay the expense of
keeping a mistress, not when he was perfectly adept at getting
his pleasures elsewhere free of charge.

∞

The grief that Lydia claimed to be so undesirous of causing was
quick to take hold in Elizabeth. She had not been oblivious to
Darcy's altered mood, his lack of concentration, and the fact
that he had hardly touched her in days. These were all
circumstances, which had been playing upon her even before
the arrival of Lydia's odious note. She spent an uneasy morning
pacing the length of the breakfast room, the bedroom, and the
main hallway. By mid-afternoon, her feet ached, and her general
disquiet was little relieved; the words from Lydia's note replaying

in her mind, and her own concerns around Darcy's behaviour nagging at her. Unable to find any peace left alone with her thoughts, Elizabeth realised she needed the comfort and good sense of a trusted confidante: she needed Jane.

℘

Elizabeth and Jane sat in a quiet front parlour waiting for tea. The warm yellow of the room raised Elizabeth's spirits, and she felt all would be well. Jane, who had no idea for the reason behind the meeting, simply sat enjoying the company of her sister and the wonderful view of the gardens. Once tea had been served, and Elizabeth had made all polite enquiries after Jane's health, the health of Mr Bingley, his sisters, and brother-in-law: Mr Hurst, Elizabeth felt at ease enough to utter, "I am afraid there is something wrong with Fitzwilliam."

Jane set down her cup and replied with no small measure of alarm, "He is not unwell? He looked the picture of health at dinner."

"No, he is not ill, Jane, you need not fear that."

Jane, tolerably calmed by Elizabeth's assurances, relaxed. "If he is not ill then why are you concerned?"

"We have not been intimate, Jane – for days – and I am concerned, for I know him to be a most passionate man."

Jane coughed, looked aghast, muttered something about the appropriateness of such a conversation, and then cast her eyes about the room, looking anywhere but at her sister.

"Oh Jane, I must talk to someone."

"But I am not certain it ought to be me."

"But we are sisters, both married, and you are my dearest confidante; if not you, then who? And you know this may be exactly the sort of conversation married women often engage in, but always cease when a single woman enters their circle."

Jane expressed her doubts on that particular notion most eloquently, but she could never refuse Elizabeth anything and so eventually relented. Although, she held tightly to the resolution that their mother, and Aunt Phillips, never talked of passions regardless of who was in the room.

"For how long have you...? I mean to say, how long has it been since...?" Jane was stumbling.

"Since Tuesday and I am concerned."

"Since Tuesday? Good Lord, Elizabeth, it is only Friday – how often does Mr Darcy impose upon you? How do you manage?"

Jane's response surprised them both and they instantly broke into laughter. With that outpouring, their unease disappeared and both women relaxed. Jane sat deeper into her chair, nibbling distractedly at the corner of a lemon biscuit, carefully considering how best to proceed.

"Elizabeth, I feel we must speak plainly. Have you found the wifely duties our mother warned us must be endured are in fact something to be endured?"

Elizabeth smiled, as Jane described one of the great pleasures of marriage as a duty, and answered with a degree of candour that she ought to have known would shock her sister. "In truth, Jane, I have not! I welcome Fitzwilliam's advances, have made advances of my own, and am as much of a participant in our love as he."

Jane blanched, and Elizabeth feared she had spoken too candidly.

"With Charles, I do enjoy our time together, it is just...it is not always as I feel it could be. We start to be intimate, and I enjoy his attentions and his kisses and then... he...well, he..."

Jane was beginning to struggle again, so Elizabeth proposed, "He completes his husbandly duty?"

"Exactly!" exclaimed Jane, relieved.

"Have you talked to your husband?" asked Elizabeth.

"I could not, could never! Elizabeth, it would be too cruel to allow him to think me disappointed; too cruel."

Both women sat, pondering the problem. Jane reached for another biscuit while Elizabeth took a turn about the room, hoping the change in position might afford a greater change in perspective. As her hand trailed the length of a dark mahogany sideboard, she recalled the way Darcy often trailed the movement of her hands on her body: where she touched, he touched – or kissed – allowing her to lead him.

"Jane, would it be possible for you to show Charles what you needed, if you could not tell him. Could you gently suggest and direct him through your actions? Touch his lips with your fingers, then kiss his lips, touch his chest with your fingers, and kiss his chest, and then perhaps touch your lips with your fingers and..."

"And lead him to me?"

"Just so! Gentle hints, letting him follow you until you are ready for..."

Elizabeth now found herself beginning to struggle, so Jane proposed, "For him to complete his husbandly duty? Why yes, I believe that would be a course I could follow, Lizzy. It would spare both Charles and me any embarrassment, and as soon as he next gives me notice, I shall spend the rest of the day preparing myself to do as you suggest."

"Gives you notice, Jane? I do not quite understand your meaning."

"Oh, do you remember when Mama talked to us of our duties as wives and part of her talk involved our duty to become mothers?"

"I confess, Jane, I do not. Even you must own that Mama talks a great deal, and so little of it is of consequence. Could anyone have listened for so long?"

"Oh Lizzy, really," was all her sister could manage by way of a scolding, "I listened. She spoke of her and Papa, and recounted one afternoon he took her – quite by surprise – and her nerves were never the same again! Well, I will not risk such a punishment, and Charles has agreed to inform me in the morning whether he should like us to share a bed that evening."

Elizabeth was so stunned by Jane's revelation, that for a moment she simply sat and stared at her sister until finally she managed, "Jane, you cannot honestly believe Mama's nerves are a result of a moment of passion some twenty years ago."

"But Lizzy..."

"No, Jane, I will not have it," said Elizabeth, a broad grin on her face. "I can assure you, if surprises in intimacy were the cause of a nervous complaint, I should daily be in peril."

It was at least a quarter-hour before Jane spoke again. "Lizzy, you have left me with much to think on, but come now, we must get to the business that brought you here, we seem to have lost our track; you say you are worried…"

Elizabeth, who had spent days feeling concerned about Darcy, had been glad of the distraction that focusing on Jane and Charles Bingley had provided, and it was with reluctance that she was drawn back into considering her own problem. "Perhaps it is nothing, Jane; perhaps I am just being fanciful."

"Lizzy, be serious. You have never been prone to flights of fancy. You are too adept at reading your husband to have formed a concern without merit. Please allow me the comfort of helping you as you have helped me – if I can."

"I was not always so proficient at knowing Fitzwilliam, you must admit," Elizabeth said, recalling the many misunderstandings that had plagued their initial encounters. "It has taken time to learn to read him, and perhaps my schooling in his ways is not complete."

Jane tilted her head a little, and regarded Elizabeth in the way she always did when she knew her sister needed to talk, but had not yet found the words, or the courage, to do so. She would wait.

Elizabeth smiled at Jane, thanking heaven for this woman who knew her so well, who could see her need to unburden her fears, and who could wait with infinite patience until she was ready. So, she drew a deep breath and began: out poured the concerns she had about Darcy, his late nights, his distracted manner, the arrival of letters that unsettled him, and finally, she produced the note that Lydia had sent.

Jane listened in silence, read the note, looked at Elizabeth, and very carefully said, "You do not mean to suggest Darcy is inconstant, that his affections have been drawn elsewhere?"

"No, Jane, I do not doubt his constancy; I believe he is true to me. I know he loves me, but there is something he is hiding. Perhaps he seeks to shield me, to protect me from a truth he fears will alarm me, perhaps…well I can imagine a hundred reasons to account for his actions of late, but until I know the actual one, I cannot rest easily, and my concern grows daily."

"Elizabeth, could you not talk to your husband as you suggested I talk to mine?"

"Oh, Jane, how easy it is to provide counsel to others, but how difficult to follow such advice oneself. I know that is what I ought to do, but I am afraid: afraid of what he might tell me and even more afraid he may tell me nothing at all."

CHAPTER 12

Elizabeth woke the next morning with a dreadful sickness in the pit of her stomach. Darcy had already risen and was dressing, preparing to leave without a word to her. His growing distraction and distance was daily adding to her disquiet. As she lay in bed listening to the sounds of him moving about the room, her disquiet began to turn to anger. She had tried to start a conversation with him the evening before, regarding his behaviour, but he had dismissed her worries with a flippancy she did not like. When she spoke with Jane, she had defended his actions, holding firm to the belief that Darcy was seeking to protect her from something, but upon further consideration, such defence began to falter.

"Am I a child to be coddled?" she wondered. "Am I not capable of reason and understanding? There can be no justification for his intentionally keeping me ignorant of matters that so forcefully intrude upon our life together."

It was the realisation that it was their life, and not merely his, which was bearing the brunt of whatever he desperately sought to hide, which forced Elizabeth from her bed.

She dressed hurriedly. Darcy had left their bedchamber about a quarter-hour before, but she hoped that he had stopped at least to drink something before leaving the house so she might yet find him in the downstairs breakfast room. When she made it down, she was informed that her husband was already gone. Elizabeth smiled at the young maid who had answered her query as to Darcy's whereabouts, and made polite enquiries as to how he had left: had he taken the carriage?

The maid, a young girl, and new in service, replied, "No, ma'am. If you please, ma'am, he walked. I overheard him say he wanted the air. Though I wasn't snooping, ma'am, just cleaning the grate in the drawing room," punctuating her answer with a bob at every "ma'am".

Elizabeth sat in the breakfast room, not eating, just pushing food around her plate. Unanswered questions troubled her, refusing to allow a moment of quiet. Any of the places she expected Darcy to visit for business were not within easy walking distance; neither were his club nor Bingley's house. She tried to quieten her suspicions: it was likely he would hire a hack once he had taken some air. The notion of a hire calmed her, but only for a moment, for the comfort was quickly replaced by another fear: he was hiring a hack to ensure anonymity! Where was he going that he did not wish to be seen in his own livery?

℘

Darcy slowed as he approached the door. He had begun doubting the wisdom of his visit and had almost determined to turn back, when the door opened and a familiar figure emerged from the dark hallway.

"Heavens! Is that Fitzwilliam Darcy I see on my step?" a surprised, but cheerful, Wickham exclaimed. "To what do I owe the honour? How does it come to pass that you should pay a call in a place such as this; on a man who is but a humble soldier?"

"I know what you are, Wickham," replied Darcy, pausing for a breath before adding, "you can scarce have forgotten who bought you your commission!"

Wickham bristled at the obvious barb, but having no ready reply remained silent, and focused all his efforts on appearing unconcerned.

Darcy had forgotten how Wickham infuriated him, but the man's charmless smile and all too pleasing manners soon brought his old feelings back with force. Uncertain of his desire to control his anger towards the man, Darcy gripped his gloves tightly, took a deep breath, and forced a charmless smile of his own.

The sight of Darcy smiling had an equally unsettling effect on Wickham, who despite himself, faltered a little, almost missed a step and had to reach for the railing to steady his body – and his nerve.

"I will not insult you with small talk, Wickham. We are too aware of the opinions we hold of each other to be slaves to convention."

"True enough, though I had hoped our newly forged bonds of brotherhood might in some measure soften those opinions, Darcy," Wickham joked.

Unwilling to rise to the bait, Darcy continued as though Wickham had said nothing at all. "I would speak with you, now, if you have no other pressing draws on your time."

The sneer with which Darcy's last comment was delivered was not lost on Wickham who, like Elizabeth, had learned to read more from the tone and manner of Darcy's address than the content. It galled him to allow Darcy even one minute of his time; true he had no planned engagements, but to admit so to Darcy – never!

"As it happens, I am most pressed today, but I believe I could spare you half an hour on Friday morning. If you insist on a meeting you may return then."

"This is a conversation that would probably best occur away from prying eyes and ears – away from your wife. Will you meet me at my club? I shall secure a private room where we will be undisturbed."

Wickham baulked at the thought of giving Darcy what he wanted, but this unexpected visit and the insistence on privacy provoked his curiosity. His concession to a meeting – where he determined some of the terms – seemed no real concession at all.

ℛ

Darcy lay in bed thinking on the meeting with Wickham, which had been agreed for that morning. There could be only one outcome: he had to be worked on to take responsibility for Maria Sinclair. Darcy would not see his happiness with Elizabeth diminished because of Wickham's mistakes. He turned to look at his wife.

"You rise rather early this morning, my love," he smiled, upon noticing she was awake. "I did not disturb you, I hope."

"No, Fitzwilliam, I feared it was I who had woken you. You have not slept well of late, my darling, is there anything the matter? I do not claim to have your mind for business or your knowledge of estate affairs, but if they trouble you then share your burden with me – I can offer a sympathetic ear at least and I hope you have not found me deficient in reason or understanding."

"Elizabeth," he responded gently, "you do not know how your words soothe me. I have been distracted of late, forgive me, but it is all in hand."

Darcy pulled her to him and kissed the top of her head. With swift smooth swirls of his hand, he caressed her back. He lay there soaking up the feel of her, the smell of her, happy in the knowledge that by the afternoon he would have dealt with Wickham. Sinclair would be a distant memory and Elizabeth would be spared any distress.

Darcy was so lost in his thoughts, he did not notice that Elizabeth was not enjoying the effect of his hands on her body; in fact, she had begun to shift uncomfortably. He only drew his attention back to her when she leapt from their bed and ran to the adjoining washroom.

When Elizabeth returned, she was pale, and her hands trembled. Darcy was by her side immediately and lifted her onto their bed.

"Elizabeth, you are not well. I shall call for someone for I must know you are being tended to. I would stay with you but..."

"But you have business at your agents?" she questioned.

"Oh, my darling, how well you know me," he said, reaching over to kiss her.

Elizabeth's eyes welled with tears; he had lied to her again. She had read it in his face; a small twinge at the corner of his mouth screamed the lie at her. Her head throbbed as the truth of his deception stood so clearly before her. He was lying to her and she could think of no good reason for it. It was no matter of business, of that she was certain. Though she would not fully allow that infidelity was at the heart of it, there was a small niggle of doubt now where once there had been certainty. Her fears were plaguing her physically: headaches and sickness were daily companions, she could not eat, and restful sleep eluded her. "And worst of all," she thought, as she lay back in bed, "he has hardly noticed how altered I am! How is it possible he is so blind?"

As she lay, too heartsick even to raise her head, things became very clear to Elizabeth; she would not suffer the indignity of ignorance any longer. Darcy would answer her questions or she would find some way to uncover his secret. The discord that had sprouted in their relationship would be rooted out, or their marriage would not survive.

Darcy left instructions for Elizabeth's care before leaving the house. He was shaken by the suddenness of her sickness and he swore that once the sorry mess with Wickham was settled, he would turn his full attention to her. He was aware her suspicions were raised, and though he maintained the story that a matter of business unsettled him, he knew he could not hope for the deception to continue. She was not being fooled, and his conscience kept him awake at night, long after he should have been sleeping soundly.

Ꙙ

Half an hour later, Darcy and Wickham stood opposite each other once more. The room at the club boasted three chairs and a large couch, but neither man sat; this was not a comfortable meeting between friends. In standing, both sought to establish dominance over the room and the other man, and for the first few minutes, the men paced about the room, circling one another in an outright display of hostility.

"So to it, Darcy! What is this all about? I must own to a degree of interest as to what could possibly induce the great Fitzwilliam Darcy to pay a call on a lowly soldier."

"I have come about May," was Darcy's only response.

"May? I thought nothing else about you could surprise me Darcy – not after I heard of your choice of bride, but this? A wife and a mistress; I am beginning to think we are not so different…"

Before he could finish, Darcy had erupted. Lunging at him, he grabbed Wickham by the throat and forced him back against a wall. "Never speak of my wife!" he threatened. The words were spat at Wickham as Darcy struggled to contain his rage.

Wickham was suddenly and undeniably afraid. He had seen this rage in Darcy when they were children: Wickham had taken to teasing the house pets at Pemberley, but once had accidentally injured a favourite of Darcy's. The young Fitzwilliam, although only a boy of ten, had attacked him with unbridled ferocity. Two groomsmen pulled Darcy away, but to this day, Wickham bore a scar as testament to what an enraged Darcy could do. Seeing the same violence, but in Darcy now with the power and strength of a man, was indeed cause to fear. Alone, and without means of escape, Wickham did not wish to provide further fuel for his anger and so he just raised his hands in surrender.

The look on Wickham's face was enough to draw Darcy back to himself, and he took his shaking hands away from the other man's throat. He fought back the urge to lash out at Wickham, whose destructive and selfish nature had too often encroached on the happiness of people he loved. He fought back the urge, for he knew if he did not, Wickham would not leave the room alive.

Wickham watched as Darcy physically struggled to control himself. He had moved away from him, around the other side of the couch. He smoothed his hair, calmed his breath, and kept his hands active by crushing the rim of his hat. Wickham was determined to give no cause to challenge Darcy's resolve.

After a few moments of silence, Darcy spoke again. "I have come here to speak to you about your relationship with May Sinclair. Do not deny your liaisons with her; I am fully aware of them."

"I am surprised May told you. I expected more discretion from a whore of her calibre."

Wickham winced as Darcy reacted to his calling May a whore. "I meant, of course, mistress. Darcy, I am a little shaken by the turn of things today, and I am still surprised she would tell you of such things."

"So you do not deny the relationship?"

"Why should I deny it? Though I risk another attack, I happily admit to plundering for free what you so generously paid for!"

Wickham edged towards the door lest the jibe cause Darcy to retaliate, but was surprised when there was no reaction, just a question.

"When?"

"Really, Darcy, does it matter? I am certain May will confess all to you."

"When?" he repeated.

With that, Wickham understood why Darcy was there, why he had attacked him, and why he would not attack him again.

"The woman has borne a child; I see it now – all that rage – Elizabeth must not find out about a child. A mistress she might forgive, but a child?"

As Darcy circled closer, Wickham warned, "Stay where you are, for I am no good to you dead, Darcy. What I do not understand is why you have not just paid May off? You can afford it. Your morality allowed you take on a mistress, now pay for the consequences."

"The child is not mine."

"Well then, you were unfortunate in your choice of bed companion, as clearly May has chosen to declare otherwise."

In frustration, Darcy yelled out that May was dead. He

recognised his error instantly, and in response could only feel tired, slumping against the heavy arms of the nearest chair, knowing his momentary weakness would cost him dearly.

Wickham now bravely moved away from the wall and spread himself along the length of the couch opposite Darcy. "So the whore is dead and the family know only of your relationship with her. What a delicate situation we find ourselves in. I can imagine the sort of favour you need from me, but you must appreciate I shall have to think this through carefully. What would it cost me to own the child? After all, there is dear sweet Lydia to consider…"

"How much?" was all Darcy could mutter.

"Oh, I really shall have to consider that…but I warn you, Darcy, honour will not come cheap."

$\mathcal{SO}$

Darcy wandered through the city after his encounter with Wickham, unable to settle on any destination, and determined to avoid any place where he might run the risk of being engaged in conversation, fearing his thoughts too forceful to be concealed from anyone who knew him. Going home and seeking the comfort he knew he needed was most impossible of all, as Elizabeth would read him instantly. It was not until well after midnight, he felt that he had gained sufficient control of himself to allow his return to Grosvenor Square after the family had retired to bed. A tray had been left for him, but he had no stomach for food. He sat alone, in the dark, focused on only two things: the sound of his racing heartbeat, and the fear he would lose Elizabeth.

He tried to counsel himself that Wickham might yet be worked upon, that the promise of money might be enough to secure his compliance, though Darcy knew that Wickham might hold destroying him in even greater esteem than coin. Perhaps Elizabeth would understand, she might eventually forgive his weakness – yet he argued, how could it be? He would be lowered in her esteem; surely, it could not be prevented. He, who had always valued his good name and character, would be reduced. If the story was allowed to be told, how long would it be before he was accused, not only of fathering a child, but of abandoning its mother to a poor house, abandoning her to her death?

He leaned against the mantel in his library and allowed his head to sink into his hands. He was suddenly struck by the thought that Wickham would be spared any public disgrace and scandal. He grimaced at the thought of Wickham gloating over his fall, but such humiliation was nothing compared to what he might suffer at the hands of Elizabeth. How would she look at him? Would she even be able to look at him at all?

The fear of this imagined rejection was the final blow in a day that had seen Fitzwilliam Darcy more beaten down than any other. In anger and fear, he yelled out and punched the marble fireplace in front of him. The servant, who had been sent to attend him, entered just at that moment and was startled by the outburst. Darcy calmly informed him that, he had stumbled in the dark and fallen against the mantel. As to why his master would fall with a closed fist, rather than an open hand, young James considered none of his business.

§

Darcy entered the bedchamber where Elizabeth was sleeping. He moved to brush the hair from her face when the sight of blood on his knuckles caused him to retreat. He took up a seat on the chair by the window and did not notice Elizabeth's waking until she was standing by him, gazing at his bruised and swollen hand.

"My love, you are hurt! What has happened? Have you any other injury?"

A dozen questions poured out at once, her concern making it impossible to wait for an answer before another question was posed. It was only when she stated, "I shall have the surgeon sent for," that Darcy managed a reply.

"No, it is nothing; just some bruising." And then, unaccountably, he begged, "Please do not leave me, Lizzy, promise me you will stay."

Elizabeth stood before him, confusion evident. "No, Fitzwilliam, I shall not leave you. If you say you do not need a surgeon, I shall certainly stay."

He grabbed at her body and pulled her to him, holding her tight; his head resting against her stomach.

Elizabeth could feel him shaking. "Fitzwilliam, what is wrong?" she pleaded now, holding his head in her hands and forcing him to look at her. "Please, you must tell me."

As he sat looking into her face, her eyes imploring him to talk to her, her face so full of concern, he knew he could not tell her. He would not see that love disappear; he would not see it replaced by disappointment, or worse, disgust.

"Nothing is wrong," he sighed. "I fell. I am shaken, nothing more, but if you hold me, my darling, I shall be well. Just hold me Lizzy, and all will be well."

CHAPTER 13

Elizabeth slept little for the rest of the night. Her fears regarding Darcy's behaviour had been worsening. His stress and fatigue were now so apparent that even Kitty had commented on how poor he looked at breakfast. For Elizabeth, his worry had become palpable. Aborted conversations and his avoidance of her direct gaze added to her insecurity. She was determined she would no longer play the dupe, but had no notion as to what should be done.

"Fitzwilliam, I was thinking, we could spend the day together," she began when they sat down to breakfast. "You have been so distracted and unsettled; I think it might do you good to enjoy the company of your wife a little."

"What a wonderful suggestion, my love," he replied. "I am sorry for my recent agitation; you have not felt neglected, I hope? I would be delighted to spend the day with you and we will do just that – tomorrow."

"Tomorrow?"

"Yes. Today I have a matter to attend to, but tomorrow I shall be all yours."

Elizabeth was about to object when it occurred to her that this might work in her favour. She expected Darcy would be seeing to the matter behind his distraction and so here was her opportunity to discover all.

"You will be concluding this tiresome matter that has kept you from me then, husband?"

"I shall, and in truth I shall be relieved to have done with it. I will be the husband you deserve once this is dealt with, my darling. I will be your Fitzwilliam again."

"Then I am content to wait one more day for you," she responded. "Do you go into town?" she added, offhandedly. "Might I take the carriage with you, for I have it in mind to visit Jane and perhaps stop later at Bertram's for lunch?"

"Of course, Elizabeth, it would be a pleasure to start my day with you, and if all goes well, I will meet you and Jane at Bertram's, later."

℘

Once Darcy had seen Elizabeth safely to Jane's, he continued on to the offices of Duddle & Thorn, his agents in London. From there, he would go to Breakmore Street, and thereafter he would be free from John Sinclair. He was so engrossed in his plans that he did not notice that the door to Bingley's house never closed behind Elizabeth.

Instead of entering, Elizabeth requested that the butler secure her a hack at once and not to worry Mr or Mrs Bingley with the information that she had called. The butler, though surprised by the request, knew better than to question Mrs Darcy, and did as commanded.

Although some minutes behind him, Elizabeth hoped Darcy's first stop would be to his agents. She instructed the driver secured by the butler to go directly to the offices of Duddle & Thorn on Dovecot Lane. Once there, she was relieved to spot Darcy's carriage, and ordered her driver to wait. He looked unsettled at the thought of lost business, but when Elizabeth handed him a full day's coin for his trouble, he sat quietly, happy to rest a few hours at the lady's expense.

Within an hour, Darcy was finished at his agents and he strode out of the office resolved to meet with Sinclair. He was armed with the name of May Sinclair's lover, and his belief that Elizabeth's curiosity would not be appeased much longer strengthened his resolve to put an end to the business. He sat back into the carriage envisioning how the meeting would go, how the meeting must go, before allowing himself the luxury of thinking of more pleasant matters, like an afternoon with Elizabeth at Bertram's.

Elizabeth's hire followed Darcy to Breakmore Street, and her alarm at the conduct of her husband increased as the streets through which he travelled grew increasingly disreputable. She had taken her hack as far as he had taken his, and alighted just down the street from him, watching as he crossed and walked along by a row of small houses. The driver had questioned whether she was sure to be safe. Elizabeth had laughed at his concerns, but standing alone and unprotected, aware of all the eyes staring at her fine dress and cape, she regretted her foolhardy dismissal of the man. Though daunted, Elizabeth remained determined to uncover what Darcy seemed so desperate to hide. She drew back her shoulders, raised her head high, and strode down the street for a better look at the house near the corner.

Darcy had not entered number twenty, Breakmore Street, but stood outside on a small patch of grass, which passed for a garden. Mr Sinclair had been called for and Darcy simply waited, every moment testing his patience further. He was determined that the matter between himself and Sinclair be ended that day: he would inform him of the identity of his sister's lover, point him to Miss Natalie DuPont who could verify his claim, and finally wash his hands of the sordid affair. What Sinclair chose to do afterwards, he cared little about; all his concerns focused on distancing himself, and Elizabeth in turn, from any scandal. The only point of pride he held in relation to his dealings with Sinclair was that Elizabeth would never have to know of any of it.

Across the street, Elizabeth stopped and looked at her husband with curiosity. What on earth had been so important that he had come here? Whom could he be waiting for? In the wake of Lydia's note, and Darcy so obviously lying to her, Elizabeth admitted a small part of her feared that he might have a mistress, but she could not countenance that he would have come to this part of town to meet a lover. If Darcy had a woman, she would have undoubtedly lived in the finer accommodations on Bow Street, and not the relative squalor of Breakmore Street.

After some minutes, a man emerged from the dingy confines of number twenty. He seemed to smile at Darcy, though judging by her husband's stance Elizabeth did not think he was pleased about the meeting. Curious about Darcy's reaction and noticing that the man held his daughter in his arms, Elizabeth could no longer contain her inquisitiveness. Knowing that she would unable to hear any part of the exchange between the two at such a distance, she first made her way across the street to stand on the corner. just beyond number twenty. Concerns she might be seen by Darcy were swept aside; even if she were, he would have no choice now, but to admit all to her, in order to explain his presence there.

Elizabeth took up a position outside number twenty-two. A large bush, which had been allowed to grow wild, provided a partial cover for her. She could just make out the men's voices. She heard Darcy refer to the other as Sinclair, and mentioned being ready to finish their business together. In response, she had heard the other laugh and follow with: "Darcy, I had not dreamed our business would come to such a speedy conclusion. I expected some attempt on your part to deny responsibility in this."

"I am not a man who sheds his responsibilities so easily," Darcy replied, "but do not think I shall play the fool for you and own a mistake, if it is not mine."

"Oh come now, Darcy, you know as well as I, you and May were lovers, and I think Maria has something of your colouring. Come, play the role of proud father; let me introduce you to your daughter."

On hearing Sinclair mentioning that Darcy had a lover, Elizabeth had stepped closer to number twenty, to see the small child being held out to her husband, just in time to hear Sinclair say, "father".

The scream that escaped her lips hung in the air between her and Darcy. She clasped her hands to her mouth to try and strangle the sound, but it was too late.

Darcy turned towards the sound, and stood rooted to the spot by the horror of his discovery.

Elizabeth's eyes darted between her husband and the young child being held out to him, unable to settle on either. Darcy did not move, but his hand reached out for Elizabeth: he seemed to be calling to her, but she could not hear him. All she heard was the sound of her own scream ringing in her ears. He had a look on his face, but she could not make it out. Was it pain? Was it fear? She hardly knew. Was he moving towards her? No, he remained in the garden, but Elizabeth felt the world spinning beneath her feet, all balance and all grounding gone.

Dizzy and sick at the discovery of her husband's infidelity, she reeled. She was desperate to escape the scene and stumbled back from his outstretched hand. Her footing unsteady and her steps faltering, she fell backwards into the street, heedless of the dangers of the road, into the path of an oncoming carriage.

❧

There was a yell from a passer-by as the carriage's horse reared after Elizabeth fell in front of it. The horse's hooves caught her body and caused her to tumble into the dirt. As the driver attempted to control the animal, its hooves came down once more, hitting hard into her. A young boy raced from the pavement and grabbed a loose rein, seeking to drive the horse and carriage back, and to avoid further injury.

Darcy was by Elizabeth in an instant. He could see that her arm was twisted at an unnatural angle, and her body had curled as if to protect itself. He turned her to him and though he could see no wound about her head, she lay almost lifeless, barely breathing. He called to a young lad and ordered him fetch a doctor. In desperation, he looked to those around him for help.

Sinclair had disappeared, but two men stepped forward to aid in carrying Elizabeth, as gently as they could, into a neighbouring house. Unwilling to carry her up any stairs, they lay her down in the kitchen, with Darcy's coat beneath her head.

As fate would have it, a doctor, unknown to Darcy, but clearly a capable man, who tended to the sick in the area on behalf of a charitable concern, was but two streets away when the accident occurred. The young boy sent to fetch assistance returned minutes later with the doctor in tow.

Darcy, knowing Elizabeth would be removed to Grosvenor Square as soon as possible, grabbed the boy by the collar and instructed him, and those of his friends who had gathered outside for their part in the excitement, to find his house, his housekeeper, his doctor and his sister-in-law, and to apprise all of Elizabeth's accident. His doctor was to be at his house when he arrived with her, and the housekeeper was to ensure all necessary preparations were in place. He tossed the boy a handful of coins and promised more if all was in order by the time he returned home. Once the boys had been dispatched, Darcy forced his attention back to Elizabeth, barely able to look at her, terrified of losing her.

Dr Fairweather, an ex-army doctor, had seen many injuries in battle resulting from the trampling of horses' hooves. He checked Elizabeth as thoroughly as circumstances would allow, set her broken arm, and ensured that there was no open wound to the head causing her unconsciousness. Once satisfied he had done all he could to secure her immediate well-being, he ordered transport be arranged to get Mrs Darcy home so that a more robust examination of her injuries could be completed.

As they waited, Dr Fairweather took Darcy aside.

"Mr Darcy, your wife is young and looks to be in good health, but I urge you, ensure your physician makes a thorough examination. By all accounts, the horse's hooves came down heavily upon her. I have seen men bleed to death from internal injuries when the soft of the belly has been hit with hooves. You must be vigilant."

"I will do as you instruct; thank you, doctor. Your care and attention to my wife will not be forgotten," was all Darcy had the heart to reply.

CHAPTER 14

Once they made it to Grosvenor Square, Darcy was relieved to see that the boys had been both quick and diligent in their service to him. All was arranged: Dr Ormsby and a surgeon were in attendance, and thankfully so was Jane, who surprised Darcy in the swift manner in which she took control of the care of her sister. While he sat being tortured by the image of Elizabeth's battered body under horses' hooves, Jane had taken care of everything. Elizabeth was in their bed, a fire lit, the doctor attending, the setting of her broken bones checked, and her small cuts and wounds cleaned.

"Doctor, will she... I mean, is she well, doctor?" Darcy asked when finally able to draw strength enough to enquire.

"Your wife has suffered a broken arm along with cuts and bruising; these will heal. What I am concerned for, however, is the possibility there may yet be damage we cannot see, there is much bruising to her stomach and I cannot tell what may lay beneath it."

"Yes," interrupted Darcy, "Dr Fairweather warned of such danger."

"However, I fear greatly for the baby, Mr Darcy," Dr Ormsby continued, "and you must prepare yourself for disappointment there."

Darcy collapsed into a chair. "A baby! Elizabeth is with child?"

"Ah…" the doctor shifted uncomfortably, "you did not know. My condolences, Mr Darcy, for I do not hold out great hope that your wife will carry the child: the injury to her stomach, you see…"

"But Elizabeth, she will recover?"

The doctor turned to Jane. The look they shared told Darcy everything – they hoped, but they did not know.

As Jane walked with the doctor to the door, Darcy entered the bedroom for the first time. Unwilling, and unable, to look at Elizabeth, he took account of the large painting that hung above the fireplace. It was Pemberley; the grand house nestled comfortably in the English countryside. The artist was talented, having included details that imbued the painting with life: the shadow of servants in the windows; a stable boy leading a horse by the lake; light wisps of smoke from the stack over the kitchen, and in the foreground, a family posing, his mother holding Georgiana. His mother, pale and fragile. His mother, smiling, though slowly dying. His mother…Elizabeth…

Darcy finally turned to look at his wife. Her face was serene, undamaged by the accident. Only the sight of the bandaged arm suggested that anything had happened. Then suddenly, movement. Elizabeth stirred, and Darcy bounded over to her side, hopeful that the day would end with her waking, their reconciliation, and his being forgiven, but she was not awake. Instead, he could see beads of sweat forming on her temples. She moved not through waking, but through dreaming, and her dreams were unsettled. When he reached to calm her, he could feel a great heat rising from her body. Fever.

℘

The fever raged, unrelenting, and heedless of every purge and potion the physician could muster. The air in the bedroom was thick with the fetid stench of sweat and sickness. The smell clung to the clothes and hair of those who entered the room, so even leaving provided no relief.

Darcy and Jane had not left Elizabeth's side, despite Jane's insistence that the sick room was no place for a man. His pronouncement: "I will be with my wife!" had ended their disagreement, and the pair had been silent for several hours.

"I saw my mother die," were the first words he spoke.

Jane stopped and looked at him. He was much calmer than she had seen him in several hours; calmer and quieter, and it unsettled her. "What an ordeal for you, you must have just been a boy. How could your father have let you witness such a thing?"

Darcy had finally settled into one of the armchairs by the fire. As Elizabeth was sleeping soundly, Jane moved to the chair opposite him in the hope that having someone near might afford him a measure of comfort.

"No one knew I was there. I heard her gasp and call for my father, saw her hand reach out towards him, and saw her hand fall before it found him. She died. She was there and then she was gone, and I just stood watching."

"But what could you have done, Mr Darcy, you were a child and your mother was so ill. No one could have helped her."

"And now, Jane, what is my excuse now? What do I do now, but stand watching?"

Jane was silent. Darcy was silent. Elizabeth slept.

"There is an animal inside of me, Jane."

Jane, though pleased Darcy had taken up their conversation again, was concerned at the turn of it. He was not making sense and his calmness was becoming disturbing.

"An animal, Mr Darcy? Good heavens, what do you mean?"

"I felt it stir when my mother died: a beast that threatened to consume all that was good and hopeful of my soul."

"You speak of grief, Mr Darcy. Grief is natural. Of course you grieved the loss of your mother – any child would – but look how you rallied again."

"I fought that grief. My father needed me; Georgiana needed me, and I knew Mother would have wanted me to keep and protect them. I beat the beast back into the darkness, but if

Elizabeth should die..."

"There are still people who need you, Mr Darcy; people who count on you."

"But I don't have the will to fight; not if she dies, Jane..."

ℰℐ

Darcy had been absent for some time. The rest that Jane hoped would replenish him, had not, and the man who now darkened the doorway of the sick room seemed even more despondent. His usual attention to dress and form abandoned, Jane hardly recognised the unkempt figure that stood in the shadows, unwilling to step into the room where Elizabeth lay.

"She will be well, Mr Darcy," Jane offered, seeking to bolster his spirits and encourage him in. "I do think she is a little better. Come in, see for yourself, and sit for a while."

He stepped into the light of the room, and the rest of her sentiment caught in her throat. Darcy, a man whose face she could never read, whose feelings and private nature had always been a mystery to her, was terrified. She could feel his fear as readily as if it were her own and even her resolve began to fail in its wake.

"I have seen this fever before, Jane. I have seen it burn through a person, leaving nothing, and only death halts it."

"The fever will break, Mr Darcy; Elizabeth is strong."

"No! Elizabeth is broken and this fever will burn her out. She will die, Jane, and I am to blame."

The force of his conviction that Elizabeth was to die, and that he was to be held accountable, was not to be undone. Pleas and platitudes failed to convince, and soon Jane fell silent, the weight of his certainty now bearing heavily on her light spirit. As Darcy's attention was drawn to the bed, Jane removed herself from the room, seeking her husband, and comfort of her own.

Darcy sat beside Elizabeth. She looked small and frail among the banks of pillows surrounding her. She did not stir on his approach, and could have been thought simply sleeping, were it not for the two spots of colour high on her cheeks, and the thick film of sweat covering her face and neck. The nightshift that had been changed by Jane not half an hour since was already wet through; the linen clinging to her breast and back. Darcy lifted her to him, grimacing as his touch brought her pain. Removing the nightshift, he reached for a cold cloth and began to bathe her burning flesh, but the relief such cooling brought was short, and as Darcy fitted a new shift, he could feel the dampness seeping through.

Elizabeth, who up until this moment had been largely unresponsive, was suddenly present. "Fitzwilliam…the girl…the girl!" was all she managed before her eyes glazed.

Darcy drew her too him. "Please, Elizabeth, you must recover. I can explain and all will be well, if you will but return to me."

He took her onto his lap and cradled her. Despite the warmth of the room and the fire that burned from Elizabeth, Darcy shivered. "Please, Elizabeth, you cannot leave me."

Darcy sat holding Elizabeth until Jane eventually returned. He did not know how long she had been away, but when Jane moved to place Elizabeth back into the bed, she could see they were both soaked in sweat. He was pale and Jane could not discern if the heat from his body was a result of the fever racking Elizabeth's body or his own.

"Mr Darcy, you must bathe and eat, change your clothes, and rest. You will be no good to Elizabeth if you allow yourself to become unwell," Jane urged, fearful now for them both.

The plea to Elizabeth's needs had some effect and Darcy withdrew from the room long enough to change his clothes. When he returned, he took up a position in their bed. Lying next to Elizabeth, he stroked her face and arms with cool cloths. Jane was gladdened when she next looked over to find that he had finally fallen asleep. With Darcy no longer in need of her, she was free to turn all her efforts to Elizabeth, determined if faith alone was to preserve her sister, then she would not fail her.

ॐ

Darcy slept, albeit fitfully, with the ghosts of old pains and the spectres of new ones haunting him. He started from sleep calling for Elizabeth...but no reply came. He looked beside him: the other half of their bed was empty, the corners pinned and tucked. The bedside chair too was empty, save for a nightshift neatly and purposefully folded. On the chaise, lay Elizabeth's favourite dress, set out, waiting...

Darcy rose from the bed, the room spinning around him. He reached for the dress and clutched it to his chest. Within him, he felt a beast stir: a ravenous, empty, pitiless animal. He would live; that was to be his punishment. He would bury his wife, he would return to his club, he would ride and fence, conduct business, and manage his estate. He would be master, brother, and friend still, but husband no longer and never again. All the joy and love a life with Elizabeth had promised would be buried with her. Darcy fell to his knees and within him, the beast howled.

Darcy knelt where he had fallen, still clutching the dress. He could see the sweat on his arms staining the fabric and was suddenly aware of a ferocious heat racing through his body. He heard his name, but in the confusion of his fever could not make out where the voice was coming from. He tried to stand, but stumbled over the dress and fell once more, this time at a woman's feet. He heard his name again; a familiar voice, now crying out for help. He reached towards the sound, it grew closer, and he became aware of a body beside him and soothing hands on his forehead.

In his delirium, he called out and reached for her. "Lizzy!"

"It is Jane, Fitzwilliam. Can you hear me?"

"Jane?"

Darcy forced his eyes to focus and before him, he could see her, a look of alarm giving sharpness to her usually soft features. "She is gone, Jane. She is gone!" he cried out. "There is nothing left," was all he could say before fever overtook him once more.

&

Dr Ormsby was surprised at the hold the illness had taken on a man as young and as fit as Darcy. The treatments that he attempted seemed to aid a little in the cooling of the fever and there was nothing else to do, but wait and pray that Darcy was strong enough to see this through.

"Talk to him, Jane," the doctor urged. "Talk to him and convince him to fight. His own will may be all that stands between the man and death."

As he drifted in and out of consciousness, Darcy was aware of others in the room, talking to him, pleading with him. He heard Georgiana crying, and sometimes words would make their way through to him: "fight"…"for Lizzy". In his quiet moments, when the fever seemed to loosen its grip, he could see her, his Lizzy, sitting by his bed, her face full of fear and concern and he would reach for her, but she would be gone.

He remained in this way for days, every passing hour strengthening the conviction of those in the house that the master would not survive. Gradually, he became aware of the talk of chambermaids as they set the fires, of maids who helped to change his linen, and of nurses who helped to tend his body, that he would not live. "Then I shall die!" he said to the silence around him.

"You shall do no such thing, Fitzwilliam Darcy!" cried a voice from the corner.

He turned and smiled at the vision of Elizabeth standing looking at him severely.

"Do not think you will escape so easily," she said. "You will most certainly live, and that will be an end to it!"

"Even now, as I lie dying, you scold me, woman. Is there no end to your determination to make me a better man? I have suffered enough, my love. I watched you die and it was enough; it was too much. Have mercy on me, Elizabeth; do not leave me now to a life without you. Take me with you." With that, he reached out his hand to the vision moving towards him. He remembered once more the sight of his mother reaching out for his father and wondered who she had seen in those last moments, who had taken her hand and lead her to the next life.

He reached out. He reached out and took hold of flesh.

"My love," the vision of Elizabeth called to him, "I have not died." As if to prove this, she squeezed Darcy's arm, and reached her other hand to his face. "I have not died and so I beg now it is you who must not leave me."

Darcy could hear pain in her voice and taking the phantom's face in his hands he stroked her cheeks and felt tears. "Lizzy?"

"Fitzwilliam, I am here, but I must get the doctor."

"No Lizzy, do not leave me. If you go now, I fear this will have all been a dream."

Elizabeth looked at her husband, his eyes were brighter than before, and the worst of the fever appeared to have passed. She took a tight grip of his hand, called out for Jane, and then turned back to him, her eyes holding his gaze. "You see, husband, I am still here. I am no ghost."

"Then hold me, Lizzy, and bid me to stay with you."

She curled up next to him on the bed and rested her head by his. "You are so bidden, Fitzwilliam."

"Then I obey," he said, before falling asleep once more.

CHAPTER 15

Darcy's recovery was slow, but with the daily ministrations of Jane, it was steady, and within two weeks he was strong enough to leave his bed. He and Elizabeth had spoken, but only briefly, and with others always at hand, so little of real meaning had passed between them. His initial happiness at the discovery of Elizabeth being alive was slowly eaten away by growing concerns regarding her coolness towards him. Her physical distance he attributed to a desire to prevent reinfection, but when it was clear that she was no longer in any danger, Elizabeth continued to keep herself separate from him. Her manner was civil. She had enquired after his health, daily, but as one would ask a passing acquaintance, and all attempts to draw her into a more intimate conversation were resisted. Her fever had left her weak and Darcy hoped it was merely her own slow recovery, which stood between them. He hoped this, but when he recalled the circumstances of her injury, he felt the absurdity of such a hope. She had witnessed Maria Sinclair being handed to him, no doubt heard him proclaimed the father, and there had been no opportunity for him to explain.

There were only a handful of residents at the house: Darcy, Elizabeth, Jane, and a small number of staff; the doctor was their only visitor. Georgiana, Kitty, and the rest of the staff had been removed to prevent any spread of infection. The Gardiners had taken in Georgiana and Kitty, much to their relief, as Kitty had dreaded the thought of sharing a house with Caroline Bingley. Jane had been a saviour to both Darcy and Elizabeth, but now he was anxious to have her gone, knowing that he and Elizabeth needed to be alone without distraction or interference.

Mercifully, Jane was of the same opinion and as soon as Dr Ormsby could assure her of the certain recovery of both patients, she felt at liberty to suggest to Darcy that it was time for the couple to be left alone to recuperate in peace. Jane did insist on a nurse being in attendance, but once all arrangements were made, she was joyous at the thought of returning to Bingley. Elizabeth was disquieted at losing Jane's company, but felt keenly the selfishness of keeping her there. It was clear that Jane missed her husband, but strong bonds of sisterly loyalty and affection had caused her to put the health and happiness of Elizabeth and Darcy above her own desires, and now Elizabeth knew that she must do the same.

With the doctor's approval, it was agreed that Darcy and Elizabeth should return to Pemberley, the country air being more conducive to rebuilding their health and vigour. The journey could only be made once all necessary arrangements were in place for their safety and comfort, but within the week, it was accomplished. Neither was yet recovered enough to be out in society, and so made their farewells to family only. Kitty and Georgiana, despite their protestations, were to remain in London to see out the rest of the season under the watchful eye of the Gardiners. Darcy was insistent they remain; this was, in a small measure, to continue the promotion of the girls, but the greater part of it lay in the fact that he knew if he and Elizabeth were to salvage their marriage, they must be alone to do it. The safe harbour of company could not be afforded them.

Although Georgiana and Kitty were sincere in their concern and willingness to return to Pemberley, there was some joy to be found in their staying. During the weeks since Elizabeth's injury, neither had been out in society; it was not deemed fitting, and neither really had the heart for socialising when there was such cause for worry at home. The Trevelyans had been dutiful in their correspondence and had enquired daily. They kept Georgiana and Kitty apprised of all the news, and declared their absence was deeply felt, not least of all by Mr Grey, who often sent his regards and best wishes. It would be good, Kitty declared, for them to join their friends once more and make the best of what still remained of the season's entertainments. It was possible that it might do Darcy and Elizabeth some good to know their sisters were in finer fettle after the depression of spirits that had lately been displayed.

℘

Elizabeth slept for much of the journey back to Pemberley, and Darcy knew he must wait until they had recovered from the travelling before any approach could be made by him. As soon as they arrived home, Elizabeth slipped away, while he ensured that all the necessary preparations for her comfort were in place. Once seen to, he went in search of his wife and found her already in bed. He called out her name, but she did not reply. Although disappointed, he left the room quietly, resolute they would talk soon enough, and that Elizabeth would finally learn the truth.

The next morning, he found Elizabeth sitting in their private breakfast room. She did not turn to him when he entered, but continued to gaze out of the window.

"You look lost in yourself, Elizabeth," he began, "what is it that so draws on your attention and furrows your brow?"

Elizabeth responded by turning her face to his, but made no effort to answer.

Darcy, still hoping to draw her out, continued, "What are you thinking upon? I can see something at work there; share it with me, Lizzy. Talk with me – please, Elizabeth."

She turned fully towards him, although still unwilling to be the first to draw into the light the matters that had darkened their marriage for weeks, she was prepared to challenge him to

143

do so.

"What has you so preoccupied, husband? That furrowed brow you say adorns my face, I have seen often enough of late on your own. If we are to talk, then lead on, Fitzwilliam; talk to me, as I have begged you to do in recent weeks. Though let there be no more lies. I will not take another lie. If the truth will wound then let it wound. It can cause no greater hurt, no greater injury than has already been suffered."

Darcy, surprised and saddened by his wife's speech, faltered, stumbling over what to say, leaving silence between them.

"Who is the baby?" Elizabeth said, filling the void.

Since his recovery had begun in earnest and they had been afforded some time together, he had seen an alteration in his wife; all light and energy was gone. Beyond her initial determination he should live, he could discern no passion towards him. He stood trying to compose himself, trying to determine how he could fix all that had gone wrong.

"Who is her mother?"

"You cannot look at me Elizabeth? Do you hate me so much?"

"Do I have reason to hate you, Fitzwilliam?" she shouted, animated at last, anger clouding her face and causing her voice to break as she spoke.

Darcy was strangely pleased at the outburst, the sudden explosion evidencing the first real sign of feeling towards him. Where there was emotion, even painful emotion, there was yet hope.

"Do you think this funny, sir? Does my pain amuse you?" glared Elizabeth, challenging him.

"No, Elizabeth, you know I could never take such pleasure. Indeed, all that has been so badly done was in the foolish attempt to spare you pain. You have reason enough, I suppose, to hate me, my love, but not for the reasons you think. The child is not mine."

"Yet, the man called you 'father'! How do you account for that? How does he know you? And I ask again, who is her mother?"

Darcy, resigned to the fact that he must share everything with Elizabeth or surely lose her, began:

"Elizabeth, you were the first woman I ever entertained the notion of marrying. Almost from our first meeting, you had a hold on my thoughts and my feelings that no other woman had inspired, but before our meeting I was a man who needed the company of a woman. I chose to meet those needs with a woman called May Sinclair. My relationship with May was a business arrangement. There was never any suggestion of our being in love, and she was aware I would never marry her. I am not ashamed of this arrangement; I was discreet in all my actions, and scrupulous to protect myself against sickness and the procreation of children, thus ensuring the Darcy name and lineage would be preserved."

"You have a mistress, Fitzwilliam?" Elizabeth's face was ashen.

"*Had* a mistress, Elizabeth. You must believe me; the relationship was over long before we married. In truth, the relationship was over almost from the day of our first meeting. The very thought of you consumed me. No other woman could have satisfied me, as a lover or a wife. The child is May Sinclair's, but not mine."

"Then how is it that the last thing I heard before the accident was you being called her father? Did I imagine it?"

"I had no idea what became of May after our time together was ended. I did not know she had taken a lover, or that she had borne him a child. Nor did I know she had died shortly after childbirth. May's brother, who had been given care of the baby, learned of our relationship, assumed the child was mine, and looked to blackmail me to keep the secret. To that end, he called me 'father'. This, I swear to you, is the truth."

Elizabeth had begun to cry, and though Darcy longed to hold her, he knew he could not, not yet.

"And it is for this secret that you have risked everything; all our present and future happiness? Why, Fitzwilliam? Why could you not tell me?"

"I knew the child was not mine, but I could not prove it.

Until I found the father, I could not risk her existence becoming known. I had to be sure I was detached from any scandal. I wanted to protect you and protect our life together."

"Was my love so fickle, it could not be trusted to hold steady in the face of scandal? Do you think so little of me, of my feelings for you? Does the passion in my heart burn less fiercely than yours? Is the devotion in my soul less constant than yours? Do you have any notion of how I have suffered?"

The words were racing from Elizabeth now, her speech broken only by sobbing.

"You broke my heart, Fitzwilliam. In that moment when I saw you with the child, you broke my heart."

Unable to say more, Elizabeth's face fell into her hands, crying racking her body as all the emotion of the last few months flooded out at once.

Distraught now, and unable to stay at a distance, Darcy knelt before her, and drawing her into his arms, pulled her down onto his lap.

Elizabeth resisted at first, angrily beating his chest with her fists, but he held firm, tightened his arms about her body, and rocked her gently.

After a time, her crying ceased, and only the sharp pull on her breath and the stains of tears on her face remained as evidence of what had passed.

Elizabeth rose from where they sat and stood looking down at her husband. "Dr Ormsby told you about our child?" she asked.

Darcy nodded.

"Did he also tell you, the child may not have lived through my fever?" she continued.

Again, Darcy nodded.

Elizabeth said nothing else, but looked at him with such inconsolable sadness, he regretted ever recovering. They had survived their illness, but he had lost her, nevertheless.

CHAPTER 16

Although Darcy's body quickly healed, his despondency of spirit continued. He left his business arrangements to his agents, did not entertain visitors, and for two weeks was hardly seen outside of his room. Mrs Reynolds did all she could to attend him. The house was kept in order, and all his favourite dishes were prepared for his meals, but he ate little, and talked less. That he and Elizabeth no longer shared a bed only added to Mrs Reynolds' concern for her master and mistress.

For the first two weeks, Darcy attended at Elizabeth's room every day: he knocked and begged admittance, and every day his pleas were met with silence. By the third week, he did not have the heart for such rejection and simply maintained a presence near her in the vain hope she would yet call out for him.

She did not. Not until the fourth week.

Darcy had finally moved from his room to the library downstairs and was idly thumbing the pages of a book when Mrs Reynolds burst into the room, in an uncharacteristic flurry.

"The mistress! The mistress is calling for you," was all she had time to utter before Darcy bolted past her, and taking the stairs two and three steps at a time, arrived at Elizabeth's door a moment later, hearing her still calling out to him.

He burst in without knocking. "Elizabeth, what is it? What is the matter?"

She was agitated and reached out for him. He approached and she grabbed at his hand and guided it to her belly.

Darcy stood, uncertain as to what was occurring, when suddenly he felt a lump emerge from just below his hand.

"A foot," cried Elizabeth, "our baby's foot! He is kicking, Fitzwilliam. He is alive!"

Darcy collapsed beside her, waiting to feel it again, fearing he had imagined it, but there it was: a little more to the left, but just as sharp as before – a kick. He stared at Elizabeth, unable to speak. She too was silent, but her hand joined with his, resting on her belly, feeling the movement of their child.

As the baby settled and the kicking ceased, the pair sat looking at one another, their fingers still interlaced. Darcy was afraid to speak; afraid that if he did, the moment would be broken and she would withdraw from him again. Yet, he was afraid that if he did not speak, he might equally lose his chance. Eventually, in desperation, he burst forth with, "Please, I beg of you, if you do not love me; if you can no longer love me, tell me, and release me from the torment of hoping you still might."

Elizabeth turned her face to his, her surprise apparent. "Is it even possible you could love me, Fitzwilliam?" she exclaimed. "After all I have risked? Can you ever forgive me? Can you ever forgive me for what I have done?"

"Good God, Elizabeth, what is there for me to forgive?" he replied, confused as to her meaning, but grateful she was willing to speak with him. "From the moment I first loved you, my feelings have only changed to deepen and grow. I do not understand what has been done? What has been risked?"

Elizabeth, in response, reached for Darcy and pulled him into a deep and desperate kiss, her mouth hungry for his.

Darcy responded with equal hunger, the taste of her so long denied to him. His hands grabbed at her with startling fierceness and unusual roughness, but Elizabeth was little concerned; her need for him just as great.

There was little of love in their first reunion; it was all of want and heat. There was a ferocity to their need of each other that overwhelmed them both, and neither could have been patient or gentle.

As Elizabeth sat atop him, Darcy's arms grasped for her, unwilling to release their hold, intent on keeping her where she was, a part of him not lost in the exhilaration of having Elizabeth once more fearing that this might yet be a dream.

Once their passions were spent, Elizabeth moved away, and looking straight at Darcy, undid the buttons of her dress and allowed it to fall to the floor.

He gazed at her naked body, his first sight of her in months, and was amazed by the changes. Her belly was round, her breasts fuller, and there was a curve to her hips that he had never seen before. Darcy doubted he had seen a more beautiful creature. She took a comfortable position on the bed, and after casting off his clothing, Darcy moved behind her, cupping her body with his. He allowed his hands to roam across her, discovering her all over again. The body he had dreamed of holding and making love to was gone, and in its place was one that was fuller and more alive than he remembered.

≪

They spent the afternoon satisfying their need for one another, knowing there was much to be said, but unwilling yet to speak. Though they could not long ignore the barrier that silence had built between them, neither knew how to move forward without hurting the other. As before, it was Darcy who eventually spoke first:

"I have ached for you Elizabeth. In these last weeks, when your refusal of me was so complete, I feared you were lost to me. My soul ached for you and I knew I would never be whole without you. The thought of you hating me…"

"I never hated you, Fitzwilliam," Elizabeth said, quietly. "I was so frightened, I lashed out at you, choosing to demonise you so I did not direct my anger where it was truly deserved – at myself!"

Darcy sat up in the bed and turned her to face him, his eyes exploring hers. "I do not understand, my darling; you were innocent in all of this. What portion of blame could you seek to claim?"

"Innocent, Fitzwilliam? Consider what I have endangered through my reckless actions! We could have lost each other, we could have lost our child, and the fault was mine. Pride – stupid, stupid pride – led me to this, to following you when I had but suspicions, to assuming your guilt when I had but half-truths. I, who knew you to be the best of men. You lied to me; my pride was wounded and what did I do? Did I confront you? Did I demand honesty of my husband? No! I engaged myself in subterfuge and still had the audacity to punish you for your deception."

"But what did you do that I did not drive you to?" he added gently, taking her face in his hands. "If misplaced foolish pride be the root of our current unhappiness, then let me claim my share. I could not bear to be lowered in your esteem, to be viewed as anything less than I believed myself to be, and so I lied and harboured secrets. Dear God, when I close my eyes, I see you still under horses hooves…" his voice broke and Elizabeth saw all colour drain from his face, "I see the small scars the accident has left on your body, and am reminded of all I have inflicted."

"My love," Elizabeth said, calling him back to her, "we must forgive each other if we are to continue. We must come back to one another and concentrate on our child. Can we be what we once were?"

"No!" said Darcy, much to Elizabeth's surprise, "I do not believe we can be as we once were." Pulling her closer to him, he whispered, "I believe we can be much more. We have come through fire, my darling, and found one another again. We will be better and stronger from now on." Looking straight into her eyes, he added, "I will never risk losing you again, Elizabeth. I could not survive it."

Neither could say more; neither was certain that more could be said, and so after kissing, as if to seal their pact, the couple finally allowed their exhausted bodies to fall asleep.

ℰↄ

Neither woke when the chambermaid entered, the next morning. She was startled by the sight of the master back in the bedchamber and ran to ask Mrs Reynolds whether to continue with the room. Mrs Reynolds instructed that there was to be absolutely no disturbance of the couple; indeed, their isolation was to be so complete that not even Darcy's dogs were permitted to wander in the hall outside the bedroom.

The Darcys' reunion was as complete as their separation had been. Their joy at discovering each other again, and in discovering their child to be alive, quickly overcame the fears that had plagued them in the weeks since Elizabeth's accident. The entire affair was laid out before Elizabeth, and although she understood that the reasons for her husband's secrecy had been pure, she was severe in her rebuke of him.

He took her reproof well and willingly. It was clear that Elizabeth was to be a partner in his life, not merely a part of it, and this was something he would have to become accustomed to. Their lives would be shared with one another, and personal notions of honour or pride would not relieve him from his obligations of openness and honesty towards her. For her part, Elizabeth also promised openness and honesty in the future, and in a playful moment, guaranteed to inform him when next she intended to have him followed.

Within a week or two, the Darcys were wholly recovered, in both body and spirit. Though Elizabeth was daily victim to the aches and fatigue induced by her ever-growing belly, she found nothing but joy in her situation. She made no complaint to her husband, but he could see her discomfort.

Darcy, although recovered, left his business to his agents, determined that until the baby was born, all his attention must be given to Elizabeth. He warned his men that only fire, flood, pestilence, or death were sufficient reasons to interrupt his care of his wife.

They spent their time, as they had done in the first weeks of their marriage, with just the two of them; Darcy's only concession to visitors being the doctor. After the turmoil of the last few months, they needed the succour that only the other could provide, and neither was willing to abandon this intimacy too soon.

୫

After weeks of indulging their need for seclusion, Elizabeth was anxious to return to London. "I wish to share our good fortune with Jane, Georgiana, and Kitty. They are so eager to see us, and I long for the comfort of my sisters."

"Then could we not invite them here, Elizabeth?" Darcy implored, despite knowing the futility of his plea. "I do not want you making such a long trip, and surely you must be close to your confinement. Would you not be more comfortable here?"

"I have no intention of hiding away just yet, Fitzwilliam, and you cannot seriously mean to take the girls away from London before the final ball of the season?"

"Foolish of me, I know. I should have guessed you would rank their need for frivolity over something as silly as concern for your welfare or social convention. Might I ask, Elizabeth, if I am ever to be allowed to make a decision again? Or shall you be doing it for me from this day forth?"

"Oh, husband," she laughed, "you will remain your own master, of course, but in matters relating to our sisters and their hopes for romance, I must insist on taking the lead."

୫

Letters outlining their planned return to London were dispatched that afternoon. They would be back in the city by the end of the week. Kitty and Georgiana were to take leave of the Gardiners and return to stay with Darcy and Elizabeth, and everyone would be expected to dine with them on Saturday.

This news was a great boon to Georgiana and Kitty, who were anxious to know, for certain, of their full recovery. Although Elizabeth and Darcy had written, both girls were troubled by how the couple had looked when last they had been together. Until they could actually see the two of them, neither would be fully convinced.

Jane was delighted at the thought of having Elizabeth back with them so soon, and even Caroline's barbed comments could not dampen her joy.

"I do hope Eliza is truly recovered and she does not rejoin us too soon," announced Caroline on hearing the news. "How pale and drawn she looked when last we saw her; you must agree, Charles? Darcy was so taken by her looks; I hope there has been no loss of bloom."

"I am sure Elizabeth would be heartened by your concern for her good health, Caroline," replied Bingley, without turning his head from his paper, "though you should not unduly concern yourself. If Darcy's love for Elizabeth is half as consuming as mine for her sister, he will care little for anything, but that she is well."

"Charles!" Caroline cried out. "I hardly think such conversation is suitable for the breakfast table."

"Caroline is absolutely right, Charles," admonished Jane. "Such talk is much more suited to after dinner!"

Caroline glowered at Jane with a look of utter disapproval, and although once it would have wounded her greatly, Jane was now able to shrug off such condemnation, having realised Caroline's approval would never truly be gained, and in fact was no longer required.

∞

By Saturday, to the happiness of all concerned, they were reunited. Georgiana and Kitty were heartened to see that Elizabeth was indeed recovered, and even Caroline grudgingly admitted to her looking very well. The excitement of a new baby added to the joy of the party.

Jane observed Darcy closely as he attended to Elizabeth in the drawing room after dinner. He ordered chairs to be moved, and fires lit; arranged for comforts and treats to be ever close at hand. He was quick to fulfil any small need, and though Jane did not doubt that his attention was largely born of love, she could not help but wonder how much of it was also born of fear. Since witnessing Darcy in the sick room, and the decimation that Elizabeth's illness had wrought on him, she had been concerned for his full recovery in spirit as well as body. Bingley had laughed at her concerns, assuring her that Darcy was a sensible fellow and would brush off the whole horrible incident admirably, but he had not been in the sick room and had not been witness to Darcy's dramatic alteration. Despite her husband's assurances, Jane wished to quiet her concerns, and though it would mean forcing an uncomfortable conversation with Darcy, she was determined to do so.

"Mr Darcy, I have a book I thought might interest you," she said, trying to draw his notice from Elizabeth.

Darcy regarded her quizzically; it was not like Jane to bring him deliberately into conversation.

"It regards treatments of fevers and all that might be done after a fever to rebuild and repair the body. It was penned by a doctor working in the Indies and I understand he had great success in recovery."

Darcy, appearing to be interested in the volume, moved Jane out of earshot of the rest of the party, fully understanding this to be her motive in approaching him, and waited for her to continue.

"Are you well, Mr Darcy?"

"Quite well, Jane. I have fully recovered and the doctor has assured me there should be no lasting damage from the fever."

"And what of your spirits? Have they recovered as completely as your body?"

"You are concerned, I assume, for how I was during Elizabeth's illness." He sighed. "I am uncertain how to speak about this painful time with you, or how to apologise for all that you were a witness to."

"I seek no apology, Mr Darcy, I simply wish to quiet concerns that plague me. I am not so foolish to think I have any talent for reading your thoughts and feelings – brother, you have long been a mystery to me – yet even I could see the dread and distress Elizabeth's illness wrought. I have no right to intrude upon your privacy, but I would rest more easily if I could be assured you were free from its grip."

"Jane, you cannot know how discomfited I have been at the thought of meeting you again, to have exposed myself to you so completely and in the manner I did. It was unforgiveable."

"Mr Darcy, you will find no censure here. My only concern is for your happiness and the happiness of you and Elizabeth."

"I was heart weary and my soul bruised when I made those revelations to you. I truly believed I would have to sacrifice Elizabeth as some sort of punishment for my sins, and the cost was too much to bear, but she is mended and restored to me, and I am made whole by it. Jane, you need worry no more."

℘

Once the general commotion had calmed, Elizabeth asked, "But now, Kitty; Georgiana; what news from you two? Aunt Gardiner tells me you have attended several parties and a play while we have been away. How did you get on? Did you meet anyone of particular interest?"

"Oh, you missed nothing of importance while you were away, Lizzy," announced Kitty, "though you have timed your return rather well for we have a number of very promising engagements next week and Lady Sackwell's ball is almost upon us."

"Really," added Elizabeth with surprise, "I had expected much news in relation to recent outings. I thought perhaps you had seen more of the Trevelyans and the charming Mr Grey."

"Do not speak to me of the Trevelyans!" exclaimed Kitty. "I can barely stand to hear their name, and it hurts me just to think of them. You simply must not ask after them."

"Heavens, Kitty, such passion, what on earth has happened? The Trevelyans were firm favourites of yours before I left. What great transgression has caused them to fall so fully out of favour?"

"They have stolen Mr Grey from Georgiana and I shall never forgive them," was Kitty's sullen response.

Elizabeth looked immediately to Georgiana, who did not seem at all distressed by Kitty's outburst, but rather amused. "Georgiana, surely Kitty does not suggest that Mr Grey has declared an intention to marry one of the Trevelyan girls?"

"She suggests nothing of the sort, Elizabeth; you will have to excuse Kitty, for she has been most displeased by what she perceives to be an unforgiveable interference in the blossoming romance between Mr Grey and I."

Elizabeth was surprised by Georgiana, whose bold talk of blossoming romance was far from the shy young girl she had left with the Gardiners.

"You smile at my mention of a blossoming romance. It is a term Kitty uses daily in her description of the handful of dances and conversations Mr Grey and I have shared, and I fear it has taken hold." She laughed, nudging Kitty in an effort to rouse her from sullenness. "Call it what you will, whatever had begun between Mr Grey and I has been interrupted by his leaving London to go to Bath with the Trevelyans."

Kitty, who could sit quietly no longer, added: "They left with no warning, and just before a ball, where I am sure Mr Grey was planning on declaring his intentions to Georgiana."

Georgiana interrupted again, to temper Kitty's tale of harsh and easy abandonment: "Mrs Trevelyan has long been plagued by a sickness. Her doctors recommended time out of the city, with cleaner air and healing waters being the best possible remedy. Mr Trevelyan – whose strength of feeling for his wife is to be commended, Kitty – refused to wait until the end of the season and removed the family to Bath at once. The girls wrote explaining all and expressing their deep regret at their forced departure. Mr Grey felt it incumbent upon him that he join them, taking account of their warm and hospitable treatment of him while in the country and here in London. I applaud the behaviour of both men and find no fault with any party."

"Well, I fail to see why Mrs Trevelyan could not have waited; her lungs have been bad for years," Kitty added, displeased with such ready forgiveness of those who had got in the way of all her romantic hopes for Georgiana.

"Ah, sister; for all you have changed, you are still my Kitty," Elizabeth joked. "It was dreadfully inconsiderate of Mrs Trevelyan, I grant you, but perhaps we might be a little gentle on the woman who will not have acted out of a deliberate desire to interfere with all your romantic machinations."

"I suppose it is of little importance now; what damage is done will not be undone. We received a letter just yesterday, informing us they will soon return to London so some comfort must be taken from that at least," Kitty admitted, ungenerously.

"I am simply grateful to have our family reunited," declared Georgiana. "The return of our friends is welcome, but all the happiness I could wish for I find here in this moment."

"Bravo, Georgiana!" applauded Elizabeth. "My heart, too, is full to the brim at being back with you all, but I trust we will all find that there is still greater happiness ahead."

CHAPTER 17

As it happened, it was two weeks more before the Trevelyans and William Grey arrived back in London; as soon as Ann and Mary were at liberty they sent a letter to Georgiana and Kitty telling of their return and making plans to meet on the morning of Lady Sackwell's ball. Their letter contained such genuine apology and sentiments of regret at their absence that even Kitty was encouraged to think well of them once more, and when at last they met, she declared herself thoroughly wretched at their absence and hailed them the truest and best of friends.

Neither William Grey nor their cousin John joined the girls, and Kitty wasted no time in enquiring after the reason for their absence. The gentlemen had returned to London, she hoped; they were both well and would be attending at the ball that evening, she pressed.

"Oh, indeed! Dear John and Mr Grey are simply running errands for Papa, you need have no cause for concern, Kitty," replied Ann.

"Oh, heavens, no!" added Mary. "They are most anxious for this evening, but Papa has his mind set on acquiring some new-fangled machine to aid Mama and would not be content until he could acquire it. Cousin John and Mr Grey, as concerned for Mama as any of us, mercifully offered to collect the thing, so

Papa could rest easily."

With Kitty's chief concern answered, she could turn her attention to pleasanter matters and was quickly questioning the sisters on all that Bath had to offer them by way of entertainment.

"Well, I hardly know what to tell you, Kitty," replied Ann, despondently, "for we were scarce outside of our house the whole time we were there, save for our trips to take the waters with Mama. We did not dine out, nor see any of the concerts. Mama's health simply would not allow it."

"Lord!" exclaimed Kitty. "What a dull time of it you must have had. I was perfectly prepared to spend the rest of the afternoon in a fit of envy at all your adventures, and now I shall be so disappointed."

"Kitty," chided Georgiana, "what a thing to say. I'm sure neither Ann nor Mary could have been happy at a concert while their mama was so ill," and turning to Ann, added, "still the company of your cousin and Mr Grey must have been a great comfort to you and added to the cheer of your evenings at home."

"Oh, heavens, no!" laughed Ann. "For John declared on his first evening, the sickroom was no place for a man, and left with Mr Grey in tow. They spent most evenings out, but then they had such wonderful tales to tell when they did stay in."

"You must ask cousin John about his lost shoe," Mary cut in, "it is such a funny tale and he will need little persuasion to recount it."

Although all four continued on, and chatted quite happily until it was time to return home to prepare to meet up again that evening, Kitty was quieter once the girls had spoken of how the gentlemen had spent their time in Bath. She was troubled by the suggestion that Mr Grey had been free to gallivant around the town with Mr Trevelyan. Although there was no suggestion from their friends that any attachments had been formed by either gentleman, she remained uneasy, knowing that relief would only be forthcoming on seeing Mr Grey and taking measure of his conduct towards Georgiana. Though she harboured some apprehension as to his fidelity, Kitty was not yet willing to abandon the hope that he was sincere in his attachment to Georgiana.

ℰℐ

In her short time in London, Kitty had amassed an impressive network of spies, or as she preferred: informed confidantes. One such confidante accosted them almost as soon as they entered the hall, with important news concerning Mr Grey and his recent attentions to a number of young ladies in Bath. Kitty's heart sank at so soon a confirmation of her fears for Georgiana's romance. Though she was loath to hear what her friend had to say, a quick look to Georgiana, who appeared entirely impassive in the wake of the news, encouraged her to listen at least to Miss Parrington, so the truth of the account could be judged.

Miss Parrington, it emerged, had heard from an unimpeachable source that Mr Grey had been quite busy during his time at Bath, having been seen in the company of three young ladies of good fortune: reading poetry with one, accompanying another on a charitable outing, and taking hold of the hand of a third while out at the theatre.

While relaying this scandal, Miss Parrington at all times closely attended to the reactions of Miss Darcy, whom she believed to have a connection to Mr Grey, but if any such connection existed, there was not a trace of it to be read in Georgiana's response to the news. She remained pleasant and mildly interested throughout, exclaimed her surprise, and tut-tutted her disapproval at just the right moments in the tale, but generally appeared unaffected. Indeed, her only comment was to propose that for a man with so many interests, it must have been of comfort to Mr Grey that he could so easily fill a day.

Miss Parrington ended her story a little disappointed. She was as convinced now that there was no great feeling between Mr Grey and Miss Darcy, as she had been convinced that there was, not five minutes before. She was robbed, therefore, of having the news of Miss Darcy's heartbreak to add to the tale upon its retelling. Her disappointment, fortunately, did not hold long, as she spied Miss Burke across the room, whom she was certain was violently in love with Mr Grey. Making her excuses, she left her companions and sought out Miss Burke before anyone else could.

Had she looked back as she crossed the room, Miss Parrington's desire for heartache would have been richly rewarded by the sight of a pale Miss Georgiana Darcy eagerly reaching out for the steadying arm of Miss Kitty Bennet before the pair escaped to a quiet couch in a secluded corner.

Before Georgiana could say a word, Kitty burst out with, "Well what a turn of events. I declare I shall never understand men! What can Mr Grey have been thinking in carrying on as he did and in so public a forum as Bath? He must have known his behaviour would be seen and reported more widely abroad. He could not have thought we would not hear of this; he must have been sensible to the feelings and disappointments he would excite."

"Why should he care? What cause had he to consider the feelings of those he left behind in London? There was no attachment here."

"No attachment!" Kitty exclaimed. "But I know that to be untrue. I know there to have been an attachment between you: I was witness to it. Perhaps it was unspoken, perhaps it was only in his implied actions, but do not tell me there was no attachment."

"Kitty, please, this does me no great service. Perhaps he might argue that any perceived attachment was on my side alone. Perhaps I allowed myself to foolishly see favour where there was none."

"Impossible, Georgiana, I know he loved you, I know it."

"Love, Kitty? What value can I place on such a love, on feelings that are so easily and freely given and to so many? I flattered myself it was love, but it seems to have been but a poor copy of the feeling."

"And you Georgiana? Did you love him?" asked Kitty after a

moment's silence.

"Knowing now what I do, I am almost ashamed to admit that I did. I did most certainly believe myself to be in love with him."

On this admission, the girls fell silent until Kitty eventually declared, "Now we must decide how we shall go about this evening. I think we must seek guidance."

"I cannot speak of this, this…this embarrassment with anyone!" gasped Georgiana, whose horror at the discovery of the fickle nature of Mr Grey was evident.

"We need not discuss the matter with anyone else, Georgiana," mused Kitty, "we need only consider: what would Lizzy do?"

℘

Georgiana sat wondering whether Kitty was right in thinking that Mr Grey would approach as soon as the earliest opportunity to find her alone presented itself, although she did not have to wait long for an answer, as no sooner had she found herself alone than a familiar figure took up a place beside her.

William Grey had in fact been attempting to secure an audience with Georgiana for some time, though he had been thwarted twice by suitors claiming a dance, and once by Kitty. So when he saw Miss Bennet accept an invitation to dance and Miss Darcy take up a seat by the window, he took his moment. He approached her with all the swagger and confidence of a man sure in what was about to happen, and took up a casual stance beside her.

Georgiana, for her part, doubtful of her own resolve 'to do as Lizzy would' maintained a steady gaze at the dancers and waited for Mr Grey to make his address.

"My word, Miss Darcy, but how brilliantly you shine this evening. I was not here ten minutes before I noticed how all others paled by comparison. I am so pleased the health of others close to us has been restored, and we both are finally free to rejoin society and the company of those we have missed. My days have seemed duller without your charm and conversation."

"Mr Grey, you flatter me, though I am not certain the companions who have helped you fill the time since our last meeting would thank you for the compliment. Indeed, in just the last two hours I saw you with a number of undoubtedly charming women and you seemed at no loss for witty conversation or distraction."

This was not the response anticipated by William Grey. Neither had it been accompanied by the expected blushes and coy glances. There was a brief silence as he considered how best to proceed.

Georgiana filled the silence. "You do not dance, Mr Grey? I believed you to be very fond of dancing, or perhaps I am mistaken. Was it poetry, or maybe the theatre you preferred?"

She now turned her full attention to him, and the boldness of her stare upset his confidence further. He took a step back, as though trying to reason whether it was, in fact, Miss Darcy that he had approached.

On seeing the space between them, Georgiana rose gracefully from her seat and with a glance that almost spoke of pity, said, "If you will excuse me, sir, I believe I shall rejoin the rest of my party. I hope you enjoy the rest of your evening."

She moved to walk away when William Grey, thoroughly uncertain as to how the course of events had veered so out of his control, made one last attempt to secure Miss Darcy's attention by reaching out to take hold of her hand.

Georgiana stiffened at the feel of him grasping for her. She withdrew her hand sharply and turned to face him. "Sir! You seem to forget yourself. We are not of an acquaintance to permit or warrant such an assault on my person."

"Georgiana…" William Grey began, before being sharply cut off.

"You will address me as 'Miss Darcy'. I must confess, Mr Grey, I am at quite a loss to understand your excessive familiarity with me. This is most improper!"

Finishing her speech with a look of disapprobation worthy of her brother, Georgiana turned her back on William Grey and crossed the hall, where she found Kitty eagerly awaiting her.

⁊⌒

Georgiana and Kitty judged it best to find Darcy and Elizabeth, for should Mr Grey take exception to his treatment, they were certain he would not risk a scene in front of them. They were unaware that anyone of their circle had witnessed the exchange and were surprised to hear Charles Bingley loudly recounting it to the entire party upon their approach.

"And I tell you, Darcy, I could not have been prouder were she my own sister! She dealt with him as only a Darcy could – even you could not have chastened the man better!"

Darcy flushed at hearing the news; Elizabeth paled, and both wondered what William Grey could have done to provoke such a rebuke from the ever-gentle Georgiana.

As neither said a word, Caroline could not yet tell whether Darcy was pleased or annoyed at this intelligence, and not wishing to fall out of favour simply added, "She was most spirited," judging such a comment would be equally appropriate whatever Darcy decided his reaction would be.

"Are you certain it was Georgiana?" Elizabeth queried.

"I think I might be trusted to recognise Georgiana," Bingley laughed. "I have known the girl since she was a babe and there was certainly no mistaking the withering look she gave poor Mr Grey, for I have seen Darcy bestow the same look on many an unfortunate creature!"

Elizabeth was amazed by the tale, but on seeing the high colour in Georgiana's face when she approached their circle, knew it to be true, and though surprised by the turn of events, and anxious that William Grey had in some way mistreated her, she, like Bingley, could not have been prouder.

"Georgiana we are all astonishment. Come, what is behind all of this?"

"It is nothing, sister; a simple misunderstanding between acquaintances."

"Acquaintances?" quizzed Darcy.

"It is as I say, brother. Mr Grey and I are but acquaintances. I hope you have not been deceived into thinking there was anything of greater substance between us."

"He danced with you on several occasions and called on you at our house, Georgiana. Assuming an attachment of some description would not be an unreasonable supposition for me, or anyone else, to make."

Georgiana, already sufficiently embarrassed by the affair, was determined to quash any speculation surrounding her affection for Mr Grey. Pulling herself up to her full height, and adopting a high-handedness more often associated with her brother, she added, "Really, Fitzwilliam, he also danced with Elizabeth; do you mean to suggest he had designs on your wife? As for his calling at the house, well, he simply escorted the Trevelyan sisters. I had not thought you prone to such wild conjecture."

Further conversation on the matter was instantly brought to an end by her reproof of Darcy, who for his part could not suppress a smile, both at an end to an affair he had never encouraged, and at the show of strength and spirit from his sister.

Still, Georgiana knew how it would be: her dismissal of Mr Grey had been public enough to make it fodder for the gossips around the ballroom. She had only to hope that her disavowal was sufficiently believable to answer rumours of an affair, an engagement, or whatever other manner of imagined impropriety was being circulated.

Bingley continued to boast at how spectacular she had been, but the ladies of the party were heard on occasion to meet reports of her supposed affair with derision.

"Mr Grey and Miss Darcy!" scoffed Caroline. "I would grant Miss Darcy more discernment in her choice of a husband. He is a charming enough fellow, I suppose, but with her fortune you must own that Miss Darcy will not likely settle for a second son."

Within half an hour, the story of Mr Grey and Miss Darcy had fallen out of favour with those chattering around the ballroom. It was true that Miss Darcy would be unlikely to show attention to a second son, and though it was remarked that Mr Grey had danced and visited Miss Darcy, it was acknowledged that he also danced and visited with Mrs Darcy, Miss Bennet, and the Trevelyans. As there was little fun to be had with such easily refuted scandal, the ladies soon turned their attention elsewhere.

℘

William Grey was ignorant of his brief moment of fame, as he had left the ball the instant his failure with Georgiana was clear. Unable to quit the scene of her disappointment so readily, Georgiana and Kitty took a turn about the room, hoping to appear unmoved by the talk that her display had inspired. As they did, they came upon two gentlemen Georgiana recognised as friends of Mr Grey's, and she slowed her walk in the prospect of overhearing some piece of information.

The two men, oblivious to the presence of the ladies at their back, were indeed just then discussing their friend and continued to laugh good-naturedly at his misfortune.

"Poor William is truly to be pitied," said one, "for you know I honestly believed he admired Miss Darcy."

"Grey's problem is that he needs the object of his admiration at hand at all times, or his admiration and his eye wanders elsewhere!" laughed the other.

"Though I tell you, I would not have risked crossing Darcy for some bit of skirt in Bath. What can Grey have meant by cavorting about the town like that, fully aware accounts of his dealings would reach us in London?"

"Oh, you know as well as I, that Grey never means anything by these flirtations. He is a fool for a charming girl with a gentle manner and an easy blush."

"Then what," his companion added, "was he doing in the company of Miss Darcy? Did you hear of the manner in which she dealt with him? Cut the legs right from under the man, or so I heard. It was quite a sight by all accounts, and I only wish I had been there to witness it myself."

"Spirit and a fortune? You know I feel inclined to seek out Miss Darcy for myself. Grey has no need of her money, but I would not pass up the opportunity to attach myself to a spirited girl with a healthy dowry."

As the two men stood laughing, Kitty and Georgiana moved away without ever being seen.

"Is it a comfort to know that Mr Grey was at least sincere in his admiration of you?" posed Kitty, when they had moved far enough away.

"What use is such sincerity if it needs my constant presence to hold steadfast?" Georgiana replied. "Is it love, if mere time and distance so easily cause it to sway? There is no comfort to be found in learning the object of my affection was so easily distracted."

CHAPTER 18

The next morning brought rain and the welcome excuse – for Georgiana, at least – to call off their planned engagements for that afternoon. In the wake of all their recent outings, she was exhausted; in truth, she was still feeling the sting of Mr Grey's betrayal. She had not the heart for gaiety and frivolity with the weight of recent doomed romance pressing so heavily upon her spirit, but she knew, too, that she could not have disappointed Kitty's hopes for diversion without good reason. Thankfully, nature had provided reason enough with a downpour, which looked set to continue the full length of the day.

Elizabeth had mentioned, in passing, a slight headache at breakfast, and Darcy had insisted that she retire at once to their bedchamber, that the doctor be called, that no noise be made in her general surrounds, and that she suffer no strain until he could be assured that she was well again. During all of this, Elizabeth had tried in vain to assure him that it was but a headache. However, on seeing his genuine concern, and fully aware memories of recent illness were still raw and vivid in his mind, she succumbed to all his fussing and attention, endured his hovering, and helped soothe him by insisting the best course of action would be for them both to share a bath and then return to bed. Darcy, mollified by the thought of a morning spent with Elizabeth, informed the household that they should not be disturbed until lunch.

Thus, Georgiana and Kitty found themselves sitting alone in the small front room, one loudly lamenting the unseasonable rainfall, and the other silently thanking the heavens for it.

Georgiana sat quietly, leafing through one of the library's many volumes, but Kitty did not find herself equal to that measure of attention. She languished on the couch, then on a chair by the table, moving next to the writing desk, before returning to the couch and sighing loudly as she sat.

"Kitty, should I move from where I sit so you may try this seat for comfort? I judge from your turn about the room, you have found the others wanting – or are you now satisfied with the couch?"

Georgiana put down her book, distracted by her companion as she flitted from chair to chair, and was now addressing the figure draped with unceremonious abandon along the full length of the couch.

"I am such a fidget today, I know!" Kitty exclaimed, and by way of explanation, continued, "Do I disturb you? Forgive me. Ignore me. I am simply too exhausted for words. I cannot settle to reading, music, or needlework. Indeed, as you have so acutely observed, I cannot settle at all. Even the exertion of picking a seat and staying in it is too much for me."

She looked so genuinely unsettled by her state of unease that Georgiana could not help but laugh. When the plan to have Kitty join them at Pemberley had first been told to her, Georgiana had been wary of having her with them for so long. As a naturally reclusive creature, she feared that she would find Kitty's rambunctious nature overwhelming, but she quickly discovered that Kitty's wildness could be tempered with sense and good nature, and only a little support was needed for Kitty to engage in better regulation of spirit. Indeed, Kitty was perfectly able to spend quiet hours in practising accomplishments, and seemed to thrive under the attention and praise Georgiana liked to bestow as encouragement. Though once she would have baulked at such a display of flighty agitation,

Georgiana was able now to smile patiently at her friend and wait for the storm to settle.

After a few moments more of self-indulgent sighing and list-lessness, Kitty raised her head, stared straight into Georgiana's eyes, and with unusual solemnity announced, "I have been thinking about love, Georgiana, and the more I think about it, the more confused I am with it all."

Georgiana moved to sit beside Kitty on the couch, and taking her hand, asked gently, "What causes such serious contemplations, Kitty? I did not think you had been affected by the young men of our acquaintance in the past weeks. Have I not heard you comment, on more than one occasion, about the lack of red coats in London? Have I been blind to an affair of the heart?"

"No, nothing so grand as that Georgiana, but – and you will forgive me for mentioning this – your disappointment with Mr Grey, as well as other recent events, have set me to contemplating the nature and expression of love."

"Good heavens, Kitty, you are being most serious indeed. Have you come to any decisions in your considerations?"

"I have," announced Kitty, sitting straight up on the couch and assuming her most adult pose. "I have come to some very important decisions. I shall tell you, though you must not laugh at me for I am in earnest in all I share with you."

With Georgiana's strictest confidence and support assured, Kitty continued, "I believe you are aware of my sister, Lydia, and the fact she married your family friend, George Wickham."

Georgiana nodded her agreement, and noticed for the first time since the discovery of their ill-fated elopement she did not feel shame, embarrassment, or even so much as the slightest discomfort at the mention of Wickham's name.

"Well, at the time, I thought theirs to be the ideal love affair. He was handsome, a military man, skilled with a horse, a fine dancer, and the embodiment of charm itself. I could not understand the objections, I then believed, so unjustly levied against their marriage, and the disapproval of Wickham, which my father and Elizabeth only barely masked. Of course, I was aware of rumours of scandal and debt on the part of Wickham, but what was past behaviour compared to present adoration and romance? When Jane married Mr Bingley, I thought it just as wonderful. He was wealthy and handsome, and I dare say as good-natured a man as I had ever met. He clearly loved Jane, and I was pleased, after her initial disappointment, that they had secured one another at last, but as for the news about Lizzy and Mr Darcy, which soon followed, well, I can hardly tell you how shocked I was – how shocked we all were – when she announced her engagement to your brother.

"You will forgive my candour, Georgiana, but I truly believed Mr Darcy to be one of the sternest, most unpleasant, and thoroughly dispassionate men I had the misfortune of knowing. The thought of Lizzy aligning herself with him – even for ten thousand pounds a year! I knew my sister to be strong-willed and passionate, and though she never confided directly in me, I overheard her speak in such disapproving terms of your brother that I feared greatly for her happiness—"

"You are very hard on my brother, Kitty!" interrupted Georgiana, her inherent loyalty and respect for Darcy unwilling to allow the slight to pass without comment.

"Oh indeed! Indeed, I am! I was, that is to say, I have since learned to view your brother so differently, I can hardly countenance how I could have been so mistaken."

With Georgiana apparently pacified by the response, Kitty was free to continue. "As I say, I feared greatly for Elizabeth's happiness and still looked to Lydia's relationship as the ideal, but since joining you, so much has happened to make me rethink all my old prejudices and perceptions. In Mr Grey, I saw Mr Wickham: the same charm and ease, that knowing self-assurance, and I was pleased for you, as I believed him to be sincere in his intentions. So imagine my surprise when he disappointed you. He showed all the signs of true interest in his notice of you, in all he said, in the way he danced with you, and sought your company; so how then could it be you would not marry? Then there was Darcy and Elizabeth: I saw him distant and, I believed, unfeeling in his attitudes towards Elizabeth. He displayed none of the sort of outward attention I associated with love and admiration..."

Kitty paused, wondering how much of what she had witnessed in the gallery to reveal.

"And have you changed your opinion about my brother?" Georgiana posed, curious as to Kitty's sudden silence.

"I have since learned: indeed, your brother loves my sister without reserve, without measure, and I daresay without comparison, certainly among my acquaintance. He has a passion for her equalled only by his respect for her. I had never thought such unity possible."

Georgiana gasped at the speech. "Kitty, this is a most unexpected declaration – now tell me what is behind it. We are together almost always, so how is it you have determined my brother's love to be so complete? I know it to be true as I have witnessed the changes in him since meeting Elizabeth, but I doubt someone generally unfamiliar with him would have noticed or indeed comprehended the significance of the changes. What have you seen? What has convinced you?"

With a moment's more reflection as to the propriety of telling Georgiana of the intimate scene she had witnessed, she broke her silence and began.

"And this is what you hope for now, Kitty?" Georgiana asked, once Kitty had finished recounting all she had seen.

"No," said Kitty, sadly, "I do not think such a love is likely for me. I do not believe all men are capable of the devotion of your brother, and I fear I am not as capable of inspiring it as my sister, but if I can find a man who loves me half as well as Darcy loves Lizzy, I believe I would be perfectly content."

Kitty was smiling again, and Georgiana was pleased to see her melancholy had not lasted long.

"My current difficulty," continued Kitty, "is in recognising it. Mr Wickham and Mr Grey showed all the signs of love, but now I doubt their actual inclinations, whereas Darcy had all of the inclination, with none of the signs. What am I to do, Georgiana? How am I to ever hope to find love if I know not what to look for?"

Georgiana was laughing at Kitty again: she, it seemed, had now abandoned all seriousness and was back to her usual self.

"Well, Kitty, a compromise must be sought. Perhaps you could look to Jane and Charles as your example? He was more reserved than Mr Grey was in his attention, but more forthright than my brother was. Shall we pair make a pact not to give our hearts away until we can be certain we have found our own Mr Bingley?"

"That is what we must do indeed," chimed in Kitty. "You know my father once threatened that I would not be allowed out again until I could prove I had spent at least fifteen minutes being serious. Well, from now on, I shall not be inclined to fancy myself to be in love until the gentleman can prove himself to be sincere in his attention and flattery in the same way."

"You only require a love of fifteen minutes, Kitty?"

"Perhaps that would be a little short – well then, fifteen days. I declare I shall be in no danger from love until a gentleman has proven his faithfulness, and feelings, for at least fifteen days!"

The two girls, aware of the silliness of the pact, collapsed back into their chairs with laughter.

When able to speak again, Georgiana added, to Kitty's surprise and amusement, "Bravo, Kitty! We shall hold the devotion of any admirers to the test of time and must hope now to secure Mr Bingleys of our own. It is such a shame Charles has only sisters, or our search would be a much easier one!"

ॐ

Later that evening, Darcy moved to stand by Kitty as she searched the library shelves for the novels Lizzy liked to hide in between the more serious volumes on display. "I believe I have you to thank for the events on the evening of Lady Sackwell's ball," he said.

"Me?" Kitty stated innocently, refusing to look away from her task. "I cannot think what you mean. I don't believe I had much time for anything but dancing. My dance card was full the entire evening!"

"Georgiana tells a different tale, but regardless, you are not in trouble. I just wished to thank you."

"Thank me?"

"I do not believe Georgiana could have managed so well without your advice."

"Mr Darcy, you are mistaken. Georgiana may have taken some notice of advice I gave, but the manner of its execution was all hers," Kitty was quick to add.

" I see…" Darcy was surprised at this and could not resist asking, "though pray, might I enquire as to what you told her to do?"

"Oh, it was all rather silly. You see, I read a fantastical tale once about a woman who could channel spirits, and when she did, she talked and acted just like them; I thought Georgiana could try something similar."

Darcy laughed out loud at the idea. "You encouraged Georgiana to channel spirits?"

"That would have been silly, Mr Darcy! Georgiana is not a medium – is she?"

"No, Kitty, she most assuredly is not!"

"No, of course not. I suggested she simply try to be like someone who would know what to do in such situations. I suggested she channel Lizzy."

"And you don't believe she did?"

"Oh no, no, no," Kitty smiled, looking directly into Darcy's face for the first time. "I believe she chose someone even more adept at subduing a foe."

Darcy raised an eyebrow.

"Ah, there is the very look, yes. It was you; it was most definitely you!"

❧

Ignorant of the fact that his rejection was still the stuff of conversation in another household, William Grey sat alone in a drawing room trying to discern how he could have so misunderstood Miss Georgiana Darcy.

"William, what are you doing in here all alone, and in the dark?" cried Ann Trevelyan on entering the room and being startled by his presence. "You scared me half to death sitting cloaked in darkness in this dramatic fashion! You are not still vexed by Miss Darcy, surely?"

"I am thinking, Ann. Is it too much to ask for five minutes quiet repose?" he replied, with a curtness underserved by his friend.

"Well, there is no need to bite so," she replied, hurt by his outburst.

William remained agitated, his sour mood refusing to relent even when faced with Ann's pouted lip. "And what if I am still vexed? I have reason enough to be so. You must have heard of her slighting of me at Lady Sackwell's ball."

"You know very well that I did," replied Ann, "and I know very well that if you were snubbed, then there was reason enough for it! Miss Darcy is too good to embarrass you needlessly and I am certain she was too fond of you to hurt you deliberately. So I must ask: what is it you have done?"

"What have I done? Oh, just like a woman to assume it is the man who has sinned."

"William," Ann interrupted, "if you are going to be intentionally hard, I shall leave."

At last, on this final challenge, William softened and stammered an apology, "I have been so foolish, Ann, so very, very foolish, and I am afraid that I have paid for my foolishness with the loss of Miss Darcy's affections."

"What have you done, William?"

"Those silly flirtations I engaged in while at Bath have, it seems, been widely reported on among our set, and you may guess that Miss Darcy was not pleased to hear of my attention being drawn to other women."

"But have you spoken to her, explained yourself, and asked for her forgiveness? She must forgive you; she was sincerely attached to you. From all I know of Miss Darcy, I do not believe she would have attached herself rashly."

"She returns my letters unopened, has avoided the outings I

would have expected to find her at, and I simply cannot attend at her house: being turned away from there would be one humiliation too many."

"Then you must be patient," Ann advised. "Miss Darcy will not hide forever. When her disappointment has passed, I have no doubt we will be sure to encounter her once more. I could send a note by her with an invitation to lunch, if you believe it would be of service."

For the first time in some days, William smiled, comforted by Miss Trevelyan's good intentions and willingness to come to his aid. "I thank you, dearest Ann, for the goodness of your heart, but I would rather that if there is to be reconciliation between me and Miss Darcy, it should not be forced. I would not have you risk the good feeling she still has for you and your sister. I will do as you suggest, and I will be patient. It is as you say: Miss Darcy will not hide away forever, and when she is ready to venture forth again I will be ready, my heart on my sleeve and a ready apology on my tongue."

CHAPTER 19

During the first weeks of their reconciliation, Darcy and Elizabeth had managed skilfully to avoid the subject of Maria Sinclair. The whole of their concentration was given to one another and the health of the next generation of Darcy that was daily growing in evidence. As she grew in confidence that their developing child was safe and well, Elizabeth turned her thoughts to the other child, and began to worry about the situation they may be abandoning her to. Her concern as to the wretchedness of the poor girl's prospects was such that she could not rest easy until she knew that Maria Sinclair was as safe and well as the child within her. Believing that Darcy would resist any broaching of the subject, she decided the best time to raise her concerns was when he was at his most vulnerable, so she waited for a quiet afternoon, after they had loved and rested, when he lay with his head next to her belly, listening for a heartbeat, waiting for a kick.

"Fitzwilliam, I have been thinking about our child," she began, "and of the bright future I hope for him."

"You remain convinced, then, our babe is a boy?" he responded.

"Oh, it simply must be," she laughed, "or I believe Mama

will never forgive me. She has counselled me most severely on the matter – I must produce an heir."

Darcy joined Elizabeth in her laughter; his affection for Mrs Bennet having grown with the distance between them. "I can well believe your mama would view it as a personal slight, and in such a case, Lizzy, have mercy on your poor papa and bear a son, or I fear it will be he who will suffer the greatest for it. I dread the nervous fit your disobedience would produce."

After a brief silence, Elizabeth began again. "This contemplation for our child's future has put me in mind of the future of another young babe, and it is of this child I wish to speak to you."

"I can guess your meaning, madam," Darcy began, moving his body so that he looked into her face, "but Maria Sinclair is none of our concern. As soon as I can be certain of your being fully recovered, I shall seek out John Sinclair and inform him of the futility of his blackmail, provide him with the identity of May's lover, and let him try his luck there."

Darcy lay on his back, signalling the end of the conversation, and distractedly began to trail his hand across Elizabeth's belly. She swiped him roughly, throwing his hand from her body and on to his face.

"And that, am I to take it, is to be the end of the matter?" said Elizabeth.

Before Darcy could recover sufficiently from the shock of finding his eye poked by his own finger, Elizabeth continued.

"You forget, at the heart of this is a child, Fitzwilliam; a child who is guiltless and faultless in this affair, yet who stands to bear the punishment. What sort of a future can be hoped for the girl, with a man such as that as her guardian? It pains me even to think about the degradations that he would have no qualms about inflicting on her."

"Hush now, my darling," Darcy soothed, "do not upset yourself. I will not have you distressed by this matter. Tell me what you would have me do, and it will be done. Tell me what future for Maria would ease your mind, and I will try to make it so, but consider: I have no claim to the child, and so I may be limited in what I can achieve. Her father will doubtless make no efforts in her regard, and though I tried, I fear I was unsuccessful in getting him to acknowledge her."

"You met with her father?"

"Yes, but it did not end well. I thought perhaps he would acknowledge Maria in return for financial reward, but it has been some time since our meeting and he has made no further approach. I can only surmise that his financial situation was not as precarious as I was led to believe, and in the end, he found greater benefit in maintaining his silence."

"Who is the man?" was the next question, and Darcy stumbled at the answer, unwilling to further expose Elizabeth to the debauchery of the man her sister called "beloved" for fear of the worry it would invite for Lydia's position.

"It is of no consequence as I cannot prove it. I have rumour and speculation only, and nothing to persuade the man as appeals to honour, and pecuniary award have already failed."

"Do you avoid my direct question on purpose, sir? I did not ask if you could prove the identity of the man – I merely asked you to reveal it."

Darcy's attempt to obfuscate had only served to heighten Elizabeth's interest, as she now assumed that his hesitance was proof that the father was a man of their acquaintance.

"You really are most obstinate, Elizabeth. Is it not enough for you to know I have reason to keep the name to myself?"

"We do not bear secrets well, my darling, as all too recent history shows us," she answered. "In some marriages, I am sure there are a wealth of secrets to be discovered between husband and wife, but I do not wish ours to be such a marriage, and I had not thought you would desire such a thing either. I accept there will be confidences that must sometimes be maintained, within the bounds of friendship or sisterhood, for example, but I cannot believe that such loyalties exist here."

Darcy sighed aloud, gave one last appealing look to his wife, and when that failed to produce any sort of reprieve, he relented, and calmly, without ceremony, detailed the parentage of Maria Sinclair, how he had come to the information, and what had occurred in his meeting with George Wickham.

Elizabeth sat, aghast. She had not dreamed that Wickham would be named the father. She burned to know more. How had they met? Had they conducted an affair? For how long had it continued? Was it before or after Wickham had been at Longbourn? Did his liaisons continue now, despite his being married?

The questions were numerous and Darcy could answer none. He could only add that Wickham had not provided any details as to the affair, beyond admitting engaging in it, and showed no signs of embarrassment or remorse as to his activities and their consequences.

"Poor, poor Lydia!" Elizabeth eventually exclaimed, overcome by the growing disappointment she felt in her sister's choice of husband. "Oh, Fitzwilliam, what sort of a man is he? Is there anything noble or worthy in him? How can it be that he feigns manners and respectability so readily when his character is clearly all defect and debasement? Lydia must be spared this humiliation, at least."

"I agree. Foolish and foolhardy as I believe your sister to be, I would not wish to see her wounded by such a scandal. She believes Wickham is all things good and honourable, and I would not disabuse her of the notion."

Elizabeth moved next to Darcy, curling up within the safety of his embrace, grateful for the comfort that could be found there. After forcing herself to turn her attentions away from Lydia and the life she had chosen, Elizabeth was more determined that even if her sister could not be saved, then Maria Sinclair must be, and though she could not yet say how they would do it, she knew they could not fail the child.

℘

Several days later, Elizabeth, under the orders of her doctor and her husband, was resting and making an entry in her journal when it struck her that May Sinclair might also have kept one. If she did, then surely she would have detailed something as important as her time with Wickham.

"Fitzwilliam, do you know where May was residing before she died?" she asked, upon entering the library.

"Elizabeth you are supposed to be resting," he replied, ignoring her question, more concerned that she was up and walking about the house.

"Fitzwilliam, I am with child, not infirm, though my feet do hurt today, so I shall sit, and you may have the honour of rubbing them while you answer me."

The couple sat on the couch. Darcy dutifully took her feet into his lap and began to knead and press her aching soles. Elizabeth sighed with the relief his touch brought, feeling the tension in her body release as his thumbs circled deep into her flesh.

"Now Elizabeth, could you please tell me what was so important that you had to ignore the doctor's orders and wander the halls of this house in search of me?"

"Fitzwilliam, I had not realised you had such a dramatic flair," she laughed. "Wandering the halls, indeed; I knew exactly where you would be, and I do not think the doctor could find too much fault in me for walking from our bedroom. I took the most direct route, I can assure you."

Darcy scowled at her glib response. "I take your health very seriously, Elizabeth, and I would appreciate it if you could do the same, if for no other reason than to satisfy me."

"You are in earnest, Fitzwilliam. Are you really so concerned? You know you need not be."

"Do I? It was not so long ago that you..." he broke off his sentence. "Please, Elizabeth, I need you to be safe and well. You must promise me, you will do all you can to follow the doctor's instructions."

Elizabeth took his hands into hers and felt a slight tremble; she had not thought him still so distressed by recent events, but there was no denying how shaken he was, and she was suddenly conscious of how vulnerable he must feel. "I will do as you wish. I will be careful and I will be safe – we shall be safe, Fitzwilliam: the baby and I. I just wish to see Maria Sinclair safe and well, also. The thought of her helpless and alone preys on my mind and unsettles me."

"Then we must see to it she is protected, for I fear I will never feel settled until you do, and I will never sleep soundly until you do. There are conditions to any further involvement in this matter, however, and if you do not abide by them, the matter ends here and I will speak of it no more – no matter what you threaten! Will you agree?"

"Name your demands, my love," Elizabeth said, happy to have her husband's agreement, whatever the bargain.

∿

Several hours later, the Darcys arrived on Bow Street at the town house that was the last known residence of May Sinclair.

"When I ended my relationship with May, I assured her the town house would remain hers until she no longer required it. I felt I owed her that much, at least. She was a good woman, Elizabeth, and I could not see her turned out on to the street, simply because I no longer needed her company," Darcy stated by way of explanation for his continuing to support his old mistress.

"Husband, there is no judgement to be found here," Elizabeth assured him. "You tell me the relationship was over from the time we met, and I trust this is the truth. I am glad you saw to the comfort of the woman; that she was not simply cast aside. I would expect such consideration of you."

A small number of staff remained at the house, and though many of the rooms had been closed off, with large white sheets covering the furnishings; the kitchen, some of the bedrooms, and the front parlour were still open. On entering, Darcy took Elizabeth to sit in the parlour before he went in search of the housekeeper.

"Where do you propose we start the search, Elizabeth?" he began on returning. "I hope you have some idea as I do not relish the thought of searching every room."

"If May was diligent in keeping her journal, she will have

wanted it close at hand. We should try the writing desk in here, and in the library, and any drawers in her room."

"You will sit, and I shall try the drawers and desks. I believe I am capable of making a thorough search. You may oversee the first search, if you like, and school me if I am lacking."

"You are decidedly playful today, Fitzwilliam. Are you enjoying the role of the mystery hunter?"

"I shall be happy when this entire business is at an end. Until then, I am simply content in being able to ensure that you do not get into further trouble. If I am required to play the mystery hunter, then so be it. Now, where is the key for the writing desk?"

As Darcy went in search of the key, Elizabeth took a turn about the room. She tried to picture May here – the house-keeper had said it was her favourite room for the evening. Elizabeth thought it must have been very comfortable, curled in one of the large chairs, sitting by the fire. There was a small stool placed in front of one, which Elizabeth assumed was May's, as it was too close to the seat to have been used by Darcy. She was struck by the notion that Darcy and May had spent time here together, and it was the first time that she allowed herself to think about Darcy and his mistress.

She was surprised as jealousy crept up on her. Elizabeth smiled at the thought she could be envious of a woman of whom she knew very little, who never had any claim to Darcy's heart, and who was a part of his life before she herself had any such claim. Yet there she stood, jealous of laughter and loving, in which she played no part. "Jealous of a ghost, Elizabeth?" she said to herself. "Really, what next?"

"What was that about a ghost?" asked Darcy, who had returned from a fruitless search of the bedroom and library.

"Oh, nothing, husband; idle silliness, nothing more."

Once the final writing desk had been searched and no book uncovered, Darcy was convinced that nothing more could be done. He suggested to Elizabeth that if May had kept a journal at all, she could have hidden it anywhere. It would have been something she would have ensured was kept private and secret.

Elizabeth agreed that May would have wanted the book to be hidden from prying eyes, and was preparing to leave with Darcy when she was struck by one possible hiding place.

"This chair, I take it, was May's? You never sat in it?"

"No, indeed not. She preferred to be closer to the fire and liked the comfort of the stool," he replied.

Elizabeth stepped to the front of the chair and placed herself squarely in the centre of the large cushion, sitting back and allowing her feet to rest upon the stool in front. "Very comfortable, such deep cushions…You know, husband, you might be surprised at what could be concealed down the side of such a cushion."

Darcy stepped forward just in time to see Elizabeth's hand emerge from the right-hand side of the chair, a leather-bound book clutched triumphantly in her fingers.

℘

Elizabeth sat on one of the couches in their library, her body sore from the strain of the day's adventure. Darcy had been called away immediately upon their return and so she was alone, knowing she would be undisturbed.

"I did not promise I would not read you," she mused, while stroking the edges of the journal, "but I wonder how Fitzwilliam would view my reading you in his absence."

Unable to resist the temptation of discovering any secrets the diary might hold, Elizabeth opened it.

The entries were usually short; the writing neat, and the style simple, without artifice. Although she had not expected to, Elizabeth found herself liking May Sinclair, who showed honesty and clarity in her writing. The early entries held accounts of her days with Darcy, and nothing salacious. She talked of gifts, trips to the theatre, and interesting conversations. Although it was apparent they were lovers, she detailed little of their lovemaking beyond the fact that Darcy was skilled, and she was glad that pleasure could be obtained from their union, despite the lack of love.

It was not until Elizabeth reached an entry stating Darcy was to be away in Hertfordshire with his friend, Mr Bingley, that Elizabeth's curiosity was piqued.

> *...Darcy is leaving London today. He tells me he will be away for some weeks having undertaken to help his friend, a Mr Bingley, establish himself in the country. His discomfort at the need to join him is evident, although it makes his willingness to help his friend all the more worthy. I confess I laughed when he complained, 'Undoubtedly there will be some manner of ball to attend! Bingley is a fool for a dance.' He professes he does not enjoy such occasions, but I believe it is more that he does not know how to be comfortable around strangers. I have witnessed him lively and gregarious among intimates, but stoic and sombre among those he does not know. He is a curious man, full of contradictions; I am most intrigued by his reserve in society, but his passionate nature in private. He stands so separate, yet I believe he yearns for somebody to draw him in. Darcy will never truly be happy or at peace until he has found a partner, in love and life, though in truth, I cannot imagine the woman who will succeed in winning his heart...*

Elizabeth sat back deeper into the couch and closed the diary. Finding an entry so close to their first meeting was thrilling, but she wondered if continuing would be advisable, given what May might reveal of Darcy's time in Hertfordshire. Her curiosity, however, outweighed her concerns, and the book reopened.

> *...Darcy has been gone a week. I received a letter informing me that he expected to be gone at least two more. In it, he decried the county, and claimed he will be relieved to return to London as soon as Mr Bingley is comfortably settled. I gather he has been subjected to much socialising and has found the company wanting, although if pressed, I would attribute his disquiet likely more influenced by his own discomfort, and less a reflection on the good people there. Poor Darcy! How the townsfolk must view him, I wager he is said to be proud and disagreeable. I can only imagine the insult he has raised, and wonder how long it will be before the*

local eligible women and their mothers determine his fortune is not sufficient to make his company sufferable...

Elizabeth smiled at this and answered out loud to the diary, "I believe it was but hours before the nature and character of Darcy had been drawn and found wanting, for my own Mama it was, but the course of an evening – his first in town!"

...Darcy has briefly returned from his stay in the country. He was here but one night and there was such an alteration in him, I would hardly have believed him to be the Mr Darcy of my acquaintance. I cannot yet be certain, but I believe some woman of recent acquaintance has caught his interest. The country, it appears, has not been quite the disappointment he was expecting! Why do I say this? He has certainly not expressed any intentions towards a woman, but he engaged me in the most curious conversation: he was musing on how bright eyes and a sharp mind can add greatly to the general attractions of a partner and how strong feelings can grow upon acquaintance where previously there were none. When he asked if I believed preservation of rank and position should take precedence over the desires of the heart, for one brief moment I thought he might be speaking of me. I stumbled in my response, unsure of how to proceed, when I noted his eyes stared far beyond me into the fire. I was not the woman who inspired his reflections; he was imagining someone else as he spoke. I do not recall ever seeing him so lost in his thoughts as when he sat in my drawing room contemplating this woman. I truly believe Darcy is in love...

The entrance of Mrs Reynolds broke Elizabeth's concentration. In the absence of her master, Mrs Reynolds had taken it upon herself to ensure the comfort of Mrs Darcy, and though Elizabeth sometimes wished her a little less diligent in her attentions, the sight of a warming pan for her feet, and hot tea, were most welcome. As soon as Mrs Reynolds was assured of her mistress' well-being, Elizabeth was left alone again, free to return to her reading.

...I have been thinking in the days since Darcy's return to Mr Bingley, about the changes I must now expect in our arrangement. There can be no doubt that he will succeed where his heart leads him. He will secure his love, I am certain of it, and I am equally certain he will not then continue with me. His fierce sense of loyalty and honour would not countenance his maintaining a mistress while courting a wife. I will not pretend to be unaffected by this thought, although I admit I do not love Darcy. I like and admire him; I take pleasure in our time together and will miss his company. I am pleased if he has found a woman to suit him. I can only hope, for his sake, she is intelligent, sharp-witted, and passionate enough to satisfy him...

The next entry was dated several days later and the script was unusually hurried. Elizabeth guessed that excitement had led to an unsteady hand.

...I have met someone! I hardly know what to write, as my mind and heart race merely at the thought of him. I had not thought it possible I should ever fall in love, but I feel I may just be in such danger. I was walking out the other day, when some pebble caused my foot to turn on the step and I stumbled. Suddenly, there was a flash of red, and I felt two strong arms about my waist. A man caught me as I fell, and secured my safety. The upset of my tumble can hardly be exaggerated and I very nearly fainted in the arms of my rescuer. On seeing me pale, he scooped me up in his arms, held me close to his chest, and with soothing words of comfort carried me back to my door. He would not be easy until he could see me settled and recovered. My protector was all attention and concern; he directed the servants with regards to my care and ordered sweet tea to steady my nerves. Before I had the chance to collect myself and to thank him properly, he was gone – a prior engagement calling him away. He promises to return tomorrow and I count the minutes until then...

A shiver ran the length of Elizabeth's spine when she read this entry. Here, at last, was Wickham. It had to be him.

...Never has a day been anticipated more than today. I scarcely slept with the excitement of my hero's expected return, but no sooner did I find myself drifting off to sweet dreams of a soldier's red coat and strong arms, than the fear he might not call gripped me and I was tormented into waking. All such worry was for nought, and as soon as decorum would allow, my hero paid his call and we were reunited. How can I write of him? My poor hand could not hope to do him justice. How can I write of his looks, his manners, and his keen attention to me, with any sufficiency? He was in all measures a gentleman; indeed although not the son of a gentleman himself, he was raised and educated as one. He was all ease and charm. Though I had feared his rejection of me once I outlined my position in the house, I knew I had to be honest. His response brings tears to my eyes even now – such understanding: 'There is no shame in what you do,' he told me. 'Life left you few options and survival is an imperative. I use my skills with a sword to preserve myself, and you, your wit and charm. We are both forced to sell ourselves in order to continue living – me to King and Country, you to the man who maintains you. We are little different, you and I.' Is it possible that a man such as this could truly love me? He promises to return. I eagerly await him...

Elizabeth stared in frustration. Although she believed it was clear that Wickham was the "hero" of May's description, she had failed to name him; without a name, there could be little use in the journal. She flicked through the pages, and there were only a handful of entries left. May had to mention him by name at least once, so Elizabeth read on.

...Darcy has finally returned from the country and it seems his friend is in the city also. I can only guess the country ultimately did not meet Mr Bingley's desires. Darcy paid me a visit me last night, and I found him much altered from our last meeting. He was quiet, almost dour, so much so I thought him ill. He talked but a little, and though he enquired as to how I had spent my time in his absence, I do not believe he heard a word of my reply. He would not be pressed into talking of his time in the

country, and he made no mention of a woman. I begin to doubt my belief that he has found love. If this is so, I fear what the future holds for my hero and me! Am I willing to leave the comfort and security that Darcy offers for the hope of a life and love of my own? Dear Lord, preserve me, but I think I might! Darcy will join me for supper tomorrow – I await his return...

Elizabeth paused a minute to refresh her tea, and take stock of all that she had read. When Darcy had initially proposed to her, he outlined his great struggle in reconciling his feelings for her with his recognition of the impropriety of their match, and the admission of this struggle had prompted her ire. After their reconciliation, Elizabeth had avoided any questions on his initial difficulties, not wanting to relive the disastrous scenes that followed, but now it seemed that fate was to afford her some insight into his time after they had first been acquainted, and so she read on with keen interest.

...How do I write of tonight with any clarity when I can hardly understand what has passed at all? When he finally arrived this evening, Darcy's demeanour could only be described as surly. He hardly ate, paced the drawing room, and barely spoke more than ten words in the first hour he was here. Eventually, I convinced him to join me in a glass of wine and this seemed to settle him somewhat – enough to sit, at least. At length, as I always supposed he would, he spoke to me, but I will not pretend to understand what he shared. He did not enjoy his time in the country; he seemed vexed at so many weeks spent in such futility, and he was determined his friend, Mr Bingley, be prevented from returning too soon. It appears Mr Bingley had begun to form an attachment to a young lady of inferior position, and Darcy wanted to ensure that any such connection be severed. It was after these revelations that I became lost in the conversation between us. In truth, I am not convinced after that point, it was a conversation between us, for as he talked of a girl from an unsuitable family, Darcy seemed lost in an internal argument about claims to propriety and claims to the heart, only voicing

snippets of the monologue running through his head. He was distracted. It was as if I were not even present, and as though he was making the argument to himself, to settle some disagreement that raged within him.

'Impossible, it is impossible to love her!' he yelled at one point, and I cannot believe he spoke of Mr Bingley and his young lady. There was such passion and wretchedness in him last evening; no bond of feeling for a friend, no matter how dear, could have inspired such torment. The love was his own, I am certain; the battle waged between his heart and his head. I know not what will happen now for Darcy left me with no word as to when he might return...

Elizabeth's heart beat fast and full in her chest. She had never dreamed that the conflict between Darcy's feelings for her and his sense of propriety had been so fervent. At the time he had revealed his struggle, she had imagined a clear-cut affair where he had, with a cool mind and a cutting logic, calmly weighed up her suitableness.

Thinking on it now, knowing the deep and passionate nature of her husband, she realised it could only have been as May described. What exertion would it have taken for him to try to master feelings for her, which would have railed against what his head told him to be right and proper, only to finally succumb to those feelings, give voice to them, and have them so easily and callously swept aside by their object?

Elizabeth winced when she allowed her thoughts to dwell on her refusal of Darcy, but not wanting to linger on her own foolishness, she quickly cast her attention back to the diary.

The next few entries detailed May's time with her hero: he had left her at points – doubtless to return to Hertfordshire and continue his seductions there, thought Elizabeth – but always bearing a trinket or gift when he returned, given with promises and heartfelt attentions. All the caution and guardedness, which May's profession naturally inspired, were quickly swept away in the passion and romance of what she believed to be her great love. Darcy was lost to her; although he had not formally ended their relationship, he never visited, and wrote rarely. She was so lonely, and here was a man who showered her with the love and attention she craved, who professed devotion, and brought the promise of a future and a life shared. May gave herself to Wickham, body and soul. It was to be the ruin of her.

...I have received a letter from Darcy. Our arrangement is over. His missive was short, and I hardly know what to make of it. There was no happiness to be found in the note, and he did not mention an engagement. I can only guess that he has not succeeded with his love, although I can scarce account for any woman refusing him, and though he has returned from a stay at Rosings, he will not call on me again. I am to have the house and staff for as long as necessary and he will allow me a stipend until I secure another arrangement. Good Lord, dare I hope to believe it; I am free!

Elizabeth turned the page. There was only one entry left, and she guessed what was to follow. Even before she read the words, she knew that there would be no happy ending for May. She was free from her arrangement with Darcy, but Elizabeth knew by this time that May would have been with child, and Wickham would never be persuaded to marry her.

Elizabeth looked at the page and spotted stains where tears had streaked the ink.

...A whore; a whore, he called me, my hero, spewing such filth from those lips that once professed love. Such venom to his words; each one like poison in my veins. The beautiful mouth that once kissed me now twisted into a vicious grin. He laughed at me when I cried, when I told him I loved him; told me the street was the only place for me now and I should look for love there. He laughed as he told me his intention had solely been to take advantage of the whore Darcy so richly paid for, and now Darcy had no more need of me, neither had he. He laughed at me. It was only then I saw my hero for what he was. I was nothing to him; our love had been but a game. What hope is there for me now? Lord, forgive me, but I hate him. If he had an ounce of

mercy in him, he would have run me through with his sword. He has ripped the very heart from chest and I hate him. My hero, George Wickham!

Finally, there it was: May's lover revealed, but Elizabeth could take no triumph in it. She closed the book.

℘

When Darcy finally returned, he found Elizabeth in the library, asleep on the couch, her cheeks stained with tears, the diary clutched to her heart.

Darcy prised the journal from Elizabeth's hands without waking her, and sat in a nearby chair to read. When he reached the final entry, he understood the tears on his wife's cheeks. There was such sadness and distress to it. Darcy grieved once more at the pain of someone important in his life serving as cannon fodder in Wickham's imaginary war.

He was determined that Maria Sinclair would not be counted as one more casualty. If Wickham could not be worked upon, there remained only one other option: Sinclair must be dealt with – reasoned with. Darcy would not claim the child as his, but he would not leave her to the mercy of either her father or uncle. He had failed May, but he would not fail her daughter. In order for him to have any hope of success, however, he needed to understand his enemy better. He would need to learn as much as he could about John Sinclair before the next visit with him, and he would need help if the venture were to succeed.

CHAPTER 20

Miss Natalie DuPont stood in her breakfast room and stared at the small gilt-edged card, which had arrived by delivery boy, stating that if she were free that afternoon, Mr and Mrs Fitzwilliam Darcy intended to pay her a call.

She could not fathom why Darcy would return to see her; she had no other details of May's love affair to offer him, and she knew he had no interest in pursuing her. This was certainly not the reason, if he was bringing his wife. Although many of her client's wives knew their husbands kept other women, none of the men would be so brazen as to flaunt their mistresses to their wives. From what she knew of Darcy, he certainly would not be capable of inflicting such humiliation.

In the wake of his last visit, she had enquired after him, and learned that he was wealthy, proud, and honourable. Indeed, there were only two things that truly set Darcy apart from the rest of the ton: the first being that while many affected responsibility and decency, Darcy embodied it. The second was in his choosing Elizabeth Bennet: the daughter of a country gentleman with no real family or connections to speak of, whose sister had a dubiously-timed wedding, as his wife. Still, she could not think to refuse them – there seemed no reason for it – and her curiosity was sufficiently raised to send a note back with the boy, declaring it would be her pleasure to have their company at three.

At exactly three o'clock, the Darcys' carriage arrived at Miss DuPont's address on Bow Street. She watched from an upstairs window as Darcy and his wife approached her door, noticing that Mrs Darcy's belly was sizeable, and surprised she was not already in confinement. For a man as fastidious about social norms, as Darcy was, this deviation was unexpected. Not for the first time, she wondered about the woman who could clearly manage the man so well.

Miss DuPont was a striking woman, and was all too aware of the power that her looks had in securing the attentions of men, even those she met in the company of their wives. So it was with some amusement that she noted, beyond his initial cordial greeting of her when he entered the room, that Mr Darcy had eyes only for his wife. Although there had been a time when she would have found such inattention rather insulting, she smiled, now heartened by the thought that such devotion existed, and even more interested in the woman at the centre of it. Once in the room, Darcy realised that they had left a tonic that Elizabeth was to take with her afternoon tea, in the carriage, and with a polite bow, he went to retrieve it, leaving the two women alone together.

Miss DuPont and Elizabeth regarded each other warily.

Elizabeth was aware of the other woman's eyes running the length of her physique, taking extra care when examining the jewellery she wore and the quality of lace that trimmed her dress. As her natural audacity was emboldened when she felt challenged, she stood straight and tall, and finally catching Miss DuPont's, queried, "Would you like me to play, or sing, for you, so you can make a more complete assessment of me?"

Miss DuPont smiled at the nerve of the woman who stood square and tall in the centre of the room, despite the fact the size of her belly could not have made the position comfortable. Mrs Darcy was not what she had expected, and yet the spirit the woman displayed certainly made her interesting.

"Do I disappoint you, Miss DuPont? Did you expect me to

be taller perhaps?"

"I will not pretend to be more than a little surprised by you, Mrs Darcy. You are, in fact, so far from what I had imagined; I am at a loss as to know quite what to make of you."

"Then suppose we dispense with the need to assess one another at all, and you invite me to sit down, for much as I hate to display weakness, I believe my back will not allow me maintain such an upright stance for a minute longer."

"Forgive my poor manners; of course you must sit. I believe I know all I need to know of you, and your back need bear no further punishment. I need scrutinise you no further."

The two women had just taken their seats when Darcy returned and their meeting began in earnest. Darcy and Elizabeth shared with Miss DuPont all they had learned since his last meeting with her, detailing in brief his meeting with Wickham and the contents of May's diary.

"And you are certain that Mr Wickham will have nothing to do with the child?" Miss DuPont enquired.

It was Darcy who responded. "I am quite certain, Miss DuPont; I doubt Wickham ever entertained true feelings for May. His sole reason for the affair seems to centre on his desire to hurt me. I am truly sorry for it; sorry that May should have paid such a high price because of her connection to me."

"So what is it you seek to learn from me, Mr Darcy? I do not see what I can add to this sorry tale. I have told you all I know of the relationship, and I doubt I shall be able to work upon Mr Wickham."

"What we seek to know from you, Miss DuPont, relates to May's brother. What do you know of him? What can you tell of him that might aid us in working upon him?"

"Beyond knowing the man to be a wastrel and a gambler, I know little of him. I met him once and I did not like him. In fact, I scarcely believed him to be a sibling of May's, so different were they in every respect. He was coarse and vulgar, where she was refined and genteel; he was lumbering, where she was graceful, and he was dull witted, where she was clever—"

"Although, there was a degree of similarity in their looks, I suppose," interrupted Darcy. "Something in a shared colouring, dark eyes and hair."

"You jest, of course, Mr Darcy," laughed Miss DuPont. "Never have a brother and sister shown so little resemblance. John was freckled and fair like his father. May believed her father never took her to be his flesh at all, so different was her look from the rest of the family, and that is why he so readily cast her out after the death of her mother."

Darcy sat puzzled by this revelation. "Indeed, Miss DuPont, I am in earnest. The man I met, the man claiming to be John Sinclair, was tall and broad, with dark hair and eyes. He had no freckles, but a slight tan to his skin. Do you mean to tell me this man was not May's brother?"

"On my life," Miss DuPont replied. "I have met John Sinclair, been introduced to him by May, and he is not the man you describe!"

The three sat in stunned silence, before Elizabeth finally asked the questions puzzling them all: "Then who is this man, and what is he doing with May's child?"

⁞

With assurances to Miss DuPont that they would contact her as soon as they had any news regarding Maria Sinclair and the imposter claiming to be her uncle, the Darcys called for their carriage and took leave of Bow Street.

"Well, do we go directly to Breakmore Street, husband?" was Elizabeth's immediate query once they were alone. "The man may still be there and we may yet resolve this situation if we act now."

"We are not going there, Elizabeth. I will see you home, then I shall call upon Charles, and he and I shall attend to the matter. If you think for one moment that I shall let you within a mile of that street again, you do not know me as well as you believe. There will be no discussion, no pleading, no cajoling, and no change of heart in this matter. I am determined."

Elizabeth had never seen Darcy so stern and unyielding, and

she doubted even her considerable influence over him could have changed his mind. Her natural response would have been to argue with him nonetheless, but as she sat in the carriage, her back and feet crying out in pain, her temples throbbing, and her belly making it difficult to sit with any real measure of comfort, she wondered what use she could have hoped to be.

"My presence would be a hindrance, of course, Fitzwilliam. I will go home and rest, and leave the remainder of the business to you and Charles. You will return to me as soon as you can, promise me. Do not leave me to fret over the fate of Maria Sinclair for too long, my love."

"Such speedy agreement, Elizabeth. I do not know whether to be grateful or concerned," replied Darcy, warily.

"I suggest gratitude to be the appropriate response, Fitzwilliam; it would be foolish though to hope me permanently altered. Today the desire to appease my curiosity must surrender to the greater desire to appease my aching back! You would be well advised, therefore, to treat this as nothing but a temporary reprieve from the worst excesses of my stubbornness."

&

After seeing Elizabeth safely home and settled, Darcy made his way directly to Charles Bingley, hoping to waste little time in getting to confront the man passing himself off as John Sinclair. Such was his haste that he did not wait to explain his need of Bingley at his home, but rather laid out the entire affair on the journey to Sinclair's lodging house.

"And Jane knew of this and said nothing to me," Bingley said, when Darcy had finished.

"Do not be hard on Jane; Elizabeth did not disclose details to her, merely suspicions concerning my behaviour, and Jane will doubtless have felt bound by bonds of sisterly affection to honour Elizabeth's confidence."

"I do not hold with the idea of her keeping secrets from me, nevertheless," Bingley replied defensively.

"Well, would you have thanked her had she requested your

interference? Would you have relished the task of questioning me about my comings and goings?" Darcy queried.

"I grant you, I would not," Bingley answered with a smile, the mere thought softening his annoyance, and in seeking to change the course of conversation, added, "So this man, Sinclair, or whoever he is, what do you plan to do with him?"

"I care little about the man. His attempts at blackmail have caused harm, that is true enough, but I want the business over. I have promised Elizabeth that the safety of Maria will be secured, and that is my sole concern."

"You would let the man go after all that has happened?" Bingley said, surprised. "I would not have expected such leniency."

"My promise to Elizabeth is what guides my actions in this matter. If allowing the man's transgressions towards me to pass will protect the child and appease my wife, my pride will simply have to bear it."

℘

Sinclair was in his bed when they arrived. Maria was in the capable hands of Bessie Hargreaves who had now been engaged by Sinclair to look after the girl. It was half an hour before Sinclair made it down to meet his guests, and Darcy was appalled by the deterioration in him: he was unkempt, unshaven, his eyes bloodshot, and the smell from him hinted at a dissipation and depravity, which neither gentleman cared to think on.

"So, you return, Darcy! I knew how it would be once your wife was well, and so I waited, perhaps more patiently than you deserved, but I waited, and I will wait no longer. You will pay for fathering Maria; only you can determine if you would rather settle the debt with money or your reputation."

"When last we met, I was here to inform you that I had uncovered the identity of May's lover and the father of her child. I was going to provide you the name of the man and let you seek recompense from him," Darcy responded.

"If you can prove you are not the father, why go to the trouble of attending here?" answered Sinclair, ill humour adding to the sourness that surrounded him.

"Because, sir, I wish to relieve you of the burden of caring for Maria. I am here to tell you that she will be removed from your custody today."

Sinclair licked his lips, and smiled at the pronouncement, although the effect was unpleasant to those witnessing it. "I see, and might I enquire what settlement you plan to make on me? You do not think I will simply hand her over to you."

"You will, in fact, do just that and you will get nothing more from me, but my guarantee that the child will be safe and well looked after."

Sinclair was on his feet at once and about to protest when Darcy abruptly reached over to him, shoved him roughly back into his seat and leaned over him to ensure he would not rise again. Although it offended every sensibility to remain in such close proximity, Darcy was determined that the full weight of his conviction would be brought to bear. Maria would be taken from the house that day and Sinclair would not profit.

"You are not John Sinclair, and I can readily prove it. I do not know how it is you came to be in possession of the facts you have surrounding May Sinclair and her relationship to me, nor do I know how you came to have custody of her child, but I promise you, this farce ends now!"

There was a moment when it appeared that the man calling himself Sinclair might yet rally for one last bout against Darcy, as his body tensed and his jaw tightened.

Bingley stepped forward, ready to aid his friend, but any opposition that might have been was brief.

With a loud exhalation, the man claiming to be John Sinclair shrunk deeper into his seat, defeated, the end to all his plans of profit taking their toll.

"My name is Nicholas Raeburn," he offered at last, "and I knew John Sinclair."

"Knew him," Bingley cut in, "then the man is dead?"

"Dead?" Raeburn looked at him as though the question were

a foolish one "Lord, yes; the man has been dead for a year."

Darcy stepped away. It was done.

Bingley was not so easily satisfied and pressed Raeburn for more: how did he know of Darcy and May? How did he come to have Maria, and what on earth had he proposed to do with the child once his blackmail was complete?

Raeburn, although not initially forthcoming, realised there was nothing to be gained by his silence, but answers might yet be paid for and so told all.

"I knew John Sinclair; we lived in India together. I would even say we were friends for a time. He liked to talk, and spoke often of his sister who provided coin for him when he was in need. He told me of her profession and of the wealthy gentleman who kept her. But even his sister's money could not secure the comfort and safety of the man. He gambled, but good fortune did not favour him. He borrowed heavily, including one hundred pounds from me, though I was not the only party importuned when he was in need, and some of his creditors were less patient than I. When Sinclair failed to pay one particular gentlemen, he was savagely beaten as a lesson to others who might be inclined to take advantage of the man's generosity. Sinclair never recovered from the beating: he was weakened and it was not long before a fever took hold and finished him."

"And you did not think to inform his family?" uttered Bingley, appalled by the cavalier manner in which the man spoke of the death of his friend.

"I owed him no duty. He died without repaying me. Was I to take on the burden and expense of finding his family, of burying the man? No, I stayed quiet. Sinclair was given the burial he deserved, in a pauper's pit dug for all those struck by the plague that carried him to his maker."

"And what of Maria? How did you come to have her?" Darcy interrupted, anxious to have answers so he could leave.

"Some time after Sinclair's death, I was forced to return to England. I used some of his old connections to set myself up when I first arrived and when an agent came looking for him, seeking the last known relative of May Sinclair, well, it was a matter of inheritance, and in it I saw my opportunity to reclaim the debts I had incurred. I did not know the largest part of that inheritance would be the damn child! I had intended to leave her at a church, though as fate would have it, on that same day, I spied a notice in the paper announcing the marriage of a Mr Fitzwilliam Darcy of Pemberley—"

"I can guess what followed next," Darcy interrupted. "You need go no further."

"And the child?" added Bingley. "If you had succeeded, what would you have done with her?"

"As I always intended, she would have been left at a church. They would see to the girl, and I would be free to travel back to India. This country no longer suits me and I long for the spiced air and warmth of my true home."

"Then go to India; die there, if that is your wish. I will take the girl," declared an irate Darcy, increasingly struck by the man's contemptibility.

Raeburn looked at Darcy through tired eyes, his spirit and body now broken by disease and debauchery, his wretchedness no longer masked by bluster and show.

"This disease that rots you, Raeburn, is there any possibility you have passed it to young Bessie?" Darcy asked quietly, knowing the answer given would determine his mercy towards the man.

"Bessie? No. I never…That is to say, we never. I have her watch Maria, that is all," was Raeburn's reply. "Sparing her my fate is probably the only decent thing I have ever done."

"Then, this is how it will be: I shall pay for you to return to India, to a place of your choosing. I shall provide you with one hundred pounds – Sinclair's debt to you – and that shall be all. You will leave this country and you will never return. You will speak of this to no one."

Raeburn did not even attempt to challenge Darcy; he did not have the will for it. His only addendum was to beg Darcy to pay, also, his landlady who had been generous enough to take pity on a dying man with a young child, and not throw them on to the street when he could no longer pay for his lodgings.

Darcy nodded, assured Raeburn that no one would suffer for his mistakes, and left the room, thankful to be free from the sights and smell within.

∮

Once Raeburn was dealt with, Darcy brought matters to an easy and quick resolution. The man was removed from Mrs Undergood's care, to be treated by a physician before Darcy secured him passage to India.

Mrs Undergood was compensated for her generosity and kindness to Maria, and was speechless at the large purse left on her kitchen table. Not one to argue with a gentleman of Darcy's standing when it came to matters of money, she gratefully received his gift and did not think it polite to point out that the sum left would have bought her the whole house and not merely paid for a room for a few months.

Bessie was last to be seen, and Darcy felt more delicacy would be required with her.

"Bessie," he said, upon sitting the girl down, "what family have you here? How is it you come to be taken in by one such as Nicholas Raeburn – well, Sinclair, as you knew him. Was there no one to protect you from the likes of the man?"

"No family here, sir, well none at least worth speaking of," she answered.

"How old are you, Bessie?" Bingley asked, struck by the innocence of the girl.

"Thirteen on my last birthday."

Bingley sat down on hearing the reply. He had expected her to be young, but just thirteen, and left to the mercy of men like Raeburn; it was more than he could stomach.

Darcy too was taken aback, and he realised there was more than one child in need of rescuing. "Bessie, I have a job for you if you are interested," he began. "I need someone to look after Maria until I find a suitable home for her. Would you be willing to take on the position?"

"Me, sir?" Bessie stared disbelievingly at him. "You wish me to look after her? Surely you cannot think me best suited?"

"It seems you have a way with the girl, and I believe it would do the infant good to have a warm and familiar face at hand."

Bessie was out of her seat at once, clapping excitedly, and hurriedly accepting the job for as long as Mr Darcy might need her.

"Well now, child, calm yourself," he added, pleased at her response. "You must understand all that will be required of you. My wife and I shall not stay long in the city with the girl, and you will have to travel to the country with us. Will you accept my offer under these conditions?"

Bessie had been silent throughout Darcy's speech. The only evidence to show that she had heard a word of what was being said was in the widening of her eyes as the full extent of the proposal was laid before her. When Darcy was finished, she fixed her dress, stood tall, and looked him straight in the eye.

"Mr Darcy, sir," she began, the seriousness of her expression belying her youth, "you have my solemn word; I shall not disappoint you."

CHAPTER 21

For a short time after his meeting with Darcy, several months previously, Wickham had considered denying paternity of Maria Sinclair and forcing Darcy to burden the responsibility. Although Darcy would undoubtedly try to persuade John Sinclair that he was not the father, he had no proof, and would likely offer to pay the uncle to conceal her parentage. Wickham was certain such a secret would not remain hidden, and that any payment made would further encourage the idea of Darcy being the father. He was warmed by the thought of Darcy forced to explain a mistress and a child to his wife. The trouble such an admission would cause him, and the injury to the great Darcy pride, was almost inducement enough to persuade him to forgo the possible advantages of owning Maria Sinclair as his.

For some days, he had enjoyed the tantalising thought of what Darcy would become in the eyes of his wife, if she were to uncover his secret. He could scarce determine what outcome pleased him more: the thought of a pathetic Darcy begging forgiveness, or a domineering Darcy remaining stubbornly unapologetic. Either man would doubtless not be a fit for Elizabeth Bennet. However, the pressures brought to bear by Wickham's various creditors were increasingly diminishing the delicious thrill that he felt at the thought of Darcy suffering so full a fall from grace. He had been obliged, just two days ago, to call into a hat shop to avoid a particular unsavoury creditor, only to be confronted by his wife who had assumed he was there was for the purpose of buying her a new bonnet. Without even flinching, and with all the charm and ease that he could muster, Wickham reached into his purse and removed almost the last of his coins as though the purchase was nothing but a trifle. Lydia was ecstatic and profuse in her expressions of gratitude and adoration for her husband, and though he sometimes found himself tired of his wife's endless prattle, he was not yet immune to her flattery. Emboldened by her praise and believing himself to be "the best and most worthy of men", he left their home later that evening secure in the belief that the world would provide for him, as the world always had, and that luck at cards, money, and the comfort of an undemanding woman would soon be his once more.

Fearing that he would encounter too many people he knew, or rather too many people to whom he owed money, Wickham avoided the better gaming rooms he could normally be found frequenting, and made his way to Cheapside to try his luck in some of the less respectable rooms there. He sold some trinkets that he had purchased for Lydia in the first flush of their marriage and prayed luck would favour him once more.

Four hours later, Wickham stumbled back out on to the street, his head sore, his heart weary, and his pockets empty. His final loss saw him fall short of the money owed and as the man took the balance in blows to Wickham's chest and gut, he realised he was finally ready to acknowledge Maria Sinclair as his. There seemed little other option open to him: he would have to content himself with knowing that Darcy would be forced to pay out a substantial sum, and guarantee to pay any monies demanded by the child's family. Though he knew it to be the right course of action, Wickham took little pleasure in it. To soothe his wounded pride, he gave over his attention to what would be demanded and tried to concentrate on all that was to be gained from the transaction, rather than all that was to be lost.

He did not join Lydia in their bed when he finally returned home, but sat up nursing his bruised body and the last of the brandy.

The following morning, he had all but decided on his final terms and recompense, when his wife, in a fit of hysteria, burst into the room just after the arrival of the first post, waving a letter and bawling about an accident, illness, and death. When he finally calmed her enough to make sense of her ramblings, Wickham learned of Elizabeth's accident and the fevers that had followed.

℘

Lydia, in writing to her mama of their great distress at the tragedy, sketched, with unusual eloquence the scene of her beloved Wickham on hearing the news. His paling due to grief, the gentle manner in which he closed his eyes and bowed his head, doubtless to offer a silent prayer, and his heartfelt hopes for their full recovery were all recounted in detail in the pages she sent.

Lydia could not have known the tender expressions and gentle prayers she attributed to her husband's good nature stemmed not from concern for his family, but from the fear that he had left his blackmail too late. He prayed for Darcy's recovery, certainly, but for his own selfish end. He would not be cheated out of what he knew he could exact from the man. His well wishes for Elizabeth, however, were genuine; with an open and honest heart, he could say to Lydia that he trusted she would make a speedy and full recovery.

Wickham ensured that Lydia kept him apprised of the Darcys' welfare; it was important he timed his approach perfectly. Darcy needed to be well enough to think and act clearly without fever addling him. His timing with regards to the health of Elizabeth was more difficult. He reasoned that an approach made while she was still weakened by her injuries might be more advantageous. Darcy would pay to protect Elizabeth from any stress, which could compromise a full recovery. The suggestion that Darcy had fathered a child with a mistress would undoubtedly do just that.

He briefly considered this course of action, but in his heart, he knew he would not endanger Elizabeth; he would not see her health threatened by his rivalry with her husband, though he had fewer scruples about threatening her happiness. He maintained a fondness for the woman who had once been an object of his affection, and felt daily the true measure of his regrets when he thought of how he had turned his attentions from her to Lydia. He had known a woman as sharp as Elizabeth would not be fooled by his manner for long, but her sister – oh, her sister – was silly enough to be fooled for a lifetime. He had made his choice and he would live with it.

Now he would wait; wait until Elizabeth was well. Darcy might consider that he had more to lose if Elizabeth were recovered. Timing, Wickham knew, was essential if he were to fully profit. He could be patient.

Weeks passed, and the drama at the Darcy household unfolded before him in the letters Lydia received from Jane, who was diligent in her correspondence so as to soothe the concerns of family. He learned of their slow recovery, their removal to Pemberley, and their eventual return to London. The announcement that Elizabeth was with child was more than he could have hoped for, and he set about recalculating what his demands would be. He smiled as he thought of the price he could demand now, and silently thanked God for giving him the fortitude to hold out against the pressure of his mounting debts and empty purse. He had waited, and he would be rewarded.

As soon as he could arrange it, he and Lydia travelled to London on the pretext of paying a call on her sister, and verifying for themselves Elizabeth's recovery, offering in person their heartiest congratulations on the highly anticipated arrival of the next Darcy heir.

Lydia was all amazement at this continued display of her husband's good and true nature. "I know not how my Wickham can be a soldier, for he has such a heart! He feels so deeply and a truer, better man has surely never graced the ranks of the regulars," she proclaimed to her circle of friends on hearing that they would be going to London.

Two of her friends were more reserved in their share of the nods and flattering sentiments then bandied about by the group in support of Lydia's commendations of Wickham. They could have cast doubt enough on the faithfulness and sincerity of the man, but their own pleasure in the recollections of their time with him, and their hopes for the repeat of such pleasures, ensured their silence.

೫

On their journey to London, Wickham imagined the upcoming meeting with Darcy. He would be gracious in his treatment of Darcy, but would ensure the man felt the full force of his obligation. He had resolved to demand a small sum of money, but greater taxes would be paid in terms of the advancement of Wickham's social standing. Being a soldier, and settled so far north, had lost its charm. He wanted a change: a move to London, and perhaps a turn at politics. Darcy had the connections that Wickham needed; he would ensure that he used every ounce of Darcy's influence to promote him.

"Husband," Lydia interrupted, not for the first time, "why do you sit so quietly there, so lost in your own thoughts? Will you not talk with me? Shall you and I not pass our journey in the shared delight of each other's company?"

He turned to look at the silly chit he had married. "Of course, my dear, and what would you like to talk about?"

"Oh, I do not know, but I am sure we might think of something…We could recount Colonel Markham's ball. I lost sight of you for a time. Where did you go? What adventures did you have?"

Wickham smirked as he thought of the evening in question and his delight at finding an hour's welcome distraction with the Colonel's wife. "Adventures, my love? Just some silly games in the billiards room; no great tales to entertain you there, but I believe you spent some time with the Colonel's wife. Tell me, what did you think of her? Is she to become one of your favourites?"

He listened with satisfaction as Lydia prattled on about her delight at meeting Gracie Markham, and being singled out by her in particular – attention to his wife no doubt secured by his own attention to the lady just a short time before. As she talked of silly conversations and instant bonds of sisterhood, he allowed his mind to wander back to the blonde curls crushed against the green felt of the billiard table, and cream silks being lifted to reveal milk-white thighs.

ℰↄ

The day after their arrival in the city, Wickham and Lydia found themselves ascending the steps to the Darcy's London home. Upon admittance, they were shown to a front parlour while the master and mistress were told of their arrival. Lydia gushed about the charm of the room, the expense of the furnishings, and about how well Elizabeth had done for herself in securing the Darcy fortune. Although it could be supposed that Lydia would be jealous of her sister, it never occurred to her. No amount of fine furnishings could make a life with Darcy comfortable, and no amount of silk and satin could make his constant company sufferable. Her devotion to Wickham was complete: she had made her choice and she was happy with it, but she could benefit from her sister's choice, and still hoped that financial and social gains could be garnered from their relation to the Darcys of Pemberley.

Elizabeth was the first to join them, and her warm hello was greeted with equal warmth and genuine congratulations on her good health and the happy announcement of her expected arrival. After the initial exchange of pleasantries, the women settled into excited chatter about baby clothes, cots, and toys.

Wickham smiled and nodded. He accepted Lydia's gentle teasing about it putting her in mind to start a family, with grace and good humour, but at all times kept a close eye on the door, eagerly awaiting the entrance of Fitzwilliam Darcy.

After a quarter-hour or so of watching Wickham's growing agitation, Elizabeth took mercy on him and said, "Wickham, you must be bored listening to us. I think you have endured enough female conversation for an afternoon. Would you perhaps like to seek out Fitzwilliam? He is in his study, I believe."

Wickham smiled graciously. Indeed, a talk with Darcy would be most welcome; how good of her to afford him the opportunity.

℀

Wickham strode into the study. He recalled that the last time he had been in the room was in the wake of Darcy's refusal to provide him the living at Kympton. The humiliation he had suffered still burned in his breast. He remembered Darcy's cold manner and damned superiority as he announced that Wickham would get nothing beyond what had already been given, and his smile as he had him shown out. Escorted from the property! As though he were a common criminal; as though he could scarce be trusted; as though he might steal the silver, if left alone. Now he moved with both swagger and arrogance. He nodded curtly at Darcy, acknowledging his presence in the room, and without so much as a "by your leave" poured himself a large brandy and casually took a seat.

"Well, Darcy, you can have no doubt as to the real reason for my visit here. We have unfinished business regarding May Sinclair's child, and I have come ready with terms you should find generous. I shall accept paternity of May's child in return for five thousand pounds."

"Five thousand pounds?"

"A modest sum, you will agree, for all the trouble my admissions will incur. You see, Darcy, I am not as mercenary as you doubtless believe. I can be reasonable. There will be some other small matters I may need your influence in: I wish to move from the North and leave the militia, and I thought perhaps a turn at politics might suit."

Darcy sat, as though considering the offer. "And what of Maria? What do you propose to do about her?"

"The child be damned! Let May's brother keep it if he wishes. I certainly won't be raising it."

"Maria!" yelled Darcy. "Your daughter's name is Maria, after May's mother."

"Good Lord, Darcy," returned Wickham, unfazed by the outburst. "You take so much trouble over the thing; one would almost believe you were the father. Well, fine, as it bothers you so – to hell with Maria!"

Darcy stifled the rage within him. He looked at the large paperweight on his desk, and for a fleeting moment considered how it would feel to drive it into Wickham's skull.

On noticing the unnerving smile spreading across Darcy's face, Wickham swallowed hard, and a cold sweat broke out across his back. "Do we have a deal, or should I go find your wife?"

The menace in his question was unmistakable, but rather than causing Darcy to tense, he seemed to relax visibly.

"That is an excellent suggestion, Wickham, although please let me spare you the trial of finding Elizabeth," Darcy responded, while ringing the library bell.

To Wickham's amazement, the young maid who answered the summons was instructed to find Mrs Darcy and have her join them.

"You jest, surely!" exclaimed Wickham. "You would risk your marriage to save a paltry five thousand pounds – such tactics will not convince me to lower the price, if that is your game."

"I play no games," Darcy retorted. "Painful lessons of late have taught me that attempting to keep secrets from Elizabeth is both pointless and foolish. She knows everything. Your claim over me is at an end."

When Elizabeth entered the room, the look on Wickham's face told her that Darcy had informed him of the futility of his blackmail and she could not suppress a smile.

"Brother, I see my husband has already spoken to you of the

change in circumstances in regards to *your* daughter, Maria."

Wickham's face contorted, angry now at the possibility Darcy would yet again gain the upper hand. Determined that the room not bear witness to a second humiliation, he burst out with, "Well, I'll be damned if I'll publicly declare the child mine. May's brother believes you the father, Darcy; how do you propose to get around that? I'll denounce the little bastard – let her be known as the daughter of a whore and the mistake of a gentleman, but the world won't know the mistake to be mine!"

Elizabeth was shocked at the violent outburst, and for the first time since Lydia's foolish decision to run away with Wickham, she felt genuine concern for her sister's safety. Until now, she had feared that Wickham might neglect Lydia in favour of the attentions of others, and squander their money, certainly, and be too reckless to secure any sort of advancement in the military, but never had she considered the possibility of his being violent. Standing in front of him, witnessing the collapse of all his plans, she was not so sure. She had enjoyed picturing him being cast out without a penny, but suddenly, the thought of unleashing him like this on Lydia filled her with dread.

Darcy, it seemed, had been as struck by Wickham's reaction as Elizabeth. His response was designed to afford him with a measure of dignity in defeat, and ultimately to secure the comfort and safety of both Maria and Lydia.

"Wickham, we have a diary written by May in which she names you as the father. If that is not enough, I can show at the necessary time I was not in London; equally, I can show that you were, but none of this matters now. I do not need you to claim the child; in fact, what I request is quite the opposite. You have named your price – five thousand pounds – then so be it. I shall pay you the sum to relinquish all claims to the girl. Will you agree?"

"Do I hear you correctly, Darcy? You wish to pay me *not* to own the child as mine? Then what do you plan to do with her? What possible use can you have for the girl, and why would you even care, as you can so clearly establish she is not yours? She is nothing to you."

"Do you really need to know, Wickham? You will have what you want – money – and the child will be no burden to you; I shall see to that. Do we have a deal?"

Wickham and Darcy stood regarding each other suspiciously. Elizabeth feared that their mutual hatred might yet jeopardise the agreement, and so intervened.

"Wickham, I have asked Darcy to do this. He does not care for the girl. As you rightly state, she is nothing to him, but I am soon to be a mother and I could not bear to see the girl become lost in this struggle. It was my suggestion to ask you to relinquish your claim as a father, and though my husband does not agree, he seeks this bargain only to satisfy me. Will you agree to it?"

Wickham began to soften a little to the idea, as there was certainly something of the female mind in the plan. "I should have guessed a tenderer heart than Darcy's was concerned in the offer," he quipped. "What do you intend for the girl? Surely, you do not plan on raising her yourself."

Elizabeth smiled. The mere suggestion that even she could convince Darcy to raise Wickham's child was ridiculous. "No, Wickham, we will not be raising her, but we know a couple who have no children and who would be wonderful parents to her. They are good people, with enough means to support her and more than enough love to see her happy and well cared for. Sign the papers. You will have your money, Maria will have a family, and Lydia need never know about this whole sorry affair."

Wickham looked at Darcy once more. The day had not gone as he had anticipated; the victory he had envisioned was denied him, but he could be a practical man when required, and he could ill afford to allow wounded pride to cost him five thousand pounds; after all, Darcy still stood to lose a substantial sum. He would be spared any percussions with Lydia, and all he had to do was relinquish a claim to an illegitimate daughter he neither wanted nor cared for.

"Give me the papers," he said. "I shall sign whatever you want!"

CHAPTER 22

Elizabeth, who was determined not to succumb to the general aches her growing mass was inspiring, increasingly found herself unwilling to rise to the exertion of joining Georgiana and Kitty on their daily ventures into the city, or their walks in one or other of its parks. Thus, the ladies found themselves free in the afternoon to walk where they may and share confidences as they pleased. They had not been at home when the Wickhams called, but had overheard two of the young maids speaking of their arrival and Mr Wickham's hurried exit. There had been some yelling from the study and one girl was sure she had heard Mr Wickham swearing in the worst way. Neither Georgiana nor Kitty felt it right to approach Darcy or Elizabeth for an account of what had passed, and thus an entreaty was made to Lydia. On the return of a letter from Lydia, the pair declared their intention of taking an afternoon walk in the park so they would be afforded sufficient privacy to pour over the contents of the letter.

As expected, Elizabeth cried off from joining them that afternoon, and the two ladies found themselves settling together on a bench at the far end of a busy park not three hours later.

"I shall read the letter," Kitty began, "for Lydia always writes so ill, you may scarce be able to make it out."

Georgiana, judging Kitty knew best, nodded her ascent, and sat patiently as Kitty picked her way aloud through the letter.

Kitty,

I can hardly tell you how thrilled I was when I received your note today, as I had thought you were writing with an invitation of some kind. So imagine my disappointment when you simply wanted an account of my visit with Lizzy yesterday! La! How is it that you should even care? Perhaps I am mistaken in the supposed excitement of your life with the Darcys if this is what catches your interest.

But out of sisterly affection, I shall tell all – though there is little enough to tell. Wickham and I arrived at the house around three. I was saddened to see you were gone out, for I had the greatest want to show you the new hat I had bought for the visit. I believe you would have quite hated me for having it! Still, Lizzy liked it well enough, and I am sure has already told you all about it. Lord, how big Lizzy is! I nearly fainted when I saw her; I did not think it possible for a belly to swell to such a size. I daresay seeing me as small as I ever was and in such a fine hat grieved her when she thought of how altered she is – and I am sorry for it, for she really was all sweetness and affability. I am gladdened she could rally such fine spirits under the circumstances.

As for the hour we passed, well, it was delightful. Lizzy, dear Wickham, and I had a most pleasant lunch of cold meats, sandwiches, and delicate sweet tarts. We talked of our home up north and our plans while in London.

Lizzy was so attentive. I had been quite put out that she had not written to invite me out, but I understand it all now. Wickham will be found charming and well liked wherever he goes, and I am not ashamed to admit that I have been quite the favourite of the wives whenever out. It would be too great a punishment to that famous Darcy pride for himself and Lizzy to be found wanting by comparison to Wickham and I, and so Darcy sees to it that we do not meet. I understand, though I am sorry for the absence from you, dearest Kitty – you know I am sure Lizzy would not mind to your joining us some evening. Lord! What fun we would have! Do mention it to Lizzy, and let me know directly when you shall join us.

As for the rest of the afternoon, Wickham joined Darcy in the library, and Lizzy was gone for some time, also, though I was so engaged in opening some gifts she had for me that I could not tell you where she was or how long she was gone for...

The remaining half of the letter merely detailed the gifts that Lizzy had given, and as there was nothing more of worth or interest to be found within, Kitty chose not to read it all aloud, but simply provided an account of the contents once she had finished reading through it. Thereafter, she sat for a moment before saying, "Was I as silly as Lydia when you first met me?"

"That is somewhat harsh on Lydia."

"No, I must protest, I believe I am right in saying it. My father always called us silly, but I never saw it until now. She talks of new hats, and of herself and Wickham as if they were the darlings of society, but after all that has happened, how can she? Even Jane baulks at being in their company, and I know she contrives to see Lydia on her own. Lydia is oblivious to this; oblivious to the general disapproval of her husband and to the fact that her marriage has not elevated her. Harsh, you say to me, Georgiana; I begin to believe I am too kind to my sister when I libel her merely silly!"

Georgiana, in seeking to console her friend, replied, "You were never quite so silly as your sister, Kitty. You were perhaps a little wilder and more flighty than you are now, but it only took a little encouragement to bring out the very best in you. I am very proud to call you 'sister'. You are quite the best friend I have ever had."

Kitty was moved by her friend's open and heartfelt expressions. For a time, the girls sat in silence, enjoying the view that their position afforded them of all the comings and goings within the park. They felt grateful that their distance from the main set now touring the lawns and main walkways provided them a measure of seclusion, and this opportunity for being alone in so public a place.

Looking to turn the conversation to a topic she had long been thinking on, Kitty took her chance and asked, "Have you decided what is to be done in relation to Mr Grey? For my part, I am determined to spurn him at any opportunity, and I shall encourage others in our circle to be just as scathing in their treatment of him."

"I beg that you would not, Kitty," responded her companion. "Thank you for the loyalty that inspires such a course of action, but I would prefer it that in the unlikely event we should ever meet him again, that you would extend him what he is due by common courtesy."

"Do I understand you? Do you genuinely wish me to be civil to the man when next we meet?"

"I do not think it likely that we should, but yes, that is exactly what I would wish. I do not want pettiness and meanness of spirit to define us. The man was foolish, he acted foolishly, so let an end to our friendship be punishment enough. Given time, I believe we could be civil should we meet."

"How much time?" Kitty interrupted hurriedly.

"What?" Georgiana asked, confused.

"How much time do we need before we ought to be capable of conversing with Mr Grey in a civil manner?"

"Kitty, what a question! What does it matter?"

"Because," Kitty continued, "unless I am very much mistaken, I see him approaching us directly, and we have but a minute before he will be upon us!"

Georgiana reddened, then blanched, and just as Mr Grey arrived at the bench, returned to her usual colour, straightened her shoulders, and turned her face towards him with a look of complete composure, if not complete happiness.

She nodded curtly at his stammered "Good day" and was prepared to simply return her attention to her companion when he continued, "Miss Darcy, I was hoping I might meet you here today; indeed, I have been walking for some time now with the expectation of us meeting."

"Well, you know that I regularly walk here on a Sunday so it can come as little surprise to you, I suppose, though why you would be so hopeful for a meeting, I cannot begin to guess."

"Indeed, you might wonder, when I think of our last meeting – nay, when I think of our last parting."

"I have no wish to speak on it, Mr Grey," Georgiana said, a high colour rising, and her back stiffening.

"I would not for the world be the source for additional upset to you, Miss Darcy, but please let me explain, if we must part..."

"We must!" interrupted Georgiana with uncharacteristic firmness.

Mr Grey slumped a little about the shoulders, but continued, "So as you say, we must part, but please let it be with openness, with all the facts of the thing laid bare. Let there be no cause for recrimination or regret. Will you hear what I have to say? Will your generous spirit afford me that, at least?"

Georgiana nodded her ascent, and though avoiding his direct gaze, she turned her head in his direction.

Kitty, wishing to be anywhere but on the bench, silently eased her way along until she reached the furthest point from the pair. Once there, she pulled out a leaflet advertising a talk to be given by one of the women's leagues and read it with a concentration and interest she would not generally muster.

"You heard, I know, of my time in Bath, and of my outings with some of the young women I encountered there," began Mr Grey. He paused; Georgiana nodded, so he continued. "Yes, I thought as much. There is no excuse, I suppose, for how I acted while away from you for so many weeks. I shall not try to absolve myself, but my sins may not be as great as you suppose, and I wonder – I hope – that perhaps you might find it in your heart to forgive the foolishness inspired by your absence."

Georgiana made no response, but the gentle tilt of her face towards him was encouragement enough for Mr Grey to continue.

"I spent time with a number of young ladies while at Bath. There were always dances and recitals to attend, and it was only natural that I would increase my acquaintance. My first friends were among the young men in Bath, but these men had sisters and cousins aplenty and there was scarce a night when I was not introduced to some young lady or other. I have always been a social creature, needing the comfort of society, and so I indulged in what I thought to be harmless flirtations, but I swear to you, they meant nothing."

"Ought that to console me, Mr Grey?" Georgiana said.

"What?" he replied, taken aback by the hardness in her voice.

"Ought I to be consoled by knowing that you risked everything between us for some flirtations that by your own account meant nothing to you?"

"No, that is not what I meant," he mumbled, increasingly disquieted by her gaze and manner.

"Then, by all means, if you wish for us to end whatever it was that had started between us with openness and honesty, tell me precisely what it is that you meant."

"What had started between us?" Mr Grey looked confused. "Georgiana, surely you must have known that I intended to ask you to marry me? You must have known this?"

At the mention of marriage, Georgiana started, and clasped her hand to her mouth. "Marriage!" she faltered, "Indeed, I had no idea of that being your intention."

"Of course, that was my intention. I am not so unworthy as you think. I did not spend time with you, encourage an intimacy, or publicly demonstrate an inclination towards you out of vanity or carelessness. How can it be that you did not know my intentions to be such?"

"If this is true; if your intentions were so honourable, then how am I to understand your actions in Bath? Can I trust the love of a man whose feelings are so capricious?"

"Georgiana," begged Mr Grey, "I was a fool. Please, please forgive me. Blame it on youth, or stupidity, or on my own misguided sense of invulnerability. I thought I was secure in your feelings; I fooled myself into thinking that I would risk nothing by indulging in a little harmless flirtation. I was wrong; I know it now. Is there any hope you might forgive me, that you might allow me to redeem myself? Tell me not that I am so far beyond redemption; please, Georgiana."

With this final imploration, he fell silent and waited for her to decide his fate.

Georgiana, almost overcome by all that had been revealed in the last few minutes, made no rush to judgement, but sat regarding Mr Grey more closely and more critically than she had ever done in all of the time they had spent together. "You are not beyond redemption," she said finally, "there is always hope."

His face grew brighter at her declaration.

"That is not to say I have forgiven you," she continued, "nor is it to say that I am willing to pursue a future with you, but you are not beyond redemption."

"Then that is enough, Miss Darcy," he smiled, his earlier look of agitation easing away. "I shall content myself with knowing that I am not completely without merit in your eyes. Yes, that will do...for now."

Their eyes met as he made this last statement.

Georgiana was surprised by the intense determination on his face, and Mr Grey was pleased by the gentle blush on hers. "And so I wish you good day, Miss Darcy, until we meet again."

"Good day, Mr Grey," she replied.

"Miss Bennet, I thank you for your tact, and wish you a very good day."

Kitty turned, as though only now aware of his presence, as though she had not just been witness to the whole of their conversation and all its thrilling revelations.

"Oh yes, indeed, Mr Grey. A very good day to you. We shall see you soon, I trust?"

Mr Grey flashed Kitty one of his most winning smiles. "You may count upon it, Miss Bennet; you may count upon it."

CHAPTER 23

Though it was still some weeks before the birth of the Darcys' baby was anticipated, Elizabeth had been suffering to such a degree with pain and stiffness that she had finally succumbed to her husband's wishes and agreed to go into confinement. The bargain was softened by her desire to see Maria comfortably settled with a family at Pemberley. If they were to make the journey to see to that, then it seemed sensible to remain there.

At least, there was distraction enough at Pemberley to make her time enjoyable: Jane would join her, and the solace of her sister's company was more than could be hoped for. Elizabeth was grateful too that Bingley would accompany Jane, for it ensured that at least some of Darcy's attention would be drawn elsewhere. Though she loved her husband, his overbearing attention to every detail of her health and comfort was stifling; his constant questions and enquiries were exhausting. Time alone with Jane offered respite from Darcy's well-meant interference.

ℴℴ

Once everyone was removed to the country, Elizabeth was anxious to see things settled with the Fosters: the family they were to approach with the plan of taking on Maria, and with luck, Bessie.

The Fosters lived in a cottage on the boundary of the large woodland to the east of the main house and gardens. Mr Foster's home and wage were large enough to support a family, but they remained childless. Mrs Foster ran a small school, looking after and teaching the younger children of Darcy's tenants, and though it was clear that she would have liked to have been a mother herself, she took great comfort in the love and care she could bestow on her pupils.

Though she could not be certain that the scheme would be a complete success, Elizabeth hoped that at least Maria would be taken in. There was no good reason to think that they would turn from the chance to raise the child as their own. Bessie's future was less certain, and Elizabeth was concerned enough about the girl to draw her aside.

"So, Bessie, how do you find the country? It is not too quiet for a city girl, I hope?"

"I have never known such quiet, ma'am. In truth, I found it frightening at first, such silence at night; so silent that I jumped when there was a sound, but I find I like it well enough now." Dropping her voice before continuing, she added, "I can honestly say, I would not for all the world go back to the city, ma'am, if I can be so bold as to hope you'll have me stay."

"Well, Bessie, of course we would love you to stay with us," Elizabeth responded, gently, "though you know Maria may soon be leaving us."

"And if she is not here, there will be no use for me. I understand just fine, ma'am, and I shall be ready to leave."

"Now, do not run away with yourself, Bessie, we have not done with you yet! You have as good as put yourself on the post-chaise back to London."

"Beggin' your pardon, ma'am, of course there's things must be paid for: my board and keep here, and my travel, and them new things you bought me, and I daresay they cost more than my time looking after Maria would pay for. Well, I pay my way, ma'am, always have done, and I shall work off the rest as you see fit."

Elizabeth considered the determined young girl who looked so squarely and honestly at her. Bessie was a strange creature, whose openness and plain speaking were disarming. Life had not been gentle on her, and Elizabeth doubted that she had been protected from the world as she should have. Though the girl never expected kindness, or hoped for better, there was no bitterness to her. Elizabeth concluded that when sadness came to Bessie, it would not last long. Bessie would, as she had always done, simply make the best of things.

"There is nothing for you to repay, Bessie. Your care for Maria can never be fully returned, and so it is Mr Darcy and I who must be indebted to you, but you know that Maria must be placed with a family and we cannot be certain they will wish to take on a grown girl as well, though of course we hope they might. If they do not feel they can take you on, would you be satisfied in accepting a position here?"

Bessie, who had always assumed that she would be turned out once her usefulness had passed, was unable to answer for a moment or two. "I would. I would indeed, ma'am. I would be grateful for any position you would see me fit for. I can clean well enough, and look after children. You know I am a useful sort of a girl, and I can be trained in almost anything. I would be no bother, honest; no bother, not one bit," she ran on.

"I know, Bessie. Mr Darcy and I know, so you must not worry. Whatever happens with the Fosters, you have a home here at Pemberley for as long as you should wish it."

Bessie, unaccustomed to such consideration, choked back a sob, but with eyes brimmed with tears, she nodded, bobbed a quick curtsey, and went back to Maria, afraid to stay longer lest her tears fall too readily.

§

Within a week of their being settled at home, Darcy and Elizabeth found themselves passing an afternoon waiting in the sitting room for the arrival of the Fosters. Darcy had called on Mrs Foster that morning with the request that she and her husband attend the house to speak with them.

Mrs Foster had spent the rest of the morning in a lather, fretting about why they had been summoned. Had she spoken out of place on her last visit? Was John to be removed from his post for some reason? Were they to lose their house as well as their position? All manner of fears were raised and set aside in favour of even greater ones. She could not remember a more unpleasant morning in all her days, and it was with dread that she approached Pemberley that afternoon; fearing darker days were yet to come.

The Fosters were shown into the small breakfast room and before Elizabeth could do anything other than motion them towards some chairs, Mrs Foster burst forth with, "My lady, why have we been called here? Have we displeased you? You will not turn us out of the house, will you? We can make amends for whatever wrong we have done you or the master."

"Good God, Darcy! What did you say to Mrs Foster to upset her so?" Elizabeth said, while taking the woman by the hand and leading her to a chair.

Darcy appeared surprised by the outburst; he drew himself up, and with a decided stiffness of manner offered in his defence that he had simply requested they attend. Elizabeth rolled her eyes at her husband; sometimes his ignorance of his intimidating manner was astounding.

"Mrs Foster, please calm yourself and have some tea. Neither you, nor your husband, are in any danger. In fact, it is because we trust and value you so highly that we have asked you here today."

Her words eased Mrs Foster considerably, but Elizabeth did not continue until she was assured that the woman was sufficiently recovered. "Now, to the reason for this meeting: I have some questions for you, Mrs Foster, and I hope you will not think me too presumptuous in asking them."

Mrs Foster nodded uncertainly, and looking at her husband, encouraged Mrs Darcy to continue.

"Is it true that you and Mr Foster have no children?"

"Yes, we have been married some sixteen years now and

have not been so blessed."

"But I believe you wished to have children?"

"Well, what one wishes for and what one gets are very different things," stated Mrs Foster. "There was a time I held such hopes, but wishing for a thing that cannot be only leads to heartache, and I have learned to stop thinking on, or hoping for, miracles. If the good Lord had wanted us to have children, then I daresay he would have provided us the means of having them."

Mrs Foster looked at her husband as she gave her reply.

Elizabeth watched her face, and though she could see traces of old hurts and sadness, there was much more of love and acceptance in her gaze.

"I cannot offer you a miracle, Mrs Foster, but perhaps God has seen fit to answer your prayers of old in an unexpected way…" She looked to Darcy as she spoke, and he rose from his seat and left the room.

"Mr and Mrs Foster, a young girl has come into our care. She is a child without family and without hope of a good future unless we can secure her a loving home."

The Fosters looked at each other. In all of Mrs Foster's wild imaginings as to the reasons for their being summoned, this had not crossed her mind.

"You wish us to look after the child?" Mr Foster said, having been silent up until then.

"I wish – I hope – you and your wife might see fit to take the child and raise her as your own,' Elizabeth responded. 'This would not be a temporary arrangement. The child – Maria – would be your daughter, as though she were your flesh and blood. We realise this request must be quite a surprise, and of course, it may be a burden you are not willing to undertake. The choice must be yours and there will be no recrimination should you feel unable to take her in. Mr Darcy is gone to fetch the girl, and we hoped you might meet her today, though please do not feel that you have to provide us with an answer so soon. You must take the time you need to make such an important decision."

As Darcy had not yet returned, Elizabeth continued. "There is also another matter we wish you to consider: the child has been taken care of by another young girl, an orphan of the city whom we could not bear to leave at the mercy of the streets. Her name is Bessie, and we convinced her to come back with us to look after Maria. We hoped you might see your way to taking in this girl, also. As she is all but grown, we would not expect you to take her on the same terms as Maria, but we thought she could be of service to you, Mrs Foster, perhaps some use about the house or school. She is a good sort of a girl and I daresay would be no trouble to you. She is wonderful with Maria and is keen to stay in the country. I trust you will be pleased with her. We would, naturally, recompense you for any extra costs."

Darcy returned just as Elizabeth finished, carrying the small basket that held Maria Sinclair. He was trailed, rather shyly, by Bessie, who seemed determined to hide behind him. Darcy placed the basket on the table at the centre of the room. No one spoke, but the sounds of contented gurgling and babbling could be heard, and two small hands could be seen above the basket's lace-covered trim.

Mr and Mrs Foster leaned forward to look upon the child. Maria, still silent, gazed back, smiling at the two faces, and reaching towards them. The Fosters reached out to her, and she grabbed at them both, her tiny hands taking a firm grip.

Elizabeth broke the silence. "I realise this must be a shock to you both. My husband and I appreciate that you will need time to make this decision."

Bessie peered out from behind Darcy and caught a glimpse of the Fosters' faces. They were as in love with Maria as she was, and she knew they would not say "no". Mrs Darcy had said that she would ask them to take her on, but Mr Darcy had warned her that the Fosters might not want the additional burden of a young girl as well as a baby. Though he promised she could stay at Pemberley, her heart broke at the thought of being separated from Maria, and at the loss of the family she had allowed herself to hope for, but then again, her own kin had not wanted her, so why would these strangers?

Mr Foster finally looked away from the basket, and said, "She's just a tiny little thing, isn't she? Is she well? Is she hale and hearty?"

Before Darcy and Elizabeth could respond, Mrs Foster was answering, "Hale and hearty? What a question, husband; of course she is! Have you ever seen a baby look better? Our daughter is just perfect." Then looking up at Bessie, she said, "And you, hiding there – Bessie, is it? Step forward."

Bessie did as she was asked without hesitation, desperate to make a good impression, to appear keen and useful, and most importantly, worthy of being kept.

"I hear you have been taking excellent care of Maria."

"I do my best, ma'am. My own family was large so there were always babies that needed minding and I like to be useful and busy. I've no patience for being idle," she replied.

"And do you read? Do you write? Can you do your sums?" Mrs Foster continued.

Bessie's face fell. Here it was: the end to all her hopes. She would be cast out for being ignorant. Lord knows she could be no good to a schoolmistress with no learning. Read! She had only held a book once and that was to look at the pictures.

"No, ma'am," she replied, downcast. "I never did get the chance, but I can still be useful, I promise you. I can still be useful."

"I daresay you can be," Mrs Foster continued, "and I daresay you are bright enough to learn, for you know, no daughter of mine will be left unable to read."

&

Maria and Bessie were removed to the cottage that afternoon. The Fosters had declined any additional payment for taking on Bessie, assuring the Darcys, with due respect, that they could well afford to look after both of their daughters. They did accept, with pleasure, the two trunks of dresses, and odds and ends that Elizabeth had purchased for the girls while they were at London. Their thanks for recognising them as worthy of such a blessing were plentiful and heartfelt.

Elizabeth, on seeing them off and promising to pay a visit as soon as she was able, was glad that the secrets and schemes that had once blighted her life with Darcy had led to a conclusion which secured the happiness of so many.

Darcy too was pleased, but the greatest share of his pleasure was in seeing the difference to Elizabeth. The worry previously evident in her face was no more, and he dared to hope that she was restored to the woman he had known before the discovery of May Sinclair's death, and all the trouble and pain that followed.

CHAPTER 24

Despite Darcy's insistence that Elizabeth remain in the house, he daily found himself out walking with her through one or other of the pleasant garden trails. However, after two weeks of confined walking, Elizabeth grew restless, and began to suggest more variation in their exercise. Mindful of the necessity of tempering the worst of Elizabeth's wilfulness, he suggested the possibility of their making comfortable a light gig so Elizabeth might travel further about the estate without the fatigue of excessive walking. Once at a pleasant spot, they could stop, walk a while, and return as they had arrived. Elizabeth agreed, and as soon as all the arrangements could be made, the couple were to be found daily taking a turn in odd corners of the estate, down by the rose garden or at points along the river, which separated Darcy's lands from those of his nearest neighbour.

The couple would sometimes be accompanied by the Bingleys. Darcy noted with a degree of satisfaction that Jane was as conscientious for Elizabeth's health and well-being as he was, and so welcomed her company, pleased to find an ally in his sister-in-law. Elizabeth was hard-pressed to go against them both when they counselled rest or an early return to the house.

"I have such a desire to be by the water today, Fitzwilliam," Elizabeth declared at breakfast. "Might we head to the riverbank for a long walk?"

The mention of a long walk did not sit well with Darcy, but the unenviable task of disappointing his wife was deftly taken up by her sister, who responded, "Oh, what a charming idea. I am sure Charles and I would love a day by the river, but Elizabeth, I feel quite unequal to a long walk after yesterday's exertions; do I ask too much to join you, but to beg a picnic and perhaps a gentle stroll instead?"

"Of course, you must join us. We could take a longer walk about the garden later this evening when we return, husband. What do you say to the plan?"

"My darling wife, as always, you and Jane appear to have the matter fixed between you, but I should be pleased to join you and know the very spot for the picnic."

Then rising to provide instructions for food and transport, he kissed Elizabeth, smiled with warmth at Jane, and thanked God for the wonderful intervention of a sister-in-law of whose true worth he was daily becoming sensible of.

§

Some hours later, the couples found themselves situated in one of the prettiest areas of the Pemberley estate. They were in a small valley at the north-west boundary, where the hills on their estate and on those of the Willowbrook estate beside them were just high enough, and the trees atop them just dense enough, that neither of the great houses could be seen. All around them was nature in abundance; the only obvious intrusion by man being the small stone bridge that crossed the river some yards down from where they had spread out their blankets.

"This is perfect," announced Jane. "I cannot imagine a more charming setting."

Bingley groaned. "Really Darcy, must you show off all the wonders of Pemberley? Are you to hold nothing back? How is Jane ever to be satisfied with the estate we purchase once she has been so thoroughly spoilt here?"

"Forgive me, Charles," Darcy replied. "How decidedly selfish of me to want to treat my guests to the best my home has to offer. I shall endeavour to be less solicitous in the future."

"Well, I would certainly appreciate any restraint on your part!"

"Charles," interrupted Jane, "you must not be so severe on Mr Darcy."

"Not so severe? Indeed, I am far too lenient on the man," he countered. "Darcy, you are unashamedly proud and boastful. Make no attempt to deny it."

"Bingley, you are fortunate I am familiar enough with your style of wit that I recognise an attempt at provocation when I see one, but you will not find satisfaction from me today, however much you goad. You shall have to make sport some other way. You should try fishing – here, I have bait and tackle, enough for the two of us."

The two men moved closer to the riverbank to cast their line, while Jane and Elizabeth settled down in a nest of blankets and cushions, enjoying the warm sunshine and the sight of their husbands happily engaged in sport and each other's company. The tranquillity of the afternoon was punctuated by an occasional passer-by or the trundling of a cart across the nearby bridge, but the couples were largely left in peace. Jane was pleased to see Elizabeth succumb to the gentleness of the day.

Such was the calm of the party, that after settling, enquiring after the gentlemen's success at fishing, their general questions in return with regards to the ladies' comfort, and a collective agreement to eat within the next hour, silence had fallen. This harmony continued undisturbed until the sounds of children laughing could be heard from a short distance away.

Elizabeth turned to the direction of the sound and could make out the figures of two young girls who were making their way from the tree-lined lane to cross the bridge.

"Are they children from your estate, Lizzy?" enquired Jane. "Ought they be out here on their own?"

"I believe they may be the Martins' girls, and I am surprised indeed that Mrs Martin would permit them to roam so freely and alone," but before she could continue, a man's voice could be heard calling to them.

Jane, relieved, said, "Oh, all is well. That must be Mr Martin I hear calling them, so there is no need for concern."

Jane, completely unaware of the bad feeling that existed between Mr Martin and Mr Darcy, was pleased, but Elizabeth paled at the thought, and before she could make clear to Jane why Mr Martin's presence should be more cause for unease than relief, the man himself cleared the trees and walked towards his daughters.

Darcy, on hearing his voice, had already cast his eyes to the treeline and Elizabeth could see his jaw tighten when Mr Martin himself appeared.

"Jane," she said hurriedly, "I must speak with Fitzwilliam. Will you fetch him to me, Jane, now; it is really quite important."

Jane, seeing the change in Elizabeth, was gone at once towards the riverbank to get Darcy back and returned with him not a minute later. Darcy and Elizabeth regarded one another without speaking at first, while Jane watched in wonder at the pair.

"I ought to have him arrested."

"But you will not, and certainly not in front of his children, will you, Fitzwilliam?"

"No, I will not."

Jane looked confused, and though she had not asked about the circumstances that would necessitate such conversation, she was soon made privy to the little history of the fire and Mr Martin's banishment so that she would not be overly alarmed by the talk of arrest.

"Should we leave them be? They seem to be in fine spirits," suggested Elizabeth.

"I suppose I should leave the man to the company of his family. Was it wrong of me to try to separate Martin from his children? I wonder now, as we come so close to the birth of our own child, what I would do if someone tried to keep either of you from me, and I doubt I could bear it."

"Well," interjected Jane for the first time, "from what you have said, you did what you believed was best for everyone. The man was a danger to himself and others. He could have killed someone in the fire, but perhaps he has come to see the error of his ways and we might hope to find him a changed man."

Darcy smiled at Jane's indefatigable goodness of spirit, and agreed to leave the family to enjoy the rest of their day, though was determined to pay a call on Mrs Martin later to reassure himself that all was in order. He checked on Elizabeth's comfort once more, touched the swell of her belly, and headed back to the riverbank and Bingley, who was in the middle of reeling in what appeared to be a capital catch.

Mr Martin, on clearing the trees, had made his way to follow his daughters and caught sight of Mr Darcy making his way back to Mr Bingley by the riverbank. He froze for a moment upon seeing him; sure that Mr Darcy would not allow him to remain. It was with genuine surprise, then, that he watched as Mr Darcy acknowledged his presence with a slight dip of his head, and instead of striding over to confront him, merely turned his attention to his friend. Mr Martin was at a loss to explain the change in Mr Darcy, and unwilling to test providence further, he tried to encourage his children that they would be happier playing elsewhere. Sadly, the girls were resolute that this bridge was the perfect spot for their favourite game and would not be moved, so he had little choice but to accept Mr Darcy's good grace; be grateful that there would be no unpleasantness in front of his children, and pray that this temporary relief might yet yield a full reprieve. For the first time since his exile, Mr Martin allowed himself to hope that he might yet be able to convince Mr Darcy to allow him to come home.

❧

Elizabeth and Jane, roused by the children's cheerfulness into more animated spirits themselves, talked excitedly about the baby as they watched the Martins' children at play. The two girls had been joined by their younger brother, and it looked as though the three were engaged in setting down leaves into the river on one side of the bridge so they could race them to the other side. After two or three attempts, it was clear that the young boy had grown tired of losing to his sisters. Longer in body and arms, the girls could reach over and place their leaves on the river, while he had to be content to have his leaf fall from his hand and drift to the water. The two women watched in amusement as the boy's frustration grew, and wondered how long he would suffer the indignity of defeat before he cried off the game altogether.

Surprising them both, however, the boy made a quick dash to his father, and, they supposed, made an impassioned plea for assistance, for before the next race was due to begin, he returned to the starting spot, only to be lifted by his father and held above the water by his ankles. The girls' advantage removed, he took to the game with even greater relish than before, and they could hear him cry, "Again! Again!" at the end of every race. Distracted by their conversation, the women looked away, their attention brought back to the party by a loud splash, which was followed by a yell from Mr Martin.

It seemed that young John Martin had slipped, or been dropped, into the water. The women laughed, Elizabeth saying that Mrs Martin was unlikely to be pleased by her boy returning home soaked to the bone, but a flash of movement from the corner of her eye suggested that her husband was taking the fall far more seriously.

"It cannot be that deep, surely, Jane?" she queried, but noting with alarm that the boy had not resurfaced.

Darcy was racing to the bridge and calling on Mr Martin to move quickly to help his son, but Mr Martin seemed rooted to the spot, unable to follow the commands that Mr Darcy was barking at him as he ran. Within a minute, Darcy's coat and vest were removed, and he paused at the bank just long enough to remove his boots.

Elizabeth was horrified at the turn the day had taken and demanded to be helped closer. With surprising speed, she reached the spot where Darcy's clothes lay, before he had even returned for air. The girls had already gone for help, and

Elizabeth called on Mr Martin to do what he could. Bingley was making to follow Darcy into the river when he was pulled back by a man the girls had met in the lane.

"Stay out of that water unless you know it, sir."

Bingley shrugged off his grip. "For God's sake, man, Mr Darcy is in there, and a boy; I shall not just stand here."

"Water looks still, but there's currents underneath likely to sweep you away if they catch a hold on you. You have to learn to swim this river; I have seen it take too many in my time."

Jane, on hearing this, grabbed Bingley and refused to release him, calling his attention to Elizabeth and the need to see to her. Elizabeth, as though colluding to keep Bingley out of the water, chose that moment to falter and Bingley took hold of her just in time.

"Where is he, Charles?" she rasped, fear strangling the words in her throat. "Why has he not come up for air?"

All three of them looked to the water, and it was as though Darcy and the boy had been swallowed up by the river. The ripples that undulated after Darcy had dived below the surface were gone and the water had returned to its seemingly steady, gentle flow.

"Why did you hesitate?" Elizabeth now turned on Mr Martin. "Why did you not go in after your boy? What sort of man stands by while his child disappears like that?"

Mr Martin looked up from the river for the first time, and Elizabeth was startled by the hollowness of his expression. In a voice broken by horror and disbelief, he could only answer, "I cannot swim. Dear God, I cannot swim."

By now, they had been joined by others at the river, and two men carried with them a length of thick rope. Bingley was moved to action at once; grabbing the rope, he ordered that one end be tied off against a tree while he secured the other end tightly about his waist. "If you feel a deliberate tug on this rope, or if I have not come up for air then pull me out; as fast as you can, you pull me out," he instructed, before being lost beneath the water.

Elizabeth and Jane were frightened by how quickly and how

far the rope was pulled downstream the minute Bingley was lost to sight, and Elizabeth struggled for composure under the certainty that Darcy was drowned. It had been three, maybe four minutes since he had been seen and she doubted even he could last without air for so long. Jane, consumed by concern for her own husband, could offer few words of consolation or solace to her sister.

Little was said among those on the bank within the tense moments that they waited for Darcy, Bingley, or young John Martin to surface, until finally there was a splash in the stillness further downstream.

Elizabeth released a cry of "Thank God!", as a man emerged, only to reel backwards on seeing that the man was not Darcy. Bingley had been forced above the water for air, and she was certain now that if Darcy were alive, he could not have lasted so long below.

The unearthly quiet that followed was only pierced by the arrival of Mrs Martin who, in a state of absolute dread, had burst on to the scene crying aloud for her boy.

Just as all hope appeared lost, there was a cry from further down the river, though at the distance what the man was yelling could not be made out. Bingley was pulled from the water and attended to by Jane while one of the men raced on ahead to bring back news on the commotion further down.

He returned – a smile full across his face – with news that Darcy had been seen to emerge from the water, a boy in hand. Both Elizabeth and Mrs Martin burst into tears of relief and joy.

"The river just took a hold of 'em and pulled 'em right down past the bend, but the master was always a strong swimmer and he knows these waters."

Elizabeth moved quickly into action, and reaching out for the nearest arm, demanded, "Help me to him," unwilling to wait for Darcy to reach her.

On seeing Elizabeth moving off, the whole party moved to walk with her. They had not gone far when the figure of a man could be seen coming towards them from around the river bend. Darcy's stride was unmistakable, and Elizabeth almost crumpled at the sight of him. Mrs Martin broke away from the group and ran towards Darcy, who carried John Martin in his arms, and everyone agreed that he must have been terrified by his ordeal and would be in need of much care and comfort in the coming days.

It was not until the boy's arm fell from his side that anyone doubted the boy being alive. His arm swung loosely, without direction or control, and the sight of it stopped Mrs Martin as she ran. Darcy paused upon seeing the woman, before resolutely steering his course towards her. As he shifted his body to change direction, John Martin's head dislodged itself from where it had rested against Darcy's chest and flopped back, lifeless.

At the sight of her son, Mrs Martin began to scream. This was the last thing Elizabeth heard before collapsing.

℅

The deep faint Elizabeth had fallen into on seeing her husband carrying the dead boy soon gave way to her being forced back to consciousness by the initial pains of childbirth. The shock of the afternoon, it seemed, had acted to quicken events, and they were not an hour back inside the house before Darcy sent for the doctor to attend at Pemberley, immediately.

The doctor soon confirmed Darcy's fears: the baby was coming and some weeks early, doubtless the result of the strain experienced by Elizabeth that afternoon.

Darcy cursed the run of events that had led them to this: one young child dead, and now Elizabeth and his own child in jeopardy. He paced the length of the room, paused to attend to any further noise from upstairs, and then continued to pace. Bingley had attempted to persuade him to read the paper, play at cards, or have a brandy, but all such distractions were refused, with Darcy eventually yelling, "Bingley! Will you cease with your damned attentions. How can you think of games and drinking while Elizabeth is in such danger?"

Jane entered at just that moment. "What a fine way to talk,

Mr Darcy. Will you have those be the first words your child hears from you?"

He leapt towards her, ignoring the chastisement. "The baby is here?"

"Not yet, Fitzwilliam, but the doctor assures me it will be soon. All looks well. Lizzy is tired, but ready for the task at hand."

From upstairs, there was a sudden scream. Jane turned on her heel and ran back to the room. Darcy paled at the sound, unsteadily dropping himself onto the nearest seat while Bingley reached for the brandy.

It was some time before Jane returned; a smile spread across her face. "Mr Darcy, would you join us upstairs? I believe Elizabeth would like the honour of introducing you to your first born."

Elizabeth was sat up in the bed, surrounded by pillows, her hair soaked in sweat. She was drawn and pale, and winced as she moved, but Darcy, who could not take his eyes off her, had never seen her look so radiant. Her smile outshone even Jane's, and he thought his heart would give out from the relief of seeing her alive and well. Indeed, such was his attention to her, he scarcely noticed the child she held tenderly to her chest.

"Fitzwilliam," she smiled, "come let me introduce you to our daughter."

He blinked, her voice calling him back from his reverie. "Our daughter?"

"You are not disappointed, Fitzwilliam, that I did not bear you a son?" A fleeting look of worry crossed her face, born more out of exhaustion than any real concern of his disapproval.

"Disappointed, my love? How could I ever be disappointed in anything you do? I am simply thankful you are well. I asked for nothing beyond your safety."

This was certainly true. In the hours of pacing, all Darcy could think about was Elizabeth's well-being. The doctor had warned that the baby's early arrival would make things more difficult, and cautioned there may yet be damage from the accident that could cause complications in the labour, posing a risk to mother and child. On hearing this, Darcy had drawn the doctor aside and in a manner that left no room for interpretation, informed him should anything go wrong, "You save my wife!"

Darcy was mindful of the need to secure the family line and he enjoyed the thought of having children as much as any man, but all he could think about was Elizabeth. All he knew was his love for her, and his need of her – until he felt small hands grab at him.

Darcy looked down, surprised. The squirming bundle beneath his hand had reached out with tiny hands of her own and gripped the first thing they encountered: the tips of her father's fingers. He was transfixed. "She...she has your eyes, my love," was all that he could utter.

§

Once the health of both mother and baby had been guaranteed, the doctor insisted that Elizabeth be left to rest, although he suggested that the nurse take the baby. Elizabeth was unhappy at so soon a separation, and their daughter – to be named Amelia Jane – was settled instead into a cot by the bed. By the time Darcy had ushered everyone out of the room, stoked the fire in the grate, and finally lowered his body into an armchair, Elizabeth had fallen asleep, and Amelia Jane, too, was resting softly.

Darcy watched his daughter sleeping in a cot that had rocked several generations of Darcy babes. The rocker at its base was smooth and well-worn from use, and as he tipped the curved foot, the cot moved into a gentle sway.

Though exhausted, he did not sleep. All the events of the day were acting upon his mind to force an unwelcome wakefulness. The wretched remembrance of holding one lifeless child, only slowly being forced out by the exhilaration of holding his own healthy newborn, full of life.

He attended to every shift from Elizabeth and every whimper from Amelia Jane, fretful that although all seemed well, something might yet be wrong. Elizabeth stirred as he was bent over the cot, checking once again on his daughter, and on hearing Elizabeth move, Darcy reached across to stroke her cheek, and cup her face with his hand.

"You are awake then, my love; not in pain, I hope?"

"I am well, Fitzwilliam. There is some discomfort, but that, I am certain, is to be expected. How is Amelia Jane?"

"She rests soundly – I believe she has born the drama of the last hours the best of us all," he said, smiling, as he sat back into the armchair.

"You can sit by me, husband," Elizabeth assured him. "I shall not break if you touch me."

Darcy reached for her hand and squeezed it, but he stayed where he was. "Your body has been most put upon, Elizabeth. I shall not give you cause to move to accommodate me. You need to rest and be still. I shall stay in this chair where I can see to you both. Amelia Jane may stir and I would not wish to jostle you while I check her."

"Should I ring for the nurse then, husband? I do not want you troubled by having her here; you will need to rest as much as I."

"No, I believe we will manage, for tonight at least. For tonight, my darling, could it be just the three of us in here together? Could I keep you both to myself for at least that long?"

"Why, Fitzwilliam, you sound positively sentimental."

Darcy stared straight into Elizabeth's eyes, and with an earnest seriousness, answered, "The moment Amelia Jane took my hand, Elizabeth, I was altered. I am no longer the man I once was. I did not think it possible to love so fiercely and completely with such immediacy. Perhaps it is sentimentality, but if it be, then I shall suffer it gladly. I had not expected such change. As I waited, all I could think of was you. Your safety was all I prayed for, but now I know my life must be spent in the service of two loves: yours and our children."

"You truly are altered, husband," Elizabeth said softly. "I see a difference in you, for there is such softness in the way you look at Amelia Jane."

"You do not think it weakness, I hope?"

"Oh, nothing could be further from the truth. Indeed, the softness towards your daughter will be amply balanced by the fierce protection that poor Amelia Jane will also be the subject of – I saw the way you growled at Charles when he held her."

"Well, he was doing it wrong. The man is steady as a rock when he handles a horse, but put a baby in his arms and he is all thumbs."

Elizabeth laughed. "Amelia Jane was perfectly safe, as well you know, and still you hovered about him, grabbing her from his arms at the first opportunity."

"Well, she is mine, after all. Have I not the right to hold my child?"

"Your child, is she? I believe I might have had some role to play in bringing her into the world," Elizabeth continued.

At that, Darcy recognised his wife's gentle brand of teasing, and he relaxed in his armchair once more. "Do you really think me too protective, Elizabeth?"

"Darling husband, you shall be both a blessing and a curse to our daughter. She will never fail to feel a boundless safety in your love, but heaven help her when she has to bring home a man to meet her father. In fact, heaven help the man!"

Darcy laughed now, low and gentle so as not to wake the baby. "Still, I need not worry about that yet. For now it will be my hand she grasps hold of, and my arms that hold her."

"And you will always have my hand to hold, Fitzwilliam, and my arms to curl into," his wife added, reaching out and stroking his leg with her fingertips.

"Then, I am complete, my love, and can ask for no more happiness than that."

Yawning, Elizabeth moved as though to sleep once more. "You will sleep, Fitzwilliam, promise me," she said, burying her head deeper into her pillow. "You will not stand guard over us all night," she continued, her eyelids closing.

"I shall sleep, my love, when you do. When I know you both to be safe and resting, then I will sleep, I promise you," Darcy whispered, stroking Elizabeth's hair and face as she drifted back into slumber.

℘

Some hours later, Darcy awoke to the piercing cry of a hungry baby.

"For all my concerns," he smiled, picking up Amelia Jane and carrying her to Elizabeth, "there is certainly nothing wrong with our daughter's lungs. She has a fine strong voice."

"A voice? Such a gentle word for the sound your daughter is making – she is screeching! Here, pass her to me that I might quiet her," Elizabeth said, reaching for the upset squirming bundle.

"Ah, so she is my daughter now, as you so rightly remonstrated not four hours ago, I believe you had something to do with her arrival into the world, my darling," teased Darcy.

"Fitzwilliam, it is quite a tiresome habit of yours: remembering what I have said and reminding me of it when it suits you! You should try to quit yourself of it. I assure you the resulting marital felicity will be reward enough," Elizabeth chided, having finally succeeded in settling Amelia Jane.

Darcy ignored her goading and moved onto the bed, unwilling to remain a spectator to the moment between his wife and daughter. He curled himself around Elizabeth, allowing her to sit back into his chest, and rest her arm on his thigh. His free hand found activity in gently stroking the soft top of his baby's head, occasionally wandering further on to Elizabeth's full breast as Amelia Jane nursed. They sat in this manner until Amelia Jane, satiated and winded, was ready to be moved to her father's arms, full, happy, and altogether quiet.

"We must write to the others and tell them our good news. They will not be expecting such tidings so soon, and it would be good to have Georgiana and Kitty here to share this with us," said Elizabeth, once they were settled.

"If you agree to rest until Amelia Jane calls for you again, I shall undertake to write the letters this very morning and have them delivered by first post, although I must ask excusal from penning one letter…"

"The letter that must be sent to Lydia and Wickham, I suppose, husband."

"No, no indeed, the one to Mr and Mrs Bennet, for I will not be responsible for breaking the news of a granddaughter to your mother!"

"Oh Lord bless me," laughed Elizabeth, "I had quite forgot I was to produce a boy!"

℘

True to his word, the happy news was dispatched by the first post and before the week was out, congratulations and gifts were flooding back in return.

In the note received from Caroline Bingley and Mrs Hurst, the ladies were profuse in their excitement at the news and eager to know when they could visit. The enthusiasm in their correspondence was in contrast to the dispassionate civility with which they had actually greeted Darcy's news. Of course, they were pleased for the couple – such good news – although a shame the child was a girl. Of course, the early arrival would mean that the Bingleys would not be returning to London on Saturday, as planned. In truth, Caroline's chief concern was that someone must remember to tell cook to change their dinner plans.

The final ball of the season was to be in a week, and in his letter to his sister, Darcy suggested that she and Kitty return to Pemberley once the ball was done and they were recovered.

Mr Grey had already appealed to Georgiana to have the honour of at least one dance at the ball, and although she had been excited at the prospect, on the receipt of her brother's letter, all her hopes were for an immediate departure to the country.

She was uncertain whether Kitty would be happy to leave before the biggest event of the season and broached the matter, tactfully, shortly after receiving the post. She was both surprised and grateful to find Kitty just as anxious to be away.

"And you will not mind missing Saturday's ball?" Georgiana asked incredulously. "For you have talked of it with such animation this last week."

"Oh, my greatest excitement for the ball lay in your being able to dance with Mr Grey, but I see now that this will be even better."

"My not dancing with Mr Grey will be better?" Georgiana replied in confusion.

"Oh yes, we must not make reconciliation too easy on the man," Kitty responded. "He should be made to suffer, at least a little, for his foolishness. A little absence should test his resolve delightfully."

Once the pair had decided to leave town, they only delayed their departure to await the arrival of Mary Bennet who had secured her father's permission for a short stay with Kitty and Miss Darcy. Mary was as excited by the news as the others, and begging only one night's rest in London was happy to be on the road to Pemberley the very next day. Kitty was thankful for Mary's happy sacrifice of the delights of London and insisted they set off as soon as they had visited a milliner, as a new bonnet was essential for a proper celebration.

The Gardiners, with whom they were travelling, were equally joyous, and ensured while at the milliners, Kitty remembered to purchase a token for the baby. Mary argued that such trifles were of little real consequence at a time such as this and was sure that the couple would have greater use for her offering: a book of sermons in which she highlighted passages of particular importance in relation to the careful regulation and instruction of children.

Mr Collins expressed his feelings in a letter of some length: his joy, their good fortune, the blessings of a child, his hope that the new arrival would heal the rift between the Darcys and his patroness, were all topics upon which he pontificated at great length in the six or seven pages he sent. The short addition from Charlotte at the end was far more gratifying to Elizabeth.

My dearest Lizzy, I was delighted to hear of the safe birth of your daughter and I am certain Amelia Jane will be a blessing to you. My heartfelt best wishes for you and your family.

In a small aside, she had added:

It might amuse you, Lizzy, to learn of Lady Catherine's reaction to the news: she simply announced that had Darcy married Ann, she would have given him a son!

Lydia was delighted by the report, and was convinced that she and Wickham would be asked to be godparents, so much so, she was excitedly planning what they would wear to the church and what they ought to provide as a gift, when Wickham yelled, "I very much doubt we shall be asked, Lydia. Darcy and I are not firm friends."

"Nonsense, he stood for you at our wedding; what better proof of friendship do you need? And we had such a lovely visit with them in London. Lizzy was quite attentive to me, ensuring my comfort and asking all about our life together. Lizzy will want me, I am sure. I was always her favourite...well, beyond Jane, of course, but I am certain she liked me better than Kitty or Mary."

Wickham, growing weary of his wife's incessant prattling, barked, "Well, she will probably ask Jane, then, and that will be that! Now stop flitting about me, woman, and leave me in peace – I have business to attend to."

Lydia burst out laughing at his chastisement. "Oh, my darling Wickham, how funny you are, and how angry you get when dealing with business. I do not know why you bother at all, as you find it so tiresome. I shall do as you ask and leave you in peace. I am off to town for I have my eye on a new hat!" she trilled as she headed for the door.

Wickham rolled his eyes to the heavens. "Good God! Another new hat?"

Upon receiving their letter, Mrs Bennet ran to her husband, exclaiming, "And what do you say to that? I always said Lizzy was a wilful child?"

"My dear, I have not the least understanding of what you mean," Mr Bennet replied. "Am I to take it that you are displeased somehow by the news?"

"I counselled her; the time I spent impressing upon her – well, I told her most strictly – that she must produce a boy. But, oh, Mr Bennet! She pays no heed of me, never has; not like Jane who has always been such a good girl and so careful to listen to her mama. I am sure she will produce a son and heir."

"Come now, Mrs Bennet, you know perfectly well, if it had been within Elizabeth's power, she would have done as you suggested and provided Darcy with a fine lad to inherit Pemberley."

"I know no such thing!" Mrs Bennet interrupted. "I am sure she has birthed a girl just to torment my nerves. She was always your favourite, to be sure, but she has far too determined a will if you ask me. And what is Darcy to do? Poor Darcy. A girl! What is he to do with a girl? What use is a girl to a man?"

Mr Bennet smiled, and fondly stroked the letter where Elizabeth had signed her name with a flourish. "Well, my dear Mrs Bennet, that very much depends on the girl!"

ℰℴ

LETTER TO THE READER

Evita O' Malley

Dear Reader,

Thank you so much for reading Doubts and Dilemmas – I really hope you enjoyed it. I swithered back and forth – a lot! – about whether to publish this, even after I had it edited, and had a cover designed. I almost decided not to hit the publish button, because, what if no one liked it?

But, just as I'd swung back to thinking that maybe I'd only publish a few copies for family and friends, and leave it there, my niece, Shan, was diagnosed with a rare form of cancer, and suddenly my worries didn't seem nearly so important.

Part sweetheart kid, part stroppy teenager (come on, Shan, you know it's true!), but all round wonderful young woman, it seemed unthinkable that she should be hit with such a battle at just sixteen, and yet she has, though she isn't battling alone. We all realise it is not going to be easy, and due to the rarity of her cancer, she will not be able to receive all her treatment in Ireland, so fundraising began almost as soon as the diagnosis was in.

Now I will, I am sure, bake, run, and bag pack with the best of 'em over the next few years in any number of fundraising efforts while Shan undergoes treatment, but I have also decided to donate half of any monies I make from the sale of this book to Shan's trust fund.

So thank you so much for buying a copy – it means more to me than I can say.

Evita

If you would like to learn a little more about the type of cancer Shan has, and the sorts of treatments available, please visit:

http://txch.org/cancer-center/histiocytosis-program/research/
http://txch.org/cancer-center/histiocytosis-program/